The Coming of the Dragon

ALSO BY REBECCA BARNHOUSE

The Book of the Maidservant

The COMING OF the DRAGON

REBECCA BARNHOUSE

RANDOM HOUSE NEW YORK

Text copyright © 2010 by Rebecca Barnhouse
Jacket art copyright © 2010 by Mel Grant

Visit us on the Web! www.randomhouse.com/kids

Educators and librarians, for a variety of teaching tools, visit us at
www.randomhouse.com/teachers

Library of Congress Cataloging-in-Publication Data
Barnhouse, Rebecca.
The coming of the dragon / by Rebecca Barnhouse. — 1st ed.
p.   cm.
Summary: Rune, an orphaned young man raised among strangers, tries to save
the kingdom from a dragon that is burning the countryside and,
along the way, learns that he is a kinsman of Beowulf.
ISBN 978-0-375-86193-2 (trade) — ISBN 978-0-375-96193-9 (lib. bdg.) —
ISBN 978-0-375-89349-0 (e-book)
[1. Heroes—Fiction. 2. Dragons—Fiction. 3. Identity—Fiction.
4. Wiglaf (Legendary character)—Fiction. 5. Beowulf (Legendary character)—Fiction.
6. Mythology, Norse—Fiction. 7. Scandinavia—History—To 1397—Fiction.] I. Title.
PZ7.B2668Com 2010   [Fic]—dc22   2009019295

Printed in the United States of America

10 9 8 7 6 5 4 3 2 1

First Edition

For

S K B

The COMING of the DRAGON

PROLOGUE

NO ONE KNEW HOW LONG AMMA HAD BEEN THERE.

When the women and children who lived in the stronghold, taking advantage of a sunny day, came down the rocky cliff path to gather bird eggs and seaweed, they saw her standing just below the high-tide line, looking out to sea.

Fulla set her basket down and approached her.

"Amma? What are you doing so far from home?" she asked, but Amma didn't answer. Instead, she stared out at the waves, eyes narrowed against the sun. Fulla turned to see what her friend was looking at, but there was nothing out of the ordinary—just gannets plummeting into the water for fish, while smaller birds swooped and skimmed above the whitecaps. She must have been there for a while, Fulla realized, looking down at the circle of dried salt at the bottom of Amma's skirt. Long enough for the tide to recede and wool to dry, at the very least, although Fulla had the impression it might have been much longer.

Gently, she touched the other woman's arm. "Amma?" Again, there was no response. "Well," she said, "I'll be here if you need anything."

She might as well have been talking to a post for all the reaction she got. She pursed her lips and picked up her basket. Glancing back at Amma every now and then, she sent her son up the rocks to hunt for birds' nests while she raked a stick through the wet seaweed, looking for the only kind worth collecting.

She raised her head just in time to see a boy hauling his arm back, ready to let a pebble fly toward Amma. She rushed over and grabbed him. "Don't you *ever* do that again," she hissed. She gave him her meanest look, then let him run away as she scanned the group for his mother.

Didn't these women have any compassion? She saw the suspicious glances they cast at Amma, who stood as still and silent as a rock, watching the water. Unusual behavior had been common for Amma ever since she had shown up seeking a place in the kingdom some six winters back. Or was it seven? Fulla couldn't recall, although she remembered the way people had treated Amma even then. Didn't they recognize grief when they saw it? And they, the wives and mothers of warriors? It was said that Amma had lost her brother, her husband, even her son in a feud, but she never talked about it, not even to Fulla. No wonder she wanted to live alone, far from the hall where nobles' sons spent their days honing their fighting skills.

Fulla looked over to see her own son climbing down from the rocks, cradling eggs in his shirt, waving away a tern that screamed and flew at him, defending her nest. It wouldn't be very many summers before Gunnar would be joining his father and his older brothers in the king's houseguard, for all that he was still a boy. Sword training started early for the youths who lived in the stronghold, and even farmers' sons traveled to the hall during the winters to learn how to wield spear and ax. She closed her eyes, indulging herself in a brief desire for a time when boys didn't have to become warriors, when feuds didn't have to be avenged, when other tribes' raiding parties didn't threaten the kingdom of the Geats.

A gray cloud rushed across the sun, blocking its light, and a gust of wind sent dried seaweed skittering over the rocks. In the west, more clouds gathered.

Fulla looked back at Amma, who still hadn't moved. What did she see out there? Shading her eyes as the cloud uncovered the sun again, Fulla stared out at the water. Was that a black speck? No, nothing. Still, uneasiness crept up her spine.

"Gunnar!" she called, and her son came running, eggs still clutched in his shirt. "Careful!"

From the way he looked down and then back up at her with his lopsided grin, she could tell that at least one egg must have broken. She smiled and shook her head as he neared her. "Two broke, but I can get more," he said.

"No need, these are fine." He held out his shirt, and she put the small, speckled eggs one by one into her basket. "I want you to do something," she said, her eye on Amma.

He craned his neck to see what she was looking at.

"I want you to run home as fast as you can and find your father. He's in the hall."

"I know that."

She suppressed a smile. All of her sons seemed to have a second sense when it came to their father's duty roster. Long before she did, they knew when he was leaving on patrol, when he was on guard at the hall entrance, when he was standing watch beside the throne or serving as the king's bodyguard. "Tell him . . ." She hesitated, not knowing quite what she wanted Hemming to know. "Tell him what Amma's doing."

He nodded and started to run.

"Wait!" she said. "Wash the egg off your shirt first."

He ran to the water's edge and dabbed some foam over his front. *Ah, well,* Fulla thought. He was sure to get plenty of other things on that shirt before the day was out. She watched until he had climbed the path up the cliff and disappeared. Once he was out of sight, her gaze shifted to the giants' mountain, looming out over the water in the distance, its top covered with mist. Amma lived out beyond the mountain's roots, alone in a hut on Hwala's farm. There was another beach near the farm, so why had she come all the way here? Fulla walked over to stand beside Amma. Shading her eyes with her palm, she looked out to sea again.

Again, she thought she saw a black speck, far out on the horizon. When she blinked, it was gone. Just waves, she realized, which have a habit of making themselves appear to be whales and sea monsters and longships.

She glanced sideways at Amma, at her dark hair and brows, so unlike the blond and brown and red hair of the Geats. Near Amma's ear, strands of gray mingled with the dark hair. Fulla unconsciously touched the hair above her own ear before concentrating on the horizon again.

There! She *had* seen something; she was sure of it. She squinted into the distance. Far out at sea, something bobbed on the water, winking in and out of existence as the waves pushed it from crest to trough. It might have been a bird or a piece of driftwood. Or it might have been something else.

She watched it for a long time, until the clouds had rolled over the entire sky, taking the sparkle off the water and turning it a hard metallic gray, like the color of chain mail.

"What is it?" someone beside her asked, making her jump—Elli, a girl Gunnar's age.

"Probably just a bit of wood," Fulla said. "Come, we'd best get home before it rains. Where's your mother?"

Elli pointed and Fulla shooed her off. When the girl was gone, Fulla whispered, "Amma? Do you know what it is?"

Without taking her eyes from the water, Amma quirked her lips, then moved her chin in the slightest approximation of a nod.

"Could you tell me?"

There was no response.

"Is it . . ." Fulla hesitated to say the word. "Is it raiders?"

Again, Amma said nothing.

It could be a longship full of warriors ready to sweep down and take the Geats captive, enslaving them. And like bait to lure them forward, defenseless women and children swarmed over the beach while gulls and terns screamed and swooped over their disturbed nests. How foolish she'd been, standing here doing nothing! Fulla gathered her skirts and ran. She called for the other women, trying to hurry them without causing panic. A few of them looked out at the water and, understanding her rush, began to help.

Just as the children had all been rounded up, the sound of hoofbeats from the cliff made Fulla turn in alarm. She let out her breath in relief when she realized it was her husband, Hemming, Gunnar in front of him on the horse. Behind them rode two other warriors, Dayraven and Horsa. They reined in their mounts, and she saw Gunnar pointing excitedly at the sea.

"Let's go," she said to the woman in front of her, who called out, "No pushing, Tor!" as she shepherded the children up the rocky path.

The children were safely at the top of the cliff and heading down the trail toward the stronghold, Elli in the lead, by the time Fulla reached her husband, who was still on his horse. Gunnar had dismounted. "It's a boat," he said.

She reached for her son, wrapping her arms around his chest, and turned back to look. She could see now that he was right; it was definitely a boat, but too small for a long-ship. Gunnar tried to shrug himself out of her grasp, but she held him and said, "I want you to go back to the strong-hold."

"I just got here," he protested.

"Let the boy stay," Hemming said. "It's nothing dangerous."

Fulla gave her husband a sharp look, but he was grinning at Gunnar, who capered to the other side of the horse, away from his mother.

Several of the women had stopped on the cliff to watch as the boat grew more defined. Fulla thought there might be someone in it, but it was still too far away to see clearly. The wind insisted on sending her hair into her eyes. She pushed it back and scanned the sky, now cloud-covered. The air had a heavy feel, but it didn't smell like rain. On the beach, Amma still hadn't moved, even though the tide had turned to creep back toward her. "If it's not dangerous, I'm going down to her."

"I'll come with you," Hemming said.

She shook her head and gestured toward Gunnar.

"He'll be all right." He dismounted and threw his reins to Gunnar. "Watch my horse, son."

Gunnar beamed and stroked the horse's neck.

Hemming looked up at the two younger warriors, who sat on their horses, scanning the horizon. Some wordless conversation seemed to take place among them before they both gave Hemming sharp nods.

A movement made Fulla turn toward the mountain. It was just a goat, standing on a rock not far away. It almost seemed to be watching them. Inwardly, Fulla laughed at herself and tried to calm her nerves. Then she made her way back down to the beach, Hemming behind her.

When she glanced up to check on Gunnar, she saw that many of the women had gathered on the cliff. Even some of the children had returned and stood watching from behind their mothers' skirts. Fulla frowned. It didn't seem wise for them to stay so close to the beach, but there was nothing she could do about it.

As she moved to stand beside Amma, she could see the boat more clearly. It wasn't very big. Unless they were flattening themselves against the bottom, it couldn't hold very many warriors.

She looked at Amma, whose lips were now parted. She leaned slightly forward, and her eyes were narrowed, not against the sun's glare but with what looked like eagerness. She was breathing quickly. Fulla's own breath quickened with anticipation and fear.

Pulled by the incoming tide, the boat drew nearer, rocking on the waves. As the prow dipped, Fulla got a glimpse of something inside—a head? But the prow rose again, blocking the view.

"Is there someone in the boat?" she asked Amma, her heart pounding.

Amma nodded, her eyes never leaving the water.

"Hemming?" Fulla turned to her husband to make sure he'd heard and saw his hand gripping his sword hilt. She glanced back at the cliff to find Gunnar, who was now sitting atop his father's horse. At least he could get away quickly if he needed to. But what about all the women and children who stood watching?

The craft drew nearer, near enough that she could see it was a rowboat, and not a very big one. There were no oars. Fulla swallowed, trying to quell her anxiety.

The prow rose, then dipped again. As it did, she saw something round—a shield. Hemming had seen it, too; he walked forward, unmindful of the waves splashing over his shoes.

The boat was no more than a furlong away now, but the nearer it got, the more its high sides shielded its contents from view. Those on the cliff would be able to see into it more easily, and Fulla glanced back in time to see Dayraven, one of the young warriors, dismounting from his horse.

When she turned around again, she realized she was alone; like Hemming, Amma had been drawn forward. Water rushed over Amma's shoes as a wave came in, then sucked at the bottom of her skirts as the wave rushed back out to sea.

Fulla moved forward, too, ignoring the icy water on her

ankles, keeping her eyes on the boat, on her husband, on Amma. She could hear the slap of the water against the boat's sides and see a line of barnacles attached to its wooden hull.

And then, coming in fast over the rocks, the boat was upon them. Amma rushed into waist-deep waves to grab a side of it as Hemming took the other, and Fulla found herself hauling at the prow, aware of a sharp reek floating on the salt air.

A wave pushed the boat forward, and she scrambled out of the way, bumping into Hemming in her hurry. The boat scraped over the rocks and sand, Amma and Hemming pulling at it as Fulla watched, hand to her chest in astonishment.

From the bottom of the boat, surrounded by a sword, a shield, and a chain-mail shirt, a wool blanket exposing its bare shoulders, a baby stared up at them with wide brown eyes.

Fulla looked from the baby to Amma, who was reaching for the child.

"Don't touch it!" a man cried out.

Dayraven strode toward them, his sword raised.

"It's just a baby, Dayraven," Fulla said.

"I said, don't touch it."

Fulla could see the fear on his face as he reached for Amma's arm, pulling her back from the boat.

The look Amma gave the warrior would have caused

Fulla to crumple if it had been directed at her, but Dayraven stood firm, putting himself between Amma and the boat.

"What's this, now? Why shouldn't she touch it?" Hemming asked, coming around to the other side of the boat.

"Look at it," Dayraven said. "Don't you see what it is? We can't interfere with somebody's offering to the gods— that would be sacrilege!"

Fulla turned her head just in time to see the baby screw its eyes closed, open its mouth, and begin to wail. Her heart hurt for the child, and she longed to comfort it. It must be so cold, so hungry, so afraid. But Dayraven could be right. The weapons and armor arranged around it did make it look like an offering to the gods.

"Get out of my way," Amma said, her voice a snarl. Unable to loosen Dayraven's grip from her arm, she tried to shoulder past him.

Dayraven jerked her by the arm.

"Dayraven!" Hemming said, his voice cold. "Let her go. Amma, stand with my wife."

Fulla saw Amma glare at him, but she shook off Dayraven's arm without trying to go to the boat. When she didn't move, Fulla went over and stood beside her, her eyes on her husband's.

"What are you suggesting we do?" Hemming asked Dayraven.

"It's obvious. Either the boat has to go back out to sea, or we have to kill the child."

Outrage filled Fulla and she couldn't stop herself. "Dayraven! We don't kill babies. We're Geats—we're civilized people!"

"Do you want to bring the wrath of the gods down on us?" he said.

She looked back at the boat and the baby crying in it and thought of Gunnar and his two older brothers. No, she didn't want the gods to punish the people she loved for taking something that had been sacrificed to them. But could they do it? Send the baby out onto open waters again? Feeling her eyes moisten, she looked desperately at Hemming.

Without speaking, Amma rushed for the boat. Her hands were almost to the baby when Dayraven pulled her back, his sword at her throat.

"Stop, both of you!" a voice commanded.

Fulla didn't need to turn to recognize it. She lowered herself into a curtsy as King Beowulf crunched over the sand and rocks.

"Unhand her, Dayraven. Amma, come to me, please."

Fulla watched as Dayraven dropped his sword and lowered his torso in a stiff bow. Amma straightened her shoulders. She did not curtsy. Instead, she stared the king in the eye for a long moment before she walked over to him, her shoes squelching.

"You knew the boat was coming," the king said.

She gave him the briefest of nods.

"You knew what was in it."

Again, the proud inclination of her chin.

Then the king bent his head toward Amma's and spoke to her in a voice so low that Fulla couldn't make out the words. A gust of wind whipped a tendril of Amma's dark hair from its knot, twisting it into a sinuous pattern that wound itself together with a strand of the king's hair, gray silvered with white. She answered him, her voice as quiet as his. Behind them, the baby howled.

The king raised his head and looked around him, and so did Fulla. For the first time, she realized how many people now stood on the beach, forming a half-moon around the boat. She saw the bard leaning over to empty sand from his shoe, and near him, several warriors standing alert, spears and swords gripped tight. Gunnar was still on the cliff astride his father's horse. She could tell he was pretending to be a warrior guarding the coast, and she tried not to think of what he might be about to witness—or what the gods would do if he didn't witness it.

"The gods," the king said, his voice calm and clear. People crowded closer to hear him, and Fulla held her breath.

"The gods have guided this boat to our shores. We are duty-bound to take this offering."

He strode to the boat, leaned down, and picked up the child, still in its blanket.

Fulla let out her breath in relief.

He wasn't going to have the baby killed.

As the king held the child high, Fulla could see a pendant hanging around its neck, disappearing into its wet and soiled blanket. No wonder the boat smelled so pungent. How long had the baby been on the waters? Where had it come from?

Then the king walked to Amma and placed the child in her arms. As he did, Fulla saw Dayraven drive his sword into the sand, fear and anger inscribed in his face.

"Fulla," the king said, and she looked at him, surprised. "Fulla, will you take Amma and the baby home with you?"

"No!" Amma said, and the king raised his brows.

"I'm taking him to Hwala's farm."

"No. I want him raised in the hall." To Fulla, the king's tone sounded as though he would brook no disagreement.

But Amma shook her head.

The king watched her for a moment. Then he sighed and looked back at Fulla. "Will you and your husband make sure they get to the farm safely?"

"Yes, my lord," Fulla said, her eyes wide. How did Amma get away with such behavior?

"But, Amma," the king said. "On this I won't be overruled. The boy will train in the hall during the winters, when he's old enough."

Amma didn't speak, but she didn't argue, either.

King Beowulf reached out and, very gently, covered the baby's head with his hand. It looked up at him and blinked. The king's hand slipped from the baby to take Amma's fingers in his own. "Take good care of him," he said softly.

Then he stepped back to allow Hemming and Fulla to escort Amma and the baby off the beach.

The crowd parted, and as Hemming led the way, Fulla could see dark looks and hear muttered oaths from people on either side of them. The king might have saved the baby's life, she thought, but he hadn't ensured that it would be an easy one. She feared that too many of the people watching them agreed with Dayraven.

She moved closer to Amma, reaching out to steady her, to protect her, even though Amma walked calmly forward, the baby quiet in her arms. Together, they climbed the rocky path.

ONE

FROM THE CORNER OF HIS EYE, RUNE SAW THE SCYTHE blade swing down. As he watched, horrified, it cut into Hwala's calf. Everything happened at once: Hwala yelled; Skoll turned, puzzled by the sound; and Skyn's mouth dropped open as he realized what he'd done. Then came the blood.

"Father!" Skoll cried, catching Hwala as he stumbled.

Skyn's scythe dropped to the ground.

Rune rushed forward to kneel beside his foster father.

From between clenched teeth, Hwala grunted, "Get Amma."

Almost before the words had been uttered, Rune was running, racing toward the farmhouse and the hut beyond it that he shared with Amma. *Gods, let her be there,* he prayed, his arms pumping as he skirted a boulder and pelted through the homefield, not taking the time to go around it. "Lady of the Vanir, I beg of you," he whispered as he burst through the hay. He skidded to a stop, but not fast enough to keep him from colliding with Amma.

"Sorry," he said, panting as he steadied her. "Hwala's hurt."

"I know. Where is he?"

In his sixteen winters, Rune had learned not to question how Amma knew the things she did. "The west field," he said.

She picked up the basket he'd knocked from her hand. "I'll need water."

Rune nodded and took off for the hut. When he caught up with her again, she was only halfway there. He took her basket in one hand, her arm in the other. The image of the blade hitting Hwala's leg, the blood welling around the wound, made him want to pull her into a run, but she was already moving as quickly as her age would allow.

How had it happened? They had come to the end of one row when Hwala had turned. Had he walked directly into the path of his son's blade? How had Skyn not seen him?

After what seemed an eternity, they reached the edge of the field. Across the stubble and the shocks of grain, Rune could see the curve of Skoll's shoulders as he bent over his father, who lay on the ground, fallen stalks of grain around him. Skyn stood a little distance away, his face gray, the fist of his shorter arm beating into the open hand of his longer one, over and over again, as if he wasn't aware he was doing so.

Rune helped Amma to sit on the ground beside Hwala. She shooed Skoll back and reached out to probe the wound with her fingers.

"Water," she said, and Rune crouched beside her, handing her the waterskin.

"Get away from him. I'll do it." Skoll's voice was as icy as his eyes.

Rune opened his mouth, then closed it and handed his foster brother the water. It sloshed and gurgled inside the leather bag.

Skoll gave him a look that made his meaning clear. Rune rose and backed away.

"I need goat wort," Amma said, and Skoll rifled uncertainly through the basket until she snapped, "Give me the whole thing." With one hand on Hwala's leg, she reached for a leather pouch and opened it with her teeth.

Rune clenched his fist. He would have had the bag of goat wort open by now and the leaves crushed between his fingers. Instead, Amma had to do it all herself, taking precious time. He turned his head so he didn't have to see the pain etched into Hwala's face.

Finally, as she finished tying a bandage tightly around the wound, Amma spoke to Hwala for the first time. "If it doesn't fester, you won't die."

He nodded wordlessly.

"How will we know if it festers?" Skoll asked.

"You'll know." She gathered her pouches and jars and placed them back in her basket. "You two." She gestured toward Skyn and Skoll. "Take your father home. Don't let him put any weight on it." Then she turned back to Hwala. "Bed for a few days at least. I'll come in the morning."

Skyn and Skoll helped their father stand. Rune winced when Hwala grimaced; the wound must hurt like elf-shot. Had the blade cut through the muscle?

"No weight," Amma said, and the three started for the farm, Hwala hopping on one foot while Skyn supported him on one side, Skoll on the other, their blond heads leaning close together.

Rune looked around him. The sun was already disappearing in the distant ash trees. He collected the abandoned tools, wiping the offending scythe on clean oat straw, but the blood was already dry. Tomorrow, Skyn would have to use it. He must already feel terrible, Rune thought, and seeing the blood again would make him feel worse. He kicked loose soil over the places where Hwala had bled on the earth and straw, then followed after the others.

Once they were home, Amma disappeared inside the hut while Rune ladled water from the rain barrel onto the scythe. He scraped at the blood and poured more water over it. Finally satisfied, he took it down the path and back to the stable beside the farmhouse, wiping it on his tunic to make sure it was dry. The last thing they needed was a rusty blade.

By the time he got back again, the light was almost gone. He needed to get inside, but first, he had to take care of Ollie. Ever since their other goat had died at midsummer, Ollie—the source of their milk and butter and some of their wool—had begun disappearing when it was time for milking and, worse, getting into the oat fields, ruining grain that was just ready to be harvested. They'd had to start tying her up for the night.

She'd worn a dirt ring around the stake and eaten everything within reach. Rune pulled it up and drove it into the ground close enough to the north wall of the hut, the one made of sod, that Ollie could reach the weeds and the yellow flowers that grew in it—but not so close that she could devour the roof thatch.

As he drew the rope through the stake, he heard her bell, the signal of their nightly dance; he would try to lure her in, and she would frisk just out of reach, making him laugh. He wasn't in the mood for it tonight. Without warning, he grabbed her by the horns and slipped the rope around her neck.

Ignoring her angry protests, he let himself inside, closing the door to the dark. Amma had already unrolled his pallet in front of the fire for him and set out strips of dried herring, bread, and skyr, the tasty cheese curds she made.

Lowering himself cross-legged to his pallet, his stomach growling, Rune picked up the bread, then stopped just before the loaf touched his tongue. Wearily, he rose again, ducking his head to keep from hitting the thatch and the beams that held it up. He went first to Thor's altar and then to Freyja's, leaving them both some of his bread, along with his thanks and an added prayer for Hwala's health.

Amma gave him a look of approval as he returned to his pallet.

"Will he heal?" Rune asked.

She gazed at the Freyja altar, at the stone with its carving of the goddess on it. "Too soon to tell."

He ate, spitting out an occasional pebble from the bread. They'd played a game, these past few years, of pretending Amma could cook, Rune trying to stay close when the porridge was boiling so he could stir and salt it. Before she poured them into the pot or kneaded them into loaves, he picked through the oats for grit and husks and insects she never bothered with. But during harvest season, when he was in the fields all day, there was no time for any of that.

At least her skyr was good. As he swallowed his last bite, he felt fatigue creeping over him. His eyelids fluttered shut, then open, then shut again. The prospect of tomorrow and the days that followed filled him with disquiet. How would they ever be able to get the harvest in without Hwala?

"I'll take care of the rest," Amma said. She inclined her head, signaling that he should lie down. "You sleep."

He didn't protest. Usually, the meal was followed by a lesson, a lay or wisdom poem that Amma wanted Rune to learn. Things hadn't gone well last night. He had been so tired that the words kept jumbling together in his head. Amma had snapped at him, saying he wasn't trying. Shamefully—he wished he could forget he'd done so—he'd snapped right back at her. Sometimes he wondered whether she had any idea how exhausting it was to work in the fields all day.

As he rolled away from the fire and pulled up his blanket, he could hear Amma moving around the little room, putting the lid on the dairy crock and closing the bread away from the mice, her metal bracelets clinking.

He was almost asleep when he heard the unmistakable sound of a sword being drawn from its sheath. His eyes snapped open. Then Amma's wooden stool creaked as she lowered herself onto it, and Rune's eyelids drooped again. He heard her opening her little pot of whale oil, and now he could smell its rancid odor, too. He didn't need to see her to know that Amma was dipping a rag into the pot and rubbing oil along the length of the blade, inspecting every crevice, every carving, checking for rust or dirt. He waited, listening for her song to start, first the humming and then the words, rhythmic and low.

It was the same song she always sang when she polished the sword, the one about the lady who'd lost her kinsmen in a feud. "Bitter breastcare hardened her heart," he heard before her voice dropped so low he could barely make out the words. But after all these years, he knew them as well as she did.

What he didn't know—what she would never tell him

when he asked—was why she spent so much time with the sword when she was dead set against fighting. If the king hadn't insisted on it, Rune knew Amma would never have allowed him to learn swordfighting during the winters, when the farm folk gathered in the hall. Hwala always stayed with the farm to care for the livestock and to repair tools, but ever since he'd been a boy, Rune had gone with Amma and his foster brothers to spend the winter in the hall. Like the other farmers, he was drilled in the proper use of ax and spear, but unlike them, he also learned the sword. It hardly made him popular, not with the other farm boys and not with the boys who lived in the stronghold. The ones whose fathers were warriors trained with their swords all year long, leaving him at a permanent disadvantage.

The fact that the king was always so kind to him, greeting him each winter when he arrived at the hall, asking him questions about himself, about Amma, about the farm, should have made things easier. Instead, it set him apart even more.

He pulled the blanket over his head and reached for the pendant he wore around his neck, rubbing his thumb over the marks incised in it, to calm himself. The last thing he saw before he fell into troubled dreams was the image of the scythe coming down on Hwala's leg.

In the morning, he woke to the sound of Amma's bracelets clinking as she kneaded bread on the stone before the hearth. He opened one eye and peered straight up through the smoke hole in the thatch. The sky was still gray, not yet pink. He stretched, yawned, and sat up.

"There's whey in the bowl," Amma said.

He yawned again, slurped down the whey, and pulled on his shoes.

"Will you finish the west field today?" She handed him a chunk of bread, and he nodded.

He knelt to leave a pinch of grain on the altar to Thor and then, taking a bite of the bread and ducking to keep from hitting his head on the lintel, emerged into the reddening dawn.

The cold morning air made him shiver as he headed to the farmhouse, where his foster brothers were just coming out of the door. Neither of them said anything about their father, so Rune didn't ask. He fell into step behind them.

They got to the west field just as the sun peeked over the horizon, the three of them walking silently, scythes in their hands, rakes over their shoulders. They spaced themselves out and bent to their work. By the time they were at the end of the first row, the sun had warmed the air. Normally, Rune loved this time of year, the clear blue of the sky, the honking calls of geese overhead, the crown of mist on the giants' mountain in the distance, the way insects bounded out of the oats ahead of him. But today, Hwala's absence made their every move fraught with the knowledge that they must complete the harvest without him. Their uneven number made the work harder, too; instead of pairing up, one person cutting while the other raked up the oats and gathered them into shocks, they had to work out the pattern with three. Finally, Rune moved to the far end of the field, cutting a row and then backtracking to rake it as well.

When Ula came out to the field with their midday meal, they all stopped and watched her approaching, none of them daring to speak. The bond servant seemed to understand their apprehension, because as soon as she was within shouting distance, the words "He's fine" drifted over the oats to their ears.

The tension went out of Rune's shoulders, and he laid down his rake, joining Skyn and Skoll in the shade of an elm as they waited for her. "Fine" seemed an overstatement to Rune when she told them more. "Sometimes he groans," she said, and Rune saw Skyn flinch. "It hurts him, but it hasn't festered." She handed Skoll the waterskin and took bread and cheese from her basket. "Yet."

After she left, they ate in silence, passing around the waterskin until it was empty. They hadn't gotten nearly as far as Rune had hoped; he'd assumed they would be moving on to another field by now.

Skoll stood to piss.

"Hey, watch it!" Rune said, scrabbling out of the way as a stream of urine spattered on the ground beside him. He stood as Skyn laughed.

"We know about you and the scythe last night," Skoll said. "What were you doing, putting a curse on it?"

"What?"

"Don't deny it. Ula saw you." Skoll turned toward him, his eyes narrowed. Taller than his father now, his muscles honed from hard farm labor, Skoll was the kind of person you'd want near you in a fight—unless he was on the other side. He'd never been on Rune's side. "When I'm in charge of this farm, you won't be bringing it down anymore with your curses."

"I was cleaning the blood off!" Rune said.

"We know why Skyn's blade slipped yesterday."

"It was an accident."

"If anything happens to my father . . ." He pointed a menacing finger at Rune.

Rune felt anger rising in him, and he clenched his fists.

"You want to fight, sword-boy?" Skoll said, his voice icy calm.

All of Amma's lessons about using his head instead of his fists, all of the tales she'd taught him about how feuds got started, everything fled him now except an overpowering desire to drive his knuckles into Skoll's jaw.

"Too bad you don't have your fancy sword with you," Skyn taunted as he rose to stand beside his brother. He might have been Rune's age, a winter younger than Skoll, but he was almost as strong as his brother.

"I'll fight you," Skoll said, raising his fists. "Come on."

The two of them stood like a wall. Rune stared at them, anger pounding behind his eye sockets. Then he dropped his fists and turned away.

"Coward," Skyn said.

Rune stalked across the field in silence, Skyn's word hanging in the air behind him. They'd ganged up on him before, and it never ended well for Rune. But that didn't make him any less of a weakling for walking away. He clenched his fists again, wishing he'd punched them both.

He knew why they hated him, but knowing didn't make it any easier.

His scythe was lying on the ground. He picked it up and started swinging.

By the time they finished the field, his anger had dulled. There was still time to make a start on another, but they didn't know which one Hwala had planned or where the grain was ripest.

"You check on the far field," Skoll said. "We'll try the east field. Meet us back there."

Rune looked at him. Instead of simply going back to ask Hwala, Skoll wanted him to go all the way out beyond the stream to the field that bordered Hwala's lands, and then come back to the field beside the farmhouse?

Then again, he thought, it would get him away from Skoll. He started walking.

When he got to the rocky path that led down to the stream, birds rose, chittering, from the branches. He grabbed smooth birch trunks and pulled himself along. Leaves tinged with gold and fiery red mingled with the greenery, whispering of the harsh winter to come. He crunched over wet brown pebbles and splashed into the stream, hopping from one rock to the next through the rushing water and then up the opposite bank.

He emerged from the trees into the far field, its slender stalks buzzing with insects and shining in the slanting sun. Dots of blue and red caught his eye from the flowers that wound their way into the oats.

A horned head rose out of the field, startling him. He laughed. "Ollie! What are you doing out here?"

The little brown goat came through the oats toward him, green stems and half-chewed blue flowers hanging from either side of her mouth. Rune shook his head in exasperation. Now he wouldn't just have to get back to the east field with his report, but he'd have to take Ollie back, too. He cringed at the damage she'd already done to the field.

He bent over to examine the oats for ripeness, feeling the moisture in the stalks, rolling the grain between his fingers. Ollie gave him an affectionate butt against the shoulder, then nibbled at the back of his neck.

"Hey, that tickles," he said, touching his neck as the goat pranced away. She turned to look at him, a glint of humor in her eye, a leather cord in her mouth. At the end of it dangled his pendant.

"That's mine!" Rune said. "Give it back!" He lunged, but she danced out of reach.

Thinking fast, he grabbed more of the blue flowers she'd been eating and held them out enticingly. She watched him but didn't come any nearer, so he laid them in the path and took a step away. He could tell she was tempted from the way she eyed them. But not tempted enough. Without warning, the goat turned and raced down the path away from the farm.

"Come back here!" Rune cried. His hand went to his neck, but of course the pendant wasn't there. Would she turn when she saw he wasn't following her? Drop it when she got bored? *Eat* it?

He looked at the oats in his hand. He needed to get back to the farm, not spend his time chasing a fool of a goat.

"Ollie!" he bellowed, but the goat kept running as if she were possessed. He squinted—she was already all the way to the tall runestone that marked the edge of Hwala's lands. There the path forked, the shield-hand side leading to the sea, the sword-hand path to the giants' mountain and, beyond it, to the king's stronghold. Ollie took the sword-hand path.

The pendant. It had been around his neck ever since Amma had found him when he was a baby. He had to get it back.

He took a last glance behind him, to the trees hiding the stream, the smoke rising from the farmhouse, the ash tree outside the hut he shared with Amma.

Then, oats dropping from his fingers, he ran.

TWO

TALL GRASSES WHIPPED AT RUNE'S LEGS. FAR AHEAD OF him, he could see the brown-haired goat bounding along, her white tail raised like a flag. She had to tire of the game soon, he told himself. As he ran, he scanned the ground for his pendant in case she had dropped it, but he knew he'd never find it that way. The path wasn't used often enough to keep it clear of vegetation, the way the ones around the farm were.

He glanced behind him. Skyn and Skoll would just have to start on the east field by themselves. He'd make up for it later. He'd work through tomorrow's midday meal if he had to; he wouldn't have them thinking of him as a free-loader. Skoll's words about what would happen to Rune and Amma when he was in charge of the farm were no idle threat. There was more than one reason to pray Hwala's wound wouldn't fester.

Rune wished he'd hit Skoll earlier. He could just feel the satisfying crunch of his foster brother's jawbone against his knuckles. But, no, he'd backed down, the way he always did. It was laughable how Amma was always warning him not to fight. If she had any idea of the truth—that he always took the coward's path—she would save her breath.

In the distance, Ollie stopped short and turned to look at him. Finally. As he drew closer to her, Rune slowed his pace, panting. The pendant still hung from the goat's lips. She watched him through the horizontal pupils of her brown eyes.

He stopped a spear length away. "Come here, Ollie," he said, forcing cheer he didn't feel into his voice. He held out his hand invitingly.

She lifted one delicate hoof as if to take a step toward him.

He smiled and kept his tone low and soothing. "There's a girl."

Without warning, she bolted, racing away again. Rune pelted after her. She was close enough that he knew he could catch her. He threw himself forward, his hands grabbing for her legs—but she slipped out of his fingers.

"Ollie!" Frustration coursed through him, and he picked himself up off the ground, brushing dirt from his elbows and staring after her.

He should just go back to the farm and hope she would

follow; he knew he should. But if he did, he might never see the pendant again. He *had* to get it back. He started running again.

As he followed Ollie, he thought about what would happen if Skoll kicked them out. No farm he knew of could afford to take in two extra mouths. Could they stay in the stronghold? Amma hated it there—"court intrigue and corruption," she always scoffed when they got to the king's hall in the winters. She might not like it, but Rune thought he would. If he could practice the sword year-round, he might get better at it. Good enough to be one of the king's hearth companions?

Ketil Flat-Nose, his only friend in the hall, had been made a hearth companion last winter. Rune imagined himself joining Ketil and the king's other warriors. If he could practice as much as they did, maybe he could learn to dance with sword and spear the way Dayraven did—Dayraven, who had killed the wild ox single-handedly. Rune and Ketil had counted Dayraven's gold armbands, gifts from the king for the warrior's prowess. No other warrior wore as many, not even Finn, the king's shoulder companion, who taught the boys in the hall.

Rune pictured himself riding alongside Dayraven and Ketil as they patrolled the kingdom's borders, fighting off raiders, defending the land, hunting the bear and the wild boar. They'd gallop into the stronghold, their harnesses jingling in time to the horses' hoofbeats. In the hall, they'd report to the king before they relaxed on the mead benches, and bond servants would bring them ale and steaming slices of meat, while the bard told tales of heroes and the women watched, their distaffs in their arms, their spindles sinking to the floor.

His pace slowed as he imagined Wyn, Finn's fair-haired daughter, looking up from her thread-making to ask him if it was really true that he had slain a water monster, just like the king had done all those years ago. He was about to tell her how he'd been kept underwater so long a lesser man would have drowned, when a glint on the ground caught his eye. His pendant!

He grabbed it. The leather thong was slimy with Ollie's saliva, but other than that, the pendant was undamaged. He wiped it on his tunic and tied it around his neck.

Now, where was Ollie? He looked around him, surprised at how far he'd come, at how dim the light was. Ahead of him, the giants' mountain loomed, the last of the sun's rays illuminating its cliffs. Before it stood the crag, the promontory looking out over the water, the only part of the mountain where humans dared venture.

Rune gazed behind him. Shadow covered the valley. The sun had already dropped behind a line of distant trees. Hwala's farm lay beyond those trees, far out of sight. He shouldn't be out here at this time of evening. Nobody should. It wasn't safe—not for him and not for Ollie. He had to find her; they couldn't afford to lose another goat.

A slight noise made him turn forward again.

A man stepped out from behind a boulder.

Rune's breath caught in his throat, and his hand went to the dagger on his belt.

"I'm no harm to you, boy," the man said, gesturing with his eyes at Rune's knife.

He was probably right; Rune could see that in a glance. The stranger wore no weapons, and his shoes, like his stained tunic, were torn and ragged, while the edges of his short cloak were frayed to a feathery fringe. His slight shoulders were stooped, and his thin strands of greasy hair made him look far from young. Yet he kept one hand hidden, holding it behind him. Rune stared at him. Who was he? There were no strangers here.

He could feel the man looking him over.

"Where'd you get that pretty thing around your neck?" There was something about the man's tone that made Rune take a step back. He reached for the pendant and shoved it under his shirt.

"Don't you speak, boy?" The man bent down and picked up a stone.

Rune pulled his dagger from his belt and dropped into a fighting stance, every muscle taut, every lesson he'd learned in the hall ringing in his skull. *Whatever you do, don't lose your nerve,* Finn always said. *Assess your opponent. Don't let him surprise you.*

Rune steadied his breath and shifted onto the balls of his feet, watching the man's hidden hand, and readied himself to whirl out of range.

The stranger appeared not to notice. Instead, he

brushed a place in the dirt clear of pebbles and weeds. Then, with the stone, he scratched marks in the dirt.

ᛈᛁᚷᛚᚠᚠᚤ

Rune straightened, staring. The marks were the same runes that were etched into his pendant.

Still crouching, the man squinted up at him. "I said, where'd you get that silver thing?"

"It's mine," Rune said.

"Whose neck did you cut it off of?" The man stayed on his haunches.

"Nobody's. It's mine. It's always been mine."

"Always is an awfully long time, boy."

"It was my father's." He spoke the words defiantly, as if he knew the truth of them. Why was he even talking to this man? Strangers had no rights here.

The man laughed, a harsh bark with no pleasure in it, and Rune could see how sharply pointed his teeth were, as if they'd been filed. "Your father's. And who might he have been?"

"It's no concern of yours."

The man stood. "Is that what you think?" Suddenly, he lunged at Rune, his hand reaching for the pendant.

Rune was ready. He pushed the man, sending him sprawling. As he danced on the balls of his feet, preparing for the man's next move, he heard a bleat. Ollie stood on the path to the crag.

He looked at the man lying in the dirt. Then he looked back at Ollie. She was so close. He ran.

Behind him, the stranger laughed, and Rune glanced back to see him still sitting on the ground. In the man's hand, he could see a glint of gold from whatever it was he had held behind his back.

Rune kept going up the crag path—he wouldn't let Ollie get away this time. He scrambled up the steep slope, slipping on loose rocks and grabbing bushes to haul himself along.

By the time he reached the top, he was out of breath and the sun was almost gone. In the half-light, wind whipped his hair into his eyes, fingering at his clothes and drying his sweat. Where was Ollie? He scanned the flat promontory, but there was no sign of her. Where could she have gone? Surely not up the mountain.

It was foolhardy for him to be here, a place no one should ever be at twilight, the Between Time, when spirits roamed freely. Giants owned the mountain—if Ollie had ventured up it, he would have to leave her to her fate. Humans had no business here, not even on the crag, at this time of day.

"Ollie!" he called, but he heard no bell, no answering bleat.

He picked up a stone and gripped it in his fist, then

threw it hard. It skittered across the shale, sending up a shower of rocks. He'd come all the way up here, and for what?

A booming sound startled him, making Rune look over his shoulder. The mountain slopes loomed black and forbidding behind him. The noise made his skin crawl.

He looked forward again. Surely a goat wouldn't fall off a cliff, would she? When he ventured far enough forward to see over the edge, the wind grew stronger, toying with him, threatening to send him over the side. Far below, the dark sea curled and crashed into white foam on the rocks. From where he stood, he could see no goat. Instead, he gazed at the two parts of the kingdom, divided by the mountain's roots, Hwala's isolated farm lost in the distant west and the more populous eastern section dotted with farms and fields. Beyond them, swathed in autumn mist, lay the stronghold and the king's golden hall.

Rune turned his back to the wind and listened for Ollie's bell, fingering his pendant as he did so. The stranger had seen it for the space of a breath, hardly long enough to read the runes, let alone commit them to memory. How had he been able to draw them in the dirt? It was as if he knew more about the pendant than Rune did. Just who was the man, anyway?

He should have challenged him, or fought him, or done *something*, instead of chasing after a stupid goat who was nowhere to be seen.

The stranger could be anybody, a harmless exile seeking

a new ring-giver, a leader he could follow. But he could just as easily be a warrior in disguise or a spy for the vengeance-seeking Shylfings. And Rune had let him go. Could he still catch him, if he ran after him now? He pictured himself subduing the man, then leading him, hands bound at his back, into the king's golden hall, all the king's hearth companions watching Rune with newfound respect. He imagined Ketil grinning him a greeting the way he used to when they were still boys training together. He could see Dayraven giving him a gruff nod of approval, the warmth in his eyes secretly welcoming Rune into the king's warband. And the king—Rune could see the old man stepping forward to thank him for his courage.

The booming sound came again. And again, there was nothing. Nothing except the relentless wind and the fear hammering through his chest. He tried not to think of the tales Amma had told him about mountain giants and their dealings with humans they caught on their lands. Sometimes they let the humans go.

Beneath his shoes, the ground seemed to tremble. Thunder rolled and rumbled. Only it couldn't be thunder, because the twilit sky still glowed blue and clear.

The earth shook again. He felt it through the soles of his feet, into his bones. It could be giants. Had they seen him? The skin on the back of his neck prickled, and now an acrid smell burned his throat, making him cough. His eyes stung and watered and his nose began to run.

Goat or no goat, he had to get out of here. *Now.*

He turned for the path—and stopped, eyes wide in horror. Something was coming toward him, some monstrous shape, some *thing* was rushing at him, flying through the air. A silent scream rose in his gorge, and again he tried to run, but it was too late. The thing was almost upon him.

He threw himself to the ground, covering his head with his arms. Hot wind battered his body, and a roaring filled his ears, deafening him. Dust swirled in the darkness as the thing blotted out the sky, the world. He was choking; he couldn't breathe. The biting smell was filling his lungs, his mouth. He was burning—he could feel the hair being seared off his arms, the clothes off his back. It was directly above him, so close he couldn't tell whether it was touching him, consuming him with its heat. On and on it came, its thunderous noise obliterating all other sound.

He screwed his eyes shut, cowering, whimpering in terror, tears and snot wetting his face.

This was death, and he hated himself for meeting it this way. Shame mingled with fear, and somewhere deep in his mind, he felt sorry for all that he would never become. Now he would never even find out who he was.

Amma! he cried out silently, and lay trembling, waiting for the final blow, the pain that would pierce his body.

He waited.

Nothing happened.

Slowly the noise and heat died away. Rune lay listening to the quiet settling around him, the scorched weeds crackling with heat, the wind—now a mere breeze—nosing around the rocks.

Gingerly, he raised his head. He was alive.

He was still alone on the crag below the mountain. His skin felt raw, but his clothes weren't burned after all.

He wiped his face on his sleeve and looked around him. In the east, golden light flickered in the air like lightning.

Still shaking too hard to stand, he raised himself to his knees, trying to comprehend what he was seeing.

Above a farm, a black shape rent the sky. Like a dark ribbon blowing in a breeze, it undulated through the air, then straightened and shot toward the farmhouse. Fire streaked from it. The thatched roof blazed in sudden flames, and two tiny figures raced from the door. The thing wheeled and turned, beating heavy wings and retching forth more fire. Both figures fell.

Rune's body turned to ice. It was the worst thing he could imagine. A dragon.

Someone had awoken a dragon.

Another roof glowed orange. Rune watched in fascinated horror, unable to turn away.

The dragon wheeled lazily through the sky, turning again, beating its wings once, twice, then gliding. Where would it go next?

Amma! Rune staggered to his feet. He had to warn her.

A field ready for harvest went up in flame.

He stopped, staring at it. The whole eastern country-side would soon be ablaze, most of the kingdom's grain for the coming year. Beyond those farms lay the stronghold. Someone had to tell the king!

The dragon soared past another farm, wide out over the eastern valley. Hwala's farm—and Amma—lay to the west, on the other side of the mountain from the dragon.

Another field blazed up and then another as the dragon casually exhaled its fiery breath.

He had to tell the king.

Whispering a plea to the gods, Rune turned, slipping over loose scree as he made his way down from the crag. As he ran, he glanced toward the west. The dragon wasn't anywhere near Hwala's farm. Amma would be safe.

THREE

UNDER THE SHADOW OF THE MOUNTAIN, DARKNESS CAME
fast. As he ran, Rune glanced behind him at every noise.
Over and over he chanted a prayer to Thor, the Hammer-
Wielder, to guard him. No one should be out in the dark
this way, especially with a dragon abroad.

A stone caught his foot, tripping him. He went down
hard, palms hitting the dirt, and lay still, breathing heavily,
feeling his stinging hands, listening for noises on the wind.
Where was the dragon? Winging silently over him, preparing to strike? He sniffed, testing the air for the creature's
acrid, choking odor. Instead, the sharp scent of fir trees
filled his nose.

If he had a horse, he could get to the king before the
darkest hour of the night, but he had no horse, only his two

feet, a dagger, and his lungs full of air. He raised himself and started running again.

The darkness deepened. No moon offered itself as a beacon, and he had to judge his way by the greater blackness of the mountain and the feel of it looming on his shield-hand side, reminding him of the giants. Did they descend at night to stalk the forests and the marshes? On he ran into the gloom, gulping air, forcing himself to keep going, his shoes pounding too loudly into the earth, alerting anything that cared of his presence.

Later, when a stitch in his side grew more painful than he could bear, he slowed to a halt, hands on his knees, to rest, to breathe. As his ragged gasps grew quieter, he began to hear the night sounds that surrounded him, pressing toward him. In the distance, a wolf howled, raising its voice in a long wail. He shuddered. If wolves found him, or giants, or the dragon, he was dead.

Nearby, something sighed in the darkness, a sound like breathing. He whirled and heard a whirring sound almost inside his ear. Barely stopping himself from crying out, he fled forward into the night.

As he came out of the firs, he could see something glowing far in the distance. Fire from the dragon—or was it the eerie flames people sometimes saw in the marshes? Had he gone the wrong way? No, the ground felt solid beneath his feet, and he couldn't smell the rancid, rotting stench of the bogs.

He kept running, stopping when he could push himself

no farther, then running again—tripping and righting himself and falling once more until his palms were bloody—asking the Thunderer for protection, for the right road to the king.

He lost all sense of time. No stars guided his way. The night was as endless as his path. Surely he should be there by now. When he went to the stronghold during the winters, they hitched the horse to the sleigh and rode or skied alongside. It couldn't have taken this long to get there, he was certain.

On he went, through stands of ash and elm, branches tearing at his clothes, up and over a rise that robbed him of his breath and made him skid his way downward, losing his footing before catching himself again.

Every step brought new terrors. He felt eyes watching him. What kinds of creatures were out in the night? Would they let him pass?

Fear made him keep going, but even fear couldn't keep him running forever. He faltered, gasping for air, his strength almost gone. He blinked. In his exhaustion, his eyes played tricks on him, making shapes in the darkness.

He blinked again. It wasn't trickery. The night was ending. The sky looked less black than gray, and boulders and bushes began to take on ghostly forms in the mist. He lifted his eyes and froze.

In the distance, something towered, a dark shape, monstrously big. He squinted, trying to understand what he was seeing.

A giant. It stood directly in his path.

He dared not breathe. If he moved, it might see him. Cold sweat trickled down his back, mingling with the hot sweat of exertion. More than anything, he wanted to turn, to hide, to bury himself behind some rock. Turning tail was what he was best at, after all, he thought grimly. But he couldn't. Not this time. Not after he'd come this far, when the message was this important. Too many lives hung by a thread, ready to be snipped off by the witch-women if he did nothing to save them. The king had to know about the dragon before it was too late.

Steeling himself, gripping his dagger tight, he took a step, then another, forcing himself to creep toward the giant. Fear walked with him, clenching his chest.

Closer he came, and closer, but the giant didn't move.

Had it seen him yet? Was it toying with him, waiting until he was near enough before it attacked?

Another step, and still it didn't stir.

Hope gleamed like sunrise. Maybe it was sleeping. Maybe he could slip past it without being seen.

Two more steps, and another. He could see a giant arm held high.

A voice called out, a harsh cry, and he jumped back, his heart in his throat.

It had seen him.

The voice called again, a throaty caw.

Rune almost dropped his dagger as he staggered in

relief, drawing in breath after breath of sweet air. It was no giant—it was a tree. And not just any tree; it was Thor's Oak, in the Feasting Field near the king's stronghold.

The raven cawed again, and now a second voice joined it. Rune let the sound wash over him as his fear fled.

Then he groaned. If this was the Feasting Field, he'd come too far by at least a mile-mark. In the dark, he had missed the path that led to the king's hall.

Weariness made him sink to the ground, his muscles jumping with fatigue, his chin bowing to his chest. Sleep. He craved sleep, and water, and food. But when he closed his eyes, images of dragonfire, of farms and fields burned to ashes, played against his lids. He opened them and remembered his prayer to the Hammer-Wielder, who had guarded him through the night and brought him to his sacred tree.

Rune stood.

The sky grew lighter, and by the time he had found the proper path, the mist had lifted. Squaring his shoulders, he turned down it.

What would he say to the king? *My lord, a calamity is upon us.* No, that sounded pompous. *Dear King, the time has come for men to honor their mead-hall boasts.* Bah. Even worse.

In the distance, across a grassy plain, he could just make out the dark shapes of buildings. Beyond them lay the king's golden hall. When the sun rose, its burnished wooden gables would gleam like fire. Rune had seen it before, but only in the winter. If he could make himself go just a step or two faster, he would see it again.

The comforting smell of wood smoke filled his nostrils, and his stomach grumbled. He hoped somebody would give him breakfast.

He passed a group of silent houses, then a farmshed, then a barn. It all looked unfamiliar to him—he'd never seen it without a cover of snow. The path turned into a rough road with wooden buildings on either side, and ahead he could see a gathering of people, men and women and children, standing in the road a few furlongs in front of him, and beyond them a high, dark barn against the gray sky.

What was going on?

He kept walking, and as he did, a figure stepped out of the group, a tall, white-haired man with a fur-trimmed cloak clasped about his stooped shoulders, a long sword sheathed by his side. He walked several steps with his head down, as if deep in thought. Then he looked up. Rune could feel the man watching him from under bushy white brows.

His mouth went dry, although he couldn't imagine it being any drier. He kept going, his eyes held by the man's fierce blue ones, eyes barely dimmed by age. Rune was vaguely aware of the murmuring of the crowd and the smell of smoke, but he felt trapped by those eyes.

A few steps now, just a few steps, he thought, and then he dropped to his knees.

The man reached out and covered Rune's bowed head with his hand. Rune could feel its warmth penetrating his scalp. The hand lifted and touched his shoulder, signaling him to rise.

"My lord, King Beowulf," Rune said, his voice gravelly with nervousness and fatigue.

The old king looked at him, and this time, Rune could see the tears glinting in his eyes. A great surge of love for the old man filled him, and gratitude for the kindness the king had always shown him, ever since Rune could remember.

Then, as the bloody sun pierced the gloom, the king turned. Rune followed his gaze and saw a beam of light hit the dark building he'd taken to be a barn.

It was no barn. It was the king's golden hall, its timbers scorched and smoking.

"The dragon," Rune whispered.

King Beowulf turned back to him.

"I'm too late." Rune's head dropped, and the full weight of his weariness fell over him, making him stagger.

The king caught his arm, steadying him. "Rune," he said. "There was nothing you could have done. Against a dragon, no warning can help. And we were warned."

A movement caused Rune to look toward the crowd. A man stepped out of it—the stranger from the path by the crag. He met Rune's eyes and barked his humorless laugh. Then one of the king's guards jerked on his arm and led him away.

Before Rune was allowed to leave, the king questioned him. But first he was taken to a bench in a nearby house, where a bond servant brought him water and bread and a wedge of salty cheese to sink his teeth into. In his exhaustion, he found himself saying more than he wanted to, admitting not only that he'd been chasing Ollie, but also that he had been on the crag at half-light, when no man should be there.

"That was courageous," the king said.

"Foolhardy, more like," said a fair-haired man with a mail coat and sword. Finn, chief of the king's hearth companions, who drilled Rune and the other boys in warcraft during the long winter months when farmwork ceased. In Geatland, every warrior became a farmer at harvest's height, and when enemy spears glinted on the horizon, every farmer a warrior.

The king turned to Finn. "And was I foolhardy when, as a youth, I fought nine sea monsters all at the same time?"

"Well, no, my king."

"Rather, say yes, Finn," the king said, "for foolhardy I certainly was. But had I not been, how would I have learned what I needed to know to fight the sea wolf, Grendel's mother? And had young Rune not been on the crag at twilight, how would he be able to tell us about the dragon?"

Finn bowed his head in acquiescence, a half-smile playing on his lips. Rune saw the look he flashed at the king and wondered if the two men had had this conversation before.

Both men glanced into the corner, and Rune realized a third man sat in the shadows. The bard. Rune shuddered. The man might have been the kingdom's knowledge-keeper, honored for his wisdom and the vast wordhoard stored in his memory, but he made Rune nervous even when he wasn't being watched by the man's single eye; the other was gone, leaving a dark hole in his face. The bard's neatly clipped beard and rich clothes somehow made the missing eye seem worse, as if it could *see* you. And worst of all, he said nothing, just stared at Rune and stroked his beard with his thumb.

The king turned back to Rune. "We were asleep when the dragon fired the hall. We shouldn't have been, but we were asleep." He closed his eyes briefly, and Rune was reminded of his great age, some eighty winters or more, Amma said. "I didn't yet understand the slave's message. Now I do."

Rune looked at him, but the king didn't explain, only shook his head. The stranger he had seen by the crag was a slave?

Finn took over. "We didn't see the dragon up close the way you did, Rune."

Rune's mouth fell open. He closed it quickly and swallowed his bread. Now the king would know the depth of his cowardice, how he had lain groveling on the rocks, weeping with terror and thinking he was dead. He hadn't seen the dragon any closer than the king had.

He felt the king watching him, and heat rose to his face. He lowered his gaze to the wooden table before him. In it, a knothole patterned like a great eye stared at him, accusing.

"Not many have survived being so close to a dragon," the king said. "Even Sigmund, the great dragon-slayer— what is it they say about his breeches, Finn?"

"Less dry than a fish's cloak, or so I've heard."

Their joke made Rune feel even worse. He might not have pissed himself, but what did it matter? Everyone knew what a coward he was, but even Skyn and Skoll, who saw it every day, would have been impressed by the new level of cowardice he had shown up there on the crag. "I—I didn't see much, my lord," he said.

"Of course you didn't," Finn said. "Only the greatest of heroes could simply stand by and watch a dragon when it was that near."

In the corner, the bard made a noise. Maybe he was just clearing his throat, but it sounded like derision. Rune saw the king glance at him before he added to Finn's words.

"There's something, it's told," he said, "that freezes a man's blood to its marrow when a dragon's overhead. The old tales say even seasoned warriors aren't spared, that they're filled with terror."

It was as if the king and Finn had seen him writhing in

horror, thinking he was dying, as the dragon passed over him. He knew they were trying to make him feel better, but it wasn't working. Both men knew what a coward he was. So did the bard. Everybody knew.

But he had come here for a reason: to tell the king about the dragon. He might have been too late to warn the king and to save the golden hall, but he could tell him everything that had happened. He owed the king the truth, at the very least.

Rune took a deep breath, then looked up to meet the king's eyes.

FOUR

RUNE JERKED AWAKE. HE HADN'T MEANT TO FALL ASLEEP. He'd only closed his eyes to convince Finn's wife, Thora, that he would get the rest she insisted on before he started for home. How late was it? Light filtered through chinks in the wall, telling him that at least he hadn't slept the whole day through. All of his muscles still throbbed from last night's journey, but he ignored them and leapt from the pallet. He had to get home as fast as he could. The dragon was still out there. He had to warn Amma, even if he'd been too late to save the king's hall.

The king. As he pulled on his shoes, he remembered how gentle King Beowulf had been as Rune had laid bare his cowardice in the face of the dragon. He groaned in embarrassment. If the king had been harsher, less understanding, it might have been easier. It had been a long time since the king was Rune's age—what did he know of the needs of a half-boy, half-man like him? King Beowulf might have been misunderstood as a boy, long thought to be without promise—this was one of Amma's favorite stories about him, one she'd told countless times as she sat working her whalebone weaving sword through the threads on her loom—but he'd proven himself so thoroughly a hero that the people who doubted him had become laughingstocks.

"What you have seen is of great value to me," the king had said to Rune, and Rune had looked away. What he had seen was the ground beneath him and the insides of his eyelids—the vision of a coward. Of what value was that to anybody?

He stood, eased the door open just enough to see that no one was in the courtyard, then slipped through.

"Rune!" The voice came from behind him.

He stopped. Thora couldn't make him stay, could she? What right did she have? He had to leave; he had to get to the farm. Gathering his arguments, he turned.

A girl stood watching him. Wyn.

"I—I thought you were your mother," he stammered, feeling his neck grow warm. He had known Wyn for years; she was one of the people who gathered in the king's hall in the winters when her father led the weapons training. And for years, he'd blushed like a girl and stumbled over his words whenever she was near. Like the last time he'd spoken to her—the memory of the way he'd reddened and stuttered made him cringe. Skyn and Skoll had seen it, and they'd hooted at him, right in front of Wyn. Worst of all, he'd seen her hide a smile behind her hand. He hoped she didn't remember any of it, but, of course, she must. How could anyone have forgotten?

"Are you leaving?" she asked, swinging her long yellow braid behind her back.

"I *have* to. I have to warn Amma—" he started, but she held up her hand to stop him.

"Did anybody tell you about the horse?"

He looked at her, confused, willing the heat in his face and neck to cool.

"I didn't think so. Come on." She turned to go, then looked back to where Rune still stood, watching her. "Hurry, before my mother sees you."

That was all he needed to hear. As he caught up, she said, "There's a horse for you—from your farm."

Rune raised his eyebrows. There was only one horse on the farm. What could it possibly be doing here?

Before he could ask, she silenced him with a finger to her lips. He followed her gaze and saw a woman with a distaff tucked under her arm, standing with her back to them. Thora, Wyn's mother.

Wyn pulled him into a narrow lane and hurried down it. "We'll take the long way. My mother means well, but I knew you'd want to get home," she whispered.

The low wooden buildings they passed surrounded the still-smoking hall. As Rune gazed around him, he realized that despite how close all the structures were to each other, only the king's magnificent mead hall had burned. The knowledge chilled him: the dragon wasn't some mindless monster. It had known what it was doing.

He pictured the inside of the hall, the king's raised dais; the images of gods and giants and monsters painted on the wooden walls and carved into the massive beams that held up the roof; the bright banners swaying high overhead; the long tables lining the fire pit, where men sat telling stories or boasting over their mead; the benches on which warriors often slept at night, especially those who had drunk too heavily or who had early-morning guard duty. Had any of them been there last night?

He sucked in his breath. "Wyn?"

He felt her looking at him, but he kept his eyes on the hall, trying not to get flustered. "Did anyone—" He took a breath and started again. "Was anyone hurt last night?"

A brief glance at her face revealed the truth. She turned away, but not before Rune saw the tears rising to her eyes. He braced himself for the answer.

"Five of the king's hearth companions died." Her voice was steady, but Rune could see her jaw clenching. "My uncle Brand was one of them." This time she couldn't hide the tears in her voice. She swallowed hard and then said, almost as if she were chanting a lay, "Modi, Thorgrim, Ragnar, Beorc the Red."

Rune caught his breath. Brand and Ragnar? Besides Finn and Dayraven, they were two of the kingdom's best warriors. The others were almost as good, especially Thorgrim, who had once single-handedly held off three Shylfing raiders before reinforcements arrived. Rune pictured good-natured Beorc the Red sitting at the mead bench, roaring with laughter at one of his own jokes. He remembered the time he'd seen Modi, a quiet man with a deadly sword, leading a troop of spearmen back from a winter patrol. The respectful way the men had watched Modi had impressed Rune as much as the look of Modi's boar-crested helmet with its fearsome face mask, his eyes glittering through its slits.

Then he realized that Wyn hadn't mentioned her older brothers. Surely they hadn't been in the hall. Before he could ask, she spoke again. "I suppose we should thank the Shylfings that more didn't die."

Thank the enemy Shylfings? He glanced at her, puzzled.

"There was only a small guard at the hall. All the other troops were out riding the borders, looking for Shylfing raiders. My brothers and my cousin Bear are with them."

Rune winced. The news of his father's death would be waiting for Bear when he returned.

"Through here," Wyn said.

His eyes widened as she led him into a stable. Despite the dimness, he could tell from the silence that almost every stall was empty. "Did the dragon kill the horses, too?"

"Anybody who wasn't already out looking for Shylfings is hunting the dragon," she said, then added, "That slave, he's up to no good. He showed up in the middle of the night on this horse." She turned to him. "They say it came from your farm."

He looked at the horse. "Hairy-Hoof! How did you get here?" The farm horse whinnied in recognition, and Rune rubbed the animal's nose in delight. He didn't know why it felt so good to see the familiar black and white horse. Hairy-Hoof seemed to feel the same way and nuzzled Rune's ear.

"So it *is* from your farm," Wyn said. "Why would they give that slave a horse?"

"I . . ." Rune didn't know what to say. "I don't think they would. Not Hwala—not during the harvest."

"Well, he was riding it," she said. She turned, then looked back. "Ride safe," she said over her shoulder as she left the stable.

A feeling of warmth flushed through him, and he stared at the stable door, allowing the image of her and the sound of her words to linger. "Ride safe," he whispered before he recalled his rush to get home. He hurried Hairy-Hoof into the yard, checking her over as he did; then he saddled her quickly, mounted, and took the path for home.

As he rode, Rune fingered the silver pendant he wore around his neck and thought about the stranger—the slave. He knew Hwala would never have lent out Hairy-Hoof at harvest time. Either the slave was no stranger at all, or, more likely, he'd stolen the horse. Who was he?

Hairy-Hoof cantered along the path. Rune didn't want

to push her too much; he didn't know how hard the slave had ridden her the previous night. Still, he couldn't quell his anxiety, his desire to be home. Hairy-Hoof must have felt the tension in his legs, because she picked up the pace.

Ahead of him to the right, the mountain loomed, and he cast a nervous glance toward it. At any minute, the dragon could emerge again. He shuddered and looked away.

The pendant felt cold against his skin. He scratched his fingernail into its markings. He didn't know what they meant, just that they were runes and that he was named for them. For them and because *rune* meant "a secret, a mystery," which was something Rune had always been.

He couldn't remember what came before he had washed ashore in Geatland in the little boat. He thought he might be able to remember the feel of wool against his cheek and the sound of waves slapping against the craft's sides, but he wasn't sure. Amma said he hadn't been old enough to walk when she'd found him, alone and naked in the boat, surrounded by a sword, a warrior's round shield, and a coat of mail—with the pendant around his neck.

If it hadn't been for the king, Amma said, he would have been killed or set out on the whaleroad in the boat again, left to drown or starve or come to some other shore. Amma hadn't told him, but he'd heard that Dayraven had wanted to kill him. Dayraven wasn't the only one who thought that letting him live would bring a curse on the kingdom.

"The king himself lifted you from the boat," Amma had told him more than once. "He held you in one hand, his sword in the other, and said, 'Whoever plans to take this child's life will have to take mine first.'"

"Why?" Rune had asked her. "Why did the king save me?"

Amma had looked at him, and Rune felt himself falling into the depths of her gaze. She knew things that other people didn't. Long before anyone showed up, Amma would know that Embla, from Sigurd's farm, or one of the women who lived past the ash grove was making her way toward the hut to have a dream interpreted or to beg for a potion for a love gone wrong. Once, Embla had told Rune that on the day he washed ashore, Amma had stood staring out at the waves as if she was waiting for something. "For you, it turned out," Embla said. Whenever Rune asked Amma about it, though, she turned the subject back to the king.

"He protected you because he remembers the legends, same as I do," Amma said.

As if that were an answer. But when Rune asked her to explain, she just shook her head. "Ask the bard if you want to know." She knew as well as he did that a boy like him wouldn't have the courage to question the one-eyed poet.

The king might have saved his life, but he could do nothing to free Rune from people's suspicion or their ridicule. Skyn and Skoll had only been mewling crib-children when the little boat came ashore, but that didn't stop them from telling Rune he'd been a shit-covered baby whose own mother didn't want him. The fact that they were probably right made their taunts cut deeper. And they were sure to repeat loudly in Rune's hearing whatever Dayraven or others said about Rune bringing a curse on the kingdom.

It had been years since anyone had mentioned the curse, and Rune hoped Dayraven had forgotten it. During weapons training, he had tried, without much luck, to impress the warrior, hoping to show him how much of an asset he could be to the houseguard. Fortunately, Dayraven rarely stayed in the hall during Finn's training sessions.

A thought struck Rune, making him jerk on the reins and causing Hairy-Hoof to toss her head and whinny. "Sorry, girl," he whispered, stroking her neck. "Do you need a rest?" He swung himself down from her back to run alongside for a while. As he did, he looked sideways at the mountain. Maybe Dayraven had been right. Maybe he *was* cursed. Could he have somehow awoken the dragon by going to the crag at the Between Time? There was so much that he didn't know about himself.

Amma knew, though; he was sure of it. At least, she knew more than she had ever told him. He had seen the way she held back when she told tales before the fire, how she wove words together until they came too close to his story. Then she stopped or took a turn into a different tale, one she'd be sure to make him learn.

Rune gripped the pendant. When he got back to the

farm, he'd ask her to tell him. No, he'd *make* her tell him. He had to know. He was old enough to be a warrior; it was time she stopped treating him like a child.

It was half-light by the time he reached the runestone that marked the edge of Hwala's lands—the same time the dragon had emerged a day before. As stiff as Rune's body was, he felt his shoulders stiffen further. He scanned the sky and kept his ears taut, sure that every sound he heard was a dragon, not the call of a bird settling in for the night.

He was glad to be near the end of the journey. Despite the trouble he'd be in from Hwala for everything he'd done, he'd welcome a warm meal and his own pallet across the fire from Amma's. He shook his head as he reviewed his transgressions: losing Ollie, going to the crag at twilight, going straight to the king instead of to the farm. He'd probably even be blamed for Hairy-Hoof's absence instead of praised for bringing her back. Even so, it would be good to be home.

He turned onto the path toward the farm. Recognizing it, Hairy-Hoof pricked up her ears and picked up the pace, eager for oats.

Ahead of him, Rune could see the line of birches that marked the stream. Beyond that, he could barely make out the farm buildings, dark in the distance. A low ray of the setting sun caught something—he couldn't tell what—and made it gleam like flame.

The smell of smoke reached Rune's nose just as Hairy-Hoof neighed nervously and pulled up short. Rune narrowed his eyes. Before the stream lay the far field—blackened by fire, wisps of smoke rising from it like ghosts.

The air drained from his lungs. He kicked Hairy-Hoof's sides, urging her into a gallop.

He was too late.

The dragon had found the farm.

FIVE

HE FOUND ULA FIRST. HWALA'S BOND SERVANT LAY FACE-down in the stream, her bucket beside the bank, her back blackened by fire. Gently, he turned her face toward his, but he didn't need to see her cloudy eyes, her blank stare, to know she was dead. The smell of her charred hair made his gorge rise. He swallowed and laid her body beside the bank, out of the water. Not allowing himself to think, he raced for Hairy-Hoof.

Small flames danced, wraithlike, in the charred timbers of the farmhouse and stable as Rune approached. He fumbled as he dismounted, his eyes searching for what he dared not find.

"Amma!" His voice cracked as he cried her name into the stillness. No answer came.

Just inside the farmhouse ruins, he stumbled on a

figure, a human body, and his hand rose to his mouth in horror. It could be Skyn or Skoll, he couldn't even tell—the figure was so badly burned. Could it be Amma?

He reached out his hand toward a glint of metal, then snatched it back, gasping—it was like sticking his hand in a fire's glowing embers. He looked again at the metal. It was a dagger, and now he could see the wolf shape etched into it. Skoll's dagger.

Rune shut his eyes tightly against the smoke, against the sight, and screamed, "Amma!"

In the answering silence, he heard only low flames licking gently at what was left of the beams.

He stepped around the body, the hot coals scorching his feet through his shoes.

Farther inside the farmhouse, Hwala lay on the floor near what had been his pallet, one leg pulled up as if he'd been trying to protect his wound from the flames.

The building wasn't large. He stared around fearfully but saw no one else.

Skyn he found in what was left of the stable, a beam across his chest, his clothes burned off, his shorter left arm stretched toward something he would never reach. Beside him lay a dead goat. The smell of its charred flesh made Rune's mouth water incongruously. Or was it Skyn's flesh?

A sound he didn't recognize rose out of his chest and escaped his lips, a whimper of dread. If all the others were dead . . .

He looked across the homefield, over the blackened hay, toward the hut he had shared with Amma for as long as he could remember. It was still standing—the dragon hadn't burned it. He ran.

"Amma!" The word came out like a cry when he saw her lying on the threshold. As he knelt beside her, she looked at him, one eye meeting his, the other drifting into the distance. She was still alive, but her burns were terrible.

He lifted her as gently as he could, but she moaned in pain until he laid her on her pallet. "I'll get you water, I'll take care of you, you'll be all right," he said, pulling the blanket over her as much to hide her wounds as to warm her.

She stared at him, her mouth working as if she was trying to speak.

"What, Amma? What is it?"

She reached a clawlike hand to his face, her metal bracelets clinking against each other. Then she brought her hand to her lips. He leaned his head toward hers, his ear near her mouth.

"Rune." Her voice was a creaking rasp.

"I'm here, Amma. I'll take care of you."

"No!" The voice had more force than she seemed to have the strength for. Again, he brought his ear to her lips.

Rune held his head still, listening to Amma's heavy, tortured breathing. Finally, she spoke again.

"Survivor of war."

He shook his head. He needed to build up the fire to

warm her, to find her water and something to eat, to dress her wounds. "It isn't war, Amma. It was a dragon."

She grimaced. "No," she rasped again. "You." She half pointed with her clawed hand, then dropped it to her chest. Heavily, her eyes closed.

"Amma?" Rune said, fear making the air catch in his throat. But as he watched, her chest continued to rise and fall. She was still breathing.

He looked in the rain barrel; soot floated on the top. He strained water through a cloth and then, cradling her head in his arms, tried to get Amma to drink, but the water dribbled down her chin.

The same thing happened when he tried to feed her the porridge he found in the pot on its tripod over the cookfire—the supper she had probably made for him. He wiped her face off, thankful that it wasn't burned like so much of the rest of her; then he sat down, leaning his trembling body against the wall, and took one of Amma's hands in his. Gently, he kneaded it, caressing her fingers the way he'd done these past few years when the stiffness in her knuckles pained her. She often sang to him when he did, choosing stories of the feuds between tribes, of the fates of the women and children when men sought vengeance. She wouldn't be singing tonight.

She was in bad shape, he knew, and he didn't know what to do to help her. *She* was the one people came to when they needed healing. Even if there had been somebody he could have gone to, it was too late now; night had fallen and the spirits of Hwala and Skyn and Skoll, even the bond servant's spirit, would be roaming. He tried not to think of their unburied bodies, but every time he shut his eyes, he saw them.

He stared into the cookfire, listening to it snap. Then, his voice low and quavering with fatigue and fear and grief, he began to chant the sorrow-filled lament Amma had sung when she polished the sword. As he chanted, he recalled the coolness of her hand on his forehead, the comforting sound of her voice singing him to sleep, the way she had when, as a child, he'd been hurt or ill.

Daylight decreed it; Wyrd agreed:
Brother and son, uncle and nephew
Lay slain in the swordplay.
That sad lady mourned in the morning
Under gray skies where she had grasped gladness.
Now bitter breastcare hardened her heart.
Hoc's blameless daughter—her kinsmen were gone.

Rune's voice choked off. Before he looked down at Amma's chest again, he somehow already knew. It moved no more.

Amma, his Amma, who had mothered him for as long as he could remember, who had taken him in when he'd been cast out alone into the world, who had taught him and disciplined him and loved him—Amma was gone.

A ragged, wordless sob tore from his chest.

It took him the entire next day to prepare the graves. He worked mechanically, feeling light-headed. His vision was as blurry as his voice was raw from the prayers he'd chanted to Thor and Freyja, asking them to guide Amma's spirit on her trip to the next world. He'd kept his fingers wound in hers all night to keep her spirit from becoming fearful—or worse, angry—when it realized the body it had lived in could no longer house it.

When he woke, Amma's fingers were stiff and cold, and he had to use one hand to free the fingers of his other from hers.

He buried Hwala and his sons and Ula first, all of them together in one pit. It took him till midday to dig it. Skyn and Skoll had made his life miserable, but he would never have wished them such a fate. And certainly not Hwala, who, though he was a hard man, had allowed both Rune and Amma food and shelter without complaint. He couldn't find Skyn's dagger, so he gave him a scythe. Hwala would meet the gods with the farm's ax.

Dully, he wondered about Ula, who had kept to herself no matter how often he had asked her to tell her story. Amma would have known. Who had her people been? Would they ever hear what had happened to her? He doubted it. He found a ceramic jug, scorched by the flames but still serviceable, to bury with her. Because she had had so little joy in her life, he wished he could search for a brooch or a bracelet for her, but he was running out of time. Amma's body was still waiting.

His shoulders aching, his hands blistered, he hefted the last shovelful of dirt onto the grave and then made his way down to the stream to rest and drink, away from the smell of ashes and death. Weak sunshine filtered through the gold-touched leaves, and the water gurgled over the rocks, reflecting the light. Then a raven croaked. Rune looked up to see it swaying on a branch too narrow to bear its weight, staring at him. It unnerved him.

Stumbling with fatigue, he returned to the hut he and Amma had shared. Her grave would be here, under the ash tree.

He wished he could build a funeral pyre for her, or even an earthen barrow to mound high over her grave, but for a pyre, there wasn't enough dry wood—the dragon had burned it all. And a barrow would take more strength than the gods had given him.

After having buried the others, he wasn't sure he had the energy for Amma's grave. But he had no choice. Again, he started to dig.

As he worked, emotion came seeping back. If only he'd come home instead of going to the king, Amma might still be alive. Each jab of the shovel into the earth brought him a fresh thorn of anger and regret. How could he have been so stupid? If only he hadn't fallen asleep after the king questioned him, he could have been home in time; if only he hadn't run after Ollie; if only he hadn't climbed the crag in the first place but had stayed to deal with that slave. Of the thousand different things he could have done, he had chosen the very worst one. He would never forgive himself. If it hadn't been for him, the dragon would never have killed Amma.

The dragon. Leaning on the shovel shaft, he lifted his face from the grave to gaze toward the mountain where the creature made its home, its top lost in a haze of clouds. Hatred seethed in his chest, renewing his strength. For the first time, he truly understood the desire for vengeance that drove tribes to fight each other, that kept feuds alive for generations. He dug his shovel into the dirt again.

Finally, when the shadows stretched long and blue across the burned fields and he deemed the grave deep enough to keep out the wolves, he lined it with soft leaves he had gathered by the stream. Then he wrapped Amma tightly in her blanket and laid her in the ground, the round stone with the image of Freyja carved in it tucked into the crook of her arm—it would tell the goddess of her coming. Her metal bracelets adorned her wrists, and in one hand Rune placed her comb, the one he had carved for her from whalebone last winter. Two of the teeth had broken while he was making it, but he remembered how proud he'd felt when the cat decoration he'd added had turned out so well. Amma had hardly said a word about it, but Rune had seen the way she looked at it, the way she held it in her palm when she didn't think he was looking.

He swallowed hard. Then, kneeling, he put his fist to his chest and lowered his head. "I will avenge you," he said. "By Thor's hammer, I swear I will find the dragon and kill it. I promise."

He had thought laying Amma in the grave would be the hardest thing he'd ever done, but he was wrong. Showering earth down on her body was even harder. As the blanket in which he had wrapped her disappeared, his anger transformed to grief again and tears coursed down his face, mingling with his sweat.

Finally, the grave filled, he covered it with flat stones from the stream. He stood beside it, panting, wondering what to do next. No holly grew near here that he could burn on the graves. Nor was there a woman to sing the song of mourning.

A sound from the hut made him turn in alarm. He smiled through his tears. Ollie stood by the rain barrel, watching him. A patch of wool had been singed from her flank—the work of the dragon.

Rune went inside and fetched a handful of grain for her. When she came forward to get it, he wrapped his arm around her neck, giving the little goat a hug. She shook herself free and nosed at the grain.

Then, exhausted and shivering as a chill breeze blew over his sweat-soaked tunic, Rune returned to the hut, threw himself down on his pallet, and slept as if he, too, were dead.

SIX

RUNE STIRRED, THEN ROLLED OVER, LONG STRANDS OF HIS dark hair falling into his face. Insects rustled in the thatch. Through closed lids, he could detect light. He squinted one eye open just enough to see through the smoke hole. Blue sky. It would be a fair day.

He pulled the scratchy goat-hair blanket over his head again and fell back into a doze, waiting for the sound of the fire snapping and the smell of bread baking in the ashes. Any minute now, Amma would start one of her low chanting prayers to Freyja.

Amma.

Rune's eyes snapped open. It hadn't been a dream. She was dead. And he was alone.

He couldn't get his breath. A terrible weight pressed against his chest, and he thought he might be sick. Unable to think, unable to move, he lay rigid on his pallet, battling the burden that threatened to drown him. The heaviness turned to helplessness, the knowledge that he had chosen wrong. *I could have saved her. I could have warned her.* Beyond all desire, he wished he had come home instead of going to the king. He saw himself standing on the crag, deciding what to do—and making the wrong choice.

Again he saw the dragon soaring through the twilit sky, belching flames at field and farm, thatched roofs lighting like torches, people running in terror—and then falling as dragonflame enveloped them. The anger he had felt while he was digging the graves still lay smoldering in his belly. Now it kindled into rage, pushing away the terrible weight of his grief.

He sat up, groaning at the ache in his shoulders, the dirt-encrusted blisters on his hands. He'd been too worn-out to even think of washing last night after he had buried Amma.

He looked around the hut he'd shared with her all these years, at the fire pit in the middle, cold and black in the dim morning light, at the altars to Thor and Freyja, the stone image of the goddess no longer in its place beside the carving of the god's wagon. Amma's loom leaned against the thick earthen wall that protected them from the north wind, stones dangling from the warp threads, a pattern just beginning to emerge in the weft. On the eastern wall hung a tapestry she'd made long ago, stories of the gods woven into it in sinuous patterns, stories she had insisted he know—Freyja and her falcon-skin cloak, Loki and his son, the wolf Fenrir. Why had he resisted her so much lately, every time she tried to teach him some new tale? The more insistent she'd been, the less willing he'd been to learn. Shame bit at him and he closed his eyes.

When he opened them, he stared across the fire pit to where Amma's pallet lay empty, bits of straw poking from a mattress seam, the goat-hair blanket gone, and felt the same emptiness filling him. He shuddered, remembering wrapping her charred body in the blanket, lowering her into the grave.

Finally, he tore himself from his thoughts and rose from his own pallet. Shoulders stooped, he looked through the hut for something to eat. It was only this season that he'd grown too tall to stand to his full height inside. He opened the door to let in light and tied his hair back with a leather cord. A chunk of oat bread sat on the board, and in the dairy crock, he found some salted butter and the remains of Amma's last batch of skyr. They tasted like soot. Still hungry, he ate the cold porridge that had congealed in the pot, grimacing at its lumpy texture and smiling a little as he bit down on a pebble. This porridge was definitely Amma's handiwork. He washed it down with the water in the bottom of the bucket, ignoring the layer of ash on its surface. Wiping his mouth on his sleeve, he turned to the west wall of the hut and stared at the space Amma had covered with goat hide. He found it hard to think, hard to know what to do.

Except that he knew exactly what he had to do.

Rune crossed the room in three paces and whipped the covering away. The wooden shield stared at him, its metal boss like the pupil in a great round eye, mocking him, asking what a spineless boy like Rune could do against a dragon.

He looked back at the empty pallet and ground his molars. The dragon had killed Amma. He had to avenge her. And for that, he needed weapons. They were his, after all. And they had been his father's. Or at least he assumed they had. Why else would they have been in the boat? Over the years, he'd heard many versions of the story. Fulla, an old woman who lived in the stronghold, had told him the one he liked best, even though it probably wasn't true— after all, what would a woman like her know about weapons and armor? Still, he liked what she said about how when the boat came rushing in over the waves, the shield had been at his head, the sword at his feet, the mail shirt along his shield-hand side, while Amma stood on the strand waiting for him.

He thought it was a good story, but he would have preferred to know the truth instead. The only things he really knew about the weapons were that Amma didn't like him touching them and that she only let him use the sword in the winter because the king said she had to. And that she had known more about the weapons—and about *him*— than she had revealed.

He reached for the mail shirt, examining its closely

linked rings. In the hall, he'd watched warriors to see how they put them on, how they cinched them to keep their sword arms free. He'd even tried on Ketil's mail once. But he'd never worn his own.

He took a deep breath and pulled it over his head. As the cold metal settled over his shoulders and fell to his thighs, it felt strange and heavy, not at all how he'd expected. He took a step back and heard the clinking sound of Amma's metal bracelets. He whirled and the mail shirt whirled with him, its rings hitting together with a metallic sound. Amma wasn't there; of course she wasn't. It was the mail shirt that made the music of her bangles—a hundred times over.

He steadied himself and turned back to the hide covering. The sword lay in its wood and leather sheath, crisscrossed with leather bands—and wound around with Amma's disapproval. The very first time Rune had joined the other boys for sword training, Amma had marched into the middle of the hall. She had put her face so close to Finn's that he took a step back. Then she told him—loudly enough that everyone in the hall could hear—that he could only teach Rune to defend himself, not to attack. Rune didn't remember the rest of the conversation, only the laughter from both the boys and the warriors standing nearby. If one of Thor's thunderbolts had struck him dead then and there, he would have been relieved. The only good thing that had come of it was that the boy across from him had caught his eye and given him a wry look, as if to say,

Women! That had been Rune's introduction to Ketil, back when his friend's nose had only been broken once.

He wasn't sure whether he'd be less awkward with the sword if his introduction to it had been more auspicious. Finn ignored Amma's admonition and taught Rune all aspects of swordfighting, but Rune always seemed to be doing something wrong: thrusting or parrying a breath too late, holding the blade too low or too high, putting his weight on the wrong foot. Ketil had encouraged him, but Rune had felt the eyes of the other boys on him, wondering why a farmer was training with a sword in the first place. He'd wondered the same thing.

The worst day had been the one when Finn stopped in front of him, shaking his head in exasperation. "It's a sword, not a scythe," he'd said, taking Rune's blade away from him. He had examined it closely, balancing it in his hand, feeling its weight, running his fingers over the patterned metal, before saying, "This is a warrior's weapon." Then he had handed Rune a wooden practice blade. In front of everyone. Even Ketil had looked away, and Rune didn't blame him. Skyn and Skoll had never let him forget the humiliation.

Rune thought of the brothers lying side by side in the grave he had dug. He closed his eyes.

Then, opening them, he grasped the sword by its hilt and slid it from its sheath. It came out easily—Amma's whale oil had seen to that—but it still felt unwieldy, as if it weren't balanced. As if it weren't made for him or he for it.

The touch of the hilt stung a blister on his palm, and he shifted the weapon to find a better grip. When he extended the blade, the sense memory of Finn's lessons came back to him. He moved the sword as if to block a heavy blow, and as he did, his legs automatically knew how to stand. His arm, too, went where it should. That was something, anyway.

Careful not to cut himself, he slid the sword back into its sheath.

Finally, he looked back at the yellow shield. This time it stared straight at him, expressionless. He hefted it, grunting at the surprising weight of the linden wood, and swung it over his back.

On his way out, he stopped in front of the altar, touching the flat stone with Thor's goat-pulled wagon carved into it. "I chose the wrong path before. May I regain my honor today," he whispered. Then, bowing his head to the statue, he said, "As Thor defeated the Midgard Serpent, so may I defeat the dragon." He turned to go, then stopped again, laying his hand flat on the lintel where the image of Freyja had been, the stone now buried with Amma. "Lady of the Vanir," he whispered, and glanced at Amma's tapestry, with its image of the goddess, her hair looped in an intricate knot, her arms outstretched as she offered her falcon-skin cloak to the god Loki. "Lady," he whispered again, the stone now warm under his hand. "Help me avenge her." Then he ducked through the door.

Outside, the air still reeked of smoke from the burned

farmhouse and fields, but a weak sun shone through the leaves of the ash tree. Rune forced himself to look at the raw grave. An orange mouser, one of the stable cats that had escaped from the fire, sat atop it, placidly cleaning its ears.

Rune watched as the sun gleamed off the animal's golden fur. It was a good omen. Freyja must have welcomed Amma into her hall—cats were sacred to the goddess.

He lowered his head in thanks.

Hairy-Hoof greeted Rune with a whinny and a toss of her mane. He hadn't taken as good care of the horse as he should have, so busy had he been burying the dead, but she seemed to forgive him. Mounting her was harder than he had anticipated, with both sword and shield to manage and his mail coat restricting his legs. After two tries, he balanced the shield in a fork of the ash tree, retrieving it when he was seated on Hairy-Hoof's back, careful to keep the horse from stepping on Amma's grave.

Together they headed away from the farm, past fire-blackened fields. A single acre of oats stood untouched, golden stalks bright against the darkness of the destroyed fields around it. It looked as if the dragon had left it alone on purpose, as a taunting threat that it might return.

They took the trail down through the birches that surrounded the stream, the trees themselves marked by fire, some of their white trunks blackened, half their green and red-gold leaves scorched. Hairy-Hoof picked her way carefully over the rocks and splashed through the stream, then climbed up the bank, out of the trees, and onto the path that led to the tall runestone. The shield banged into Rune's back as the horse's hooves clopped over the dirt, sending up flurries of ash. Rune stared stonily ahead, refusing to look at the burned fields on either side of him, but he couldn't keep the smell of smoke from filling his nostrils.

Far in the distance, the giants' mountain loomed dark and forbidding. Amma had warned him never to go there. The crag was only the footstep of the mountain, and it was dangerous enough. But the mountain itself? He shivered. Yet, if he was to find the dragon, he would have to climb it.

He rode on, eyeing the steep slopes, wondering how he would ever find the dragon's lair. Countless years the monster must have dwelt there, sleeping on its hoard, yet no one had even known about it. Why had it emerged now? And what made him think he could find it?

He had been on the crag when the dragon had flown over him. As he drew nearer, he scanned the rocky heights. Maybe its cave was nearby. Maybe not, but he couldn't think of any other place to start.

He shrugged and heard his mail shirt clink with the sound of Amma's bracelets. He took it as a sign.

When he finally got to the bottom of the crag, he stopped. Hairy-Hoof would never make it up slopes that steep and rocky. Careful not to drop the shield or let the sword trip him, he dismounted, grateful that there was no one nearby to see his lack of grace.

He was settling the shield more firmly on his back

when his eye fell on the runes the stranger had scratched into the dirt. They were still there. He reached for his pendant and held it for a moment before he began climbing.

He had taken only a few steps when something made him turn. Below him, two shapes like shadows darkened the patch of dirt. Ravens. Where had they come from? He watched as they hopped on the dirt, pecking at it. He couldn't be sure from this distance, but it looked as if the birds had wiped out the stranger's marks.

The hair on his arms prickled. The king's hearth companions had a saying: "Fate often protects an undoomed man, if his courage is good." Courage had never been Rune's companion, and he felt as though doom walked alongside him. It didn't matter. To avenge Amma, all he had to do was kill the dragon. He didn't have to survive.

He began climbing again.

At the top of the crag, he stopped to catch his breath and readjust his sword and shield. He hadn't considered how much harder mountain climbing would be, encumbered by such weight. At least the air was still today, so he wouldn't have to worry about the wind buffeting him as he climbed. He stared up the slopes at the mountain's beard of spruce and firs. Surely he should be able to see where the dragon had emerged. He shuddered, remembering just how huge it had been, how long it had taken to thunder over him. Although it had probably only been the space of a few breaths, it had seemed like a lifetime.

Above the tree line, the mountain was strewn with

boulders, but Rune could see no place where the monster had trampled trees or bushes, no burn marks on the ground. "A dragon must live in a barrow, old and proud of its treasures." He whispered the adage, one of the hundreds Amma had taught him. But where was there a barrow? He'd never heard of any old grave mounds near here, nor caves full of bones and treasure. It would have to be a sizeable cave if the dragon was to get into it, although people said the creatures could flatten themselves the way a mouse does to crawl into tight places.

He scanned the mountain for cave mouths but saw nothing promising. How would he ever find the dragon?

Footsteps sounded behind him. He whipped around, hand tight on his sword hilt.

A goat balanced on a rock, watching him.

Rune let out his breath in a whoosh of relief. He gazed at it; the goat must have been twice as big as Ollie. Its coat was pure white, and there was something strange about its eyes. For a goat, he thought, that was saying something. It gave a nasal bleat, then sprang off the rock and ran lightly up the mountainside. As Rune watched, another goat pranced out from behind a boulder, and the two animals clashed horns lightly. The first goat looked back at him before both of them dashed farther up the mountain.

They could be ordinary mountain goats, he thought, but they didn't look like it. Could the Thunderer have sent them as guides? It was a chance he would have to take. He started after them.

The goats had disappeared by the time he made it to the boulder. He grasped at a tree root that offered itself like a handle and pulled himself up to rest on the stony surface, lowering his shield from his back. Until today, he'd never realized just how big and cumbersome a warrior's shield could be—the round wood stood half as high as Rune, and in places, the metal edges and fittings dug into his flesh. He was sure he had a pattern of ring-shaped bruises where the shield had pressed his mail coat into his back.

From where he sat, he could see the goat trail disappearing into the clouds that covered the mountaintop, but he saw no cave. He wrapped his arms around himself, wishing he'd worn his cloak against the cold. Far in the distance, serpentine rock shapes rose out of the dark seawater. At least, he hoped they were rocks.

When he looked back up the mountainside, a sudden movement caught his eye. The goats? No, not goats—it was a tendril of smoke curling through the air.

Smoke! The dragon's smoky breath?

Steeling himself, he picked up his shield again and started climbing fast, keeping his eyes on the smudge in the air.

There was no straight path; he dodged around scraggly trees and bushes, climbed over rocks, slipped on loose pebbles, and zigzagged his way up the slope, his heart hammering with effort and fear. His feet crunched on something, and he looked down to see a skeleton, some animal he didn't recognize, its rib cage whitened with age. Beside it, an indentation in the ground was shaped like a giant's footprint. He shuddered and hurried onward.

Now his swordbelt, too loose to keep the sheath stable on his left side, slipped down over his hips, making the rings of his mail shirt bite into bone. Irritably, he yanked it up. A boulder rose before him, and, still tugging at his belt, he edged around it and through a stand of fir trees. He burst through them—and stopped short, teetering, his heart in his throat.

Below him, the mountain dropped away in a sheer cliff. One more step and he would have gone over the side.

Barely daring to breathe, he drew his foot back. Steadying himself, grasping the boulder for balance, he looked down. Far below him, an eagle hovered on a current of air. He heard it shriek, a faint sound carried on the wind. It was a long way to the bottom.

Edging back to the other side of the boulder, he began his ascent again, more carefully this time. But as he scanned the heights, he could no longer see the trail of smoke, nor the boulders that had been near it. Instead, a gray cloud hung over the mountaintop, obscuring them.

Higher and higher he climbed, blinking away mist. He kept going, wiping dampness from his face and focusing on his path, watching for sudden drop-offs. When he reached forward to steady himself on a rock, he stopped, amazed to see his arm disappear into the air. Mist swirled around him, cutting off sound and light, chilling him. Water droplets formed in his hair, on his clothes and skin. If he kept climbing, he might go straight past the dragon's lair without seeing it. Or he might come to another cliff—but this time, he wouldn't know until it was too late.

Above him, below him, on his sword-hand side, on his shield-hand side, the air was solid, a white-gray mass that no human eye could penetrate.

There was nothing he could do. He lowered himself to the ground beside the rock.

He was trapped.

SEVEN

BEADS OF MOISTURE SETTLED ON RUNE'S EYELASHES. HE
hunched his shoulders against the fog and wished for his
cloak, the one Amma had woven for him. He thought of
her sitting at her loom, chanting songs as she worked, stories of gods and giants and heroes, of King Beowulf's battles, of the feuds between the tribes, the Shylfings and the
Frisians, the Geats and the Danes. People said Amma
could out-chant the bard, she knew so many tales. Much as
Rune liked the stories, he'd never seen the point of having
to learn them himself. And especially not all the histories
of the tribes and their leaders or the wisdom poems, like
the one about what was expected of king and queen, earl
and churl. A churl—a farmer like him—hardly needed a
poem to know how to harvest a field.

Shivering, he wrapped his arms around himself and

stared at the mist. Never still, it eddied and purled like stream water. Sometimes he thought he could see shapes moving within it—giants going about their business? He sat frozen, hunched like a boulder, hoping that giants couldn't see through the gray air any better than he could.

Now he thought he could discern sounds, vague and muted. A wordless voice seemed to float toward him through the mist. For a moment, he thought it sounded like Amma's voice.

Sudden anger welled in Rune, anger at himself for leaving the farm unprotected, for not warning Amma about the dragon. The dragon! Such rage as he had never felt before flooded through him. If he had to crouch here, unmoving, on this mountainside for even one more heartbeat, he would explode.

Maybe it was too dangerous to walk, but he could crawl, couldn't he? Whatever it took, he would find the dragon, and he would take his vengeance for Amma, for Hwala and his sons, for Ula, for the fields of ripened grain, for the burned gables of the king's golden hall. For the king's hearth companions.

He dropped to hands and knees and slung his shield onto his back. His sword dragged and the shield slid forward, hitting the ground and making his going slow, but nothing would stop him now, not the rocks biting into his hands and knees, nor the mist that seemed to thicken with every move he made.

That voice again—he seemed to hear it ahead of him

now, leading him on, almost pulling him up the steep slope. He rose to his feet for speed, keeping his hands to the ground like a bear, the shield falling forward until finally he rose to his full height. Let the mist try to slow him. He wanted the dragon *now*, while he was white-hot with fury.

Shapes rose before him in the mist, boulders hunched like trolls, fir trees standing like spears, but he scarcely noticed. He grabbed hold of one to pull himself upward, then stumbled, righted himself, and stumbled again. This time, he caught hold of a bush whose thorns pierced his hand.

The pain fueled his anger and pushed him blindly on. As long as he was heading up the mountain, he must be going the right way.

Until a wall stopped him, a cliff face. In the fog, there was no way for him to see how high it was. He reached for handholds but found no way to scale it. As he stood before the wall, a muted sound pierced the solid air. Rune stood stock-still, listening. Again he heard it, the sound like a voice, coming from his sword-hand side.

"Amma?" Rune said softly, and strained his ears for a reply.

None came, nor any sign.

He swallowed hard. Then, one hand on the rock wall, he began edging to the right, each foot stretching out to feel for solid ground.

Suddenly, his hand met air and he pulled back. But his feet told him the ground was still there. He reached down to feel scraggly bushes and, beside them, a path that seemed to go around the cliff face.

He was right—the voice *was* leading him. Was it Amma's spirit helping him to avenge her death? Or some malign presence luring him to his doom?

The path, probably a goat trail, led him higher and farther to the sword-hand side. It seemed like the right way, but in the fog, he had no idea where he was or where the curl of smoke had been, the smoke that had looked like the dragon's breath.

The thought of the dragon lying smugly on its treasure hoard made his anger flame. He grasped at his sword hilt but let it go as a root tripped him, sending him sprawling. As he fell, his hands reached out, touching . . . *nothing.*

He lay still for a moment, listening, breathing. Then, cautiously, he pulled himself forward on his belly, feeling the ground in front of him and the air beyond, where mountain gave way to cliff. Still splayed on the ground and blind in the mist, he searched with his hand until he found a loose stone and dropped it over the edge, listening for its landing. No sound answered. For all he could tell, the cliff might plunge all the way to the sea.

He reached behind him and took hold of the root that had tripped him, saving his life.

Shakily, Rune started again, crawling this time, heading away from the cliff edge. The farther right he went, the better he felt. For some reason he couldn't name, it seemed like the way to the dragon.

He smiled grimly. "Thought you'd send me over the cliff, did you? Not this time." The mist swallowed his words, turning them pale and making them sound less hearty than he'd intended.

He rose to his feet, gripped his sword hilt, and stared upward. Was the fog beginning to thin up ahead? He blinked and stared again. He wasn't sure, but he thought he could see the shapes of three monstrous boulders. Eagerly, he started toward them, and as he did, he found himself walking directly out of the mist, as if he were stepping out of the sea. When he looked down, his legs were still covered in the thick white air, but above his waist, it thinned into nothing.

He stepped forward, watching the fog dissipate around him, leaving him on an island above an ocean of cloud.

He squared his shoulders and increased his pace. As he did, thunder rumbled below him. He stopped to listen. The ground trembled, the rumbling resonating in the soles of his feet, in his legs, in his chest.

He knew that sound—he'd heard it before.

Drawing his sword from its sheath and heaving his shield into position, he dropped into a fighting stance and tried to steady his breath. This time, he would be ready.

Now came the smell, the acrid odor that dried his tongue and made his eyes water, his nose run. A hot wind roused the mist into swirling eddies.

Heart in his throat, sword in his hand, Rune scanned the gray air. Where was the dragon?

"Come on, show yourself!" he shouted, but his voice sounded as thin and shrill as a child's.

The rumbling grew louder, the smell stronger. He wiped his eyes and squinted, searching for a sign.

Without warning, the dragon shot out of the mist below him, its monstrous bulk churning toward him as he turned, shield raised to protect his body, sword poised to strike.

As the dragon neared, Rune could see how low it was, maybe low enough to stab with his sword. His breath came in shallow gasps, and now he felt horror overtaking him. *"No!"* he cried out. "Vengeance!"

The word died in his throat as he staggered backward, but his anger buoyed him, keeping him from falling.

Then the dragon's red eye flicked toward him. The creature reared up. As it did, Rune caught a glimpse of a white spot on its chest, a circle of darker, bronze scales surrounding it. In the split second it took him to raise his shield, a stream of fire spit forth from the monster's jaws.

The wooden shield burst into flames. Rune dropped it and fell to his knees, his hands over his head, a silent cry of terror in his throat as the dragon screamed over him, its body as big as a longship, the heat from its scales scorching him, the wind whipping rocks and grit into his mouth, his nose, his ears, even his tightly shut eyes. He scrabbled over the ground like a rat, half crawling, trying to flee the dragon's flames, its hurricane roar. Suddenly, he found himself toppling over a rock, then rolling over and over, unable to check his fall, stones bruising his shoulders, his thighs, his head; trees and bushes scratching his limbs; his world a whirl of white-gray mist and pain.

EIGHT

THE SOUND OF BLEATING WOKE HIM. SLOWLY, HE OPENED one eye. Light seemed to pierce his brainpan. He shut his eyes tight.

After a little while or a long time, he wasn't sure which, he heard another *baa*.

Carefully, he opened his eyes again, squinting against the brightness. He was lying on his back. Far above him, the sky shone white-blue, a single feather of cloud floating across his view. When he turned his head to the right, a pair of eyes startled him. A large white goat balanced on a boulder, flicking its ears and watching him. He blinked— one of its eyes looked yellow, the other one blue. That couldn't be right. He looked away.

He sat up slowly, every muscle a mass of pain, every bone a bruise, and tried to think. He was still on the mountain, but how far he'd fallen, he didn't know. The mist had lifted. The dragon—where was the dragon?

Surveying the ground for scorch marks revealed nothing; nor could he hear the telltale rumble of a dragon in flight.

Gingerly he stood, the rings of his mail coat clinking as they settled into place. His sheath was still strapped to his belt, but his sword was gone.

Rune gave a low cry and lowered his head to his hand. His shield burned, his sword gone, the dragon nowhere to be seen, and for the second time, he'd been no more than a coward. Worst of all, he hadn't avenged Amma.

He searched the ground around him for the sword, then followed his trail of broken trees and disturbed bracken upward, looking for it, but the path petered out and the sword remained hidden. So did any sign of the dragon.

Below him, the goat sprang off its boulder and bounded down a path only it could see.

Aching and miserable, Rune followed it down the mountain.

He had almost made it to the bottom when he found the body. The smell of burned flesh made him gag. He forced away the memories of the bodies he had buried and then, cringing at what he feared to discover, edged toward the charred remains, more work of the dragon.

The corpse was too badly burned for him to recognize.

All he could tell was that it had been a man, a warrior wearing mail and a helmet, and that he had died faceup, his mouth open as if he had been screaming in defiance, his sword in his hand.

Rune dropped to his knees and looked at the sword hilt, its interlacing patterns surrounding a fire-red garnet. Finn's sword.

"No!" he cried, and pounded his fist into the earth.

Finn, the king's shoulder companion, his dearest friend, his heir; Finn, who had taught Rune to wield a sword, who had patiently guided his hand on the hilt, who had always treated him fairly and sometimes even with kindness.

He thought of Wyn finding out her beloved father was dead. He thought of the king, whose eyes had filled with tears when his golden hall burned. Now his best warrior was gone, and the dragon was still alive.

They would be glad that Finn had died fighting. Already the warrior maidens would be winging their way here to escort him to an exalted seat in Valhalla. He would need his sword there.

Even if Rune had had the strength, he had no tools to dig a grave. Instead, he looked skyward and said the ritual words that would send Finn on his way. Later, perhaps the king would place a runestone here to mark Finn's fight.

A few paces away, he saw a huge linden shield, its leather handgrips faceup, as if Finn had flung it away. He must have realized what Rune himself had been too stupid to see—fire burns wood, even wooden shields. He shook his head. He had been so close to the creature. If only he had raised his sword instead of his shield, the dragon might be dead by now.

He laid the shield by Finn's side.

As he did, something near the warrior's head caught his attention, a piece of fire-blackened metal. The Thor's hammer amulet Finn had worn around his neck, its leather thong burned to ashes. Rune reached for it and pulled his hand back in surprise—it was still warm.

He looked at it, thinking of Finn, then dropped it into the pouch he wore on his swordbelt. Wyn would want it.

The moment his feet finally hit flat ground, he heard the jingling of a bridle and the clopping of hooves. A rider was coming around the mountainside, whistling a complicated melody as he rode.

Rune relaxed his shoulders in relief—he'd know that sound anywhere. Ketil Flat-Nose.

As the young man rode into view, he pulled his horse to a halt, looked at Rune, and turned his tune into a long, low whistle. "By the hammer, what happened to you?"

Rune glanced at his bruised and bloody arms. He wondered if he looked as bad as he felt. "I—I fell," he said.

"From the top of the mountain?" Ketil's eyes widened with disbelief.

"Just about," Rune said. He cringed inwardly. Since Ketil had been made one of the king's hearth companions last winter, the two years between them had seemed like much more, as if Ketil had become a man while Rune was still a boy. A boy who couldn't even handle his own sword. "What are *you* doing here?"

"Dragon-hunting," Ketil said, grinning and slapping his sword. Then his face turned somber. "Well, scouting, really. I was just at your farm. Did anyone—?"

Rune shook his head and looked at the ground.

"It's a bad business," Ketil said. "Yours wasn't the only burned farm I found."

"I know." It was far worse than Ketil realized, but suddenly Rune found it hard to find words for what he needed to say.

"The king sent out scouts; we're supposed to see who survived and to tell able-bodied men to join him. I saw Sigurd; he's on his way to the king right now."

Rune looked down, gathering his breath. "Ketil," he said, more loudly than he meant to. He looked steadily up at his friend, who stared back at him in surprise. "Ketil," he said again, his voice dropping low. "I found Finn."

"Found?" Ketil gave him a puzzled look. "Oh." He let out his breath as the realization hit him. "Oh, not Finn." He closed his eyes briefly. "Where?"

Rune gestured behind him. "Up the mountain. Four or five furlongs. He died well."

"The dragon?"

Rune nodded.

Ketil stared up the mountain. "He was the best of us. Next to the king, he was the very best."

They stood for a moment in silence before Rune said, "I saw the dragon."

"I heard—the other morning when you came running into the stronghold."

"No, I mean today."

Ketil's eyes widened again, and again Rune got the impression the older youth didn't believe him.

"Up on the mountain. That's why I fell," he added. He hung his head. "I lost my shield—and my sword."

Ketil kept staring at him. Finally, he spoke. "If you saw the dragon, why aren't you burned?"

"I *am*, I mean, my shield is. I don't think it was trying to kill me." He hung his head as shame filled him. "I don't think it saw me as a threat."

"What were you doing up there?"

"Trying to kill it." Rune caught Ketil's eye again. "To avenge Amma."

Ketil looked him up and down, as if he were a seasoned warrior judging an errant boy, the way Finn had looked the time he took away Rune's sword.

"I'll see to Finn," Ketil said in a different voice, a dismissive one. "There was a horse grazing around the bend. Yours?"

Rune nodded.

Ketil watched him for a moment longer, as if deciding something. "You need to go to the king, you know. He wants all able-bodied men." Then he kicked his horse's sides and urged it up the mountain.

Able-bodied? Men? Rune snorted in disgust.

Hairy-Hoof's neck felt warm as Rune leaned his head into it. She nickered at him, reaching around to nuzzle for a treat, but he had nothing to give her. "Sorry, girl," he said, and then pulled himself onto her back. *"Ow."* His tailbone was as bruised as the rest of him. If it hurt this much to sit, how would he ever ride?

By lying flat on his stomach, it turned out. It was the only way he could stay on. He tried various other positions first, but none of them worked, and he thought he would have to make his way on foot to the king's hall again. Then, in defeat, he collapsed forward, hugging the horse's neck, and found that the pain wasn't as bad that way. When he urged Hairy-Hoof forward, she tossed her head as if to ask him why he was being a fool, but finally she began to trot.

As Rune flopped up and down on the horse's back, his mail jingling, he cringed at the thought of somebody seeing him this way, especially Ketil or one of the other warriors. Or worse, Wyn. She might not say anything, but she could convey deadly scorn with the simplest glance. But now . . . he remembered the Thor's hammer amulet and the reason he was carrying it. Wyn would have other things to think about than him.

The ride seemed endless, and several times Rune sat up, enduring the pain so he could get a better sense of direction. It was fully dark by the time he came to the path that led to the stronghold. As he came out of the trees, he gasped.

Fires, everywhere. Where was the king? Heart in his throat, Rune urged Hairy-Hoof into a gallop, ignoring his aching tailbone.

The closer he got, the more flames he saw, as if the dragon had scorched the entire settlement—houses, stables, *everything*. Now, closer by, he saw light—a torch?

"Halt!" A man's voice came hurtling out of the darkness.

Rune reined Hairy-Hoof in, breathing hard and blinking as a man as tall and thin as a spear stepped forward, holding a torch high, his sword unsheathed.

"Show yourself!" the man commanded.

"Gar?"

"Who's there?" It was definitely Gar's voice.

"It's me, Rune. Ketil said we were supposed to—"

"All right, all right, go on."

"But, Gar, what's happening? Did the dragon—"

Again Gar cut him off. "I'm a guard, not a messenger." He motioned impatiently with his torch. "Hurry up."

Rune nudged Hairy-Hoof forward, and suddenly the sight before him resolved itself in his tired eyes and brain. The settlement wasn't on fire after all—those were campfires he was seeing. Of course. The king's hall had been burned, so people must be gathering outside.

He felt relief wash over him and was glad he hadn't said more to Gar.

The closer he got, the more foolish he felt. As he dismounted and led Hairy-Hoof to the stables, men who stood talking in groups beside the campfires glanced at him, firelight making weird shadows on their faces. Somewhere meat was sizzling, and it made his mouth water. He hadn't eaten since early morning.

Outside the stables, he heard the unmistakable sound of a blacksmith hammering. At this time of night?

Once he'd settled Hairy-Hoof and found her some oats, he stood in the lane, listening, watching. He heard a man saying something in a low voice, and then a woman answering, saying, "No, he's not back yet."

It was Thora, Finn's wife. She didn't know.

Rune dug in his pouch for Finn's amulet. He stood looking at it, feeling its weight in his palm, remembering Finn's blackened body on the mountainside. Then he started forward.

Thora stood in her doorway, looking at something in the distance, the light from a nearby campfire shining off her eyes. She turned, startled, as Rune approached.

"Finn," he said.

"He's not here."

"I know," Rune said, his head down. He took a ragged breath, then raised his eyes to hers.

Her eyes widened, and he saw her nostrils flare before

she shot out her hand to grip his forearm. "He's dead. Isn't he?"

He swallowed, then lowered his face in a half-nod. It made it easier to turn away from her terrible gaze. He couldn't make himself look up again.

"Tell me," she said, her nails digging into his skin.

As he looked up, he realized that Wyn had glided forward out of the shadows to stand behind her mother. "He died fighting the dragon. I—I wasn't there. I found him. Here." He reached out his hand, and Thora took the hammer-shaped amulet from him, staring at it as if she didn't recognize it.

Then she looked back at him, rage written across her face. "You took this from him? You took my husband's goods from him?"

"Mother."

Over Thora's shoulder, Rune saw Wyn, her eyes huge in a face drained of color.

"You—you carrion crow! He needed this!" Thora shouted, shaking her fist at him, the amulet locked within her grasp.

"I thought you would—" Rune started at the same time Wyn spoke.

"Mother, stop." She met Rune's eyes. "Leave us." She turned and led her mother into the dwelling, shutting the door behind her.

As he stood in the darkness, his skin prickling with

horror, Rune heard Thora crying out, *"Finn!"* in a long, trailing wail.

A hand clapped his shoulder and he whirled.

The king.

He started to kneel, but the king stopped him, staring at him in the dark, asking him a question as distant firelight reflected on the whites of the old man's eyes.

Rune's eyes filled with tears and he nodded once.

The king let out his breath in a long shudder, closed his eyes briefly, then stepped past Rune and disappeared into Finn's house.

NINE

HUNGER WOKE HIM, AND THE SMELL OF ROASTING MEAT.
Rune opened his eyes to the gray mist of early morning.
His campfire had gone out. Shivering, he pulled his knees
to his chest. The movement awoke the sharp pain of his
tailbone and the duller aches of his other bruises. He suppressed a moan.

Around him, he could hear other people stirring, somebody walking between sleepers, a horse whinnying, and
somewhere nearby, the crackle of a fire. He sniffed the cold
air, his mouth watering at the aroma of mutton cooking.
As he sat up, a cloak fell off his shoulders. His own was still
at the farm, so someone must have thrown this one over
him. Who?

He looked around and saw Ketil sitting on his heels
before a cheerful fire on the other side of the campsite.

When he saw Rune, he held up a stick, and Rune could see a piece of meat on the end of it.

Carefully, mindful of every bruise, he rose. His mail shirt lay on the ground beside him. He glanced back at Ketil and caught a glimpse of the mail under his cloak. Rune pulled on his own, cinched it, then picked his way around sleeping men and cold fires to join Ketil, who grunted and handed him a second stick, a piece of meat skewered on its end.

Rune grunted back and hunkered down, letting the fire warm his aching limbs. As he watched the mutton sizzling in the flames, his stomach rumbled. Finally, unable to wait any longer, he ate it half-raw, burning his fingers and his tongue.

Ketil laughed and tossed him half a loaf of black bread, then walked away. Rune had just taken a huge bite when Ketil returned and laid something on the ground between them before settling back onto his haunches.

Rune's mouth fell open. "My sword," he said, and then, "My sword!" He gazed at Ketil, who gave him a lopsided grin, his face misshapen by his thrice-broken nose.

"Wolves'll get your bread."

Rune snapped his mouth shut, then opened it again. "Where did you find it?"

Ketil's grin disappeared. "Where do you think?"

On the mountain, near where Finn had died. Near where Rune had acted the fool, where he had failed to avenge Amma. His shoulders slumped.

He reached for the sword, examining the hilt, the blade. It seemed unharmed. He stood to sheathe it. As he did, he saw Ketil watching him. *He thinks I don't deserve such a blade,* Rune thought. *He's right.*

All his pleasure at the sword's return vanished. He gave Ketil a quick thanks, then headed for the stables, where he could find Hairy-Hoof—and solitude.

He was currying the horse, having a quiet talk with her, when a horn sounded and a man's voice called from afar, urging people to attend the king.

Giving Hairy-Hoof a final slap, he hurried out of the stable and followed behind a man who was heading down the narrow lane between buildings. The path led to the campsite where Rune had slept—the king's hall, now that the dragon had destroyed his golden one.

Many others had already arrived. Rune took a place outside the ring of people, some standing, some sitting on logs or stools, a group of bond servants crouching on the ground. He recognized some of them: Elli, Gar's wife, held their baby to her breast, and near her, two little boys played a game in the dirt—Ottar's sons, their older cousin Gerd watching them. She was a plump, bossy girl whose braid could never tame her blond curls.

At the head of the circle, guarding the seat that had been made for the king, stood battle-scarred Dayraven, his armbands gleaming in the light.

Rune's fingers touched his sword hilt, and as they did,

shame flooded through him. Had Dayraven heard that he'd lost his sword? That he'd failed against the dragon, not once but twice? Ketil was one of the king's guard now—would he have told the others?

He didn't know why it mattered or why he should care so much what Dayraven thought, especially since the warrior had no love for him—or for Amma. She hadn't liked Dayraven any more than he had her. *Do you think he really believes I turn people's butter sour or make their love go awry?* he remembered her saying, her voice filled with scorn. She refused to understand what a good warrior Dayraven was. Early on, Rune had given up trying to explain it to her. Those were the kind of conversations he saved to have with Ketil. They weren't the only boys who hoped for a nod of recognition from Dayraven. Even now, Rune couldn't help but wish for the warrior's approval, despite the uncomfortable sensation it gave him of disloyalty to Amma.

He moved back a step to take Dayraven's shining armbands out of his line of sight. As he did, he realized someone was speaking to him: Fulla, Hemming's wife, who had lost all three of her sons to the Shylfings and now had only her husband left. Rune remembered when they'd brought her youngest son back. Rune had been in the hall with the other boys when the sound of thundering hooves brought them all running to the door, eager to see the returning troop. None of them had expected to see Hemming ride in with a young warrior before him on his horse, Gunnar's lifeless body slumped against his father's. People said Hemming and Fulla had both aged ten years on the day Gunnar died.

Now Fulla reached for Rune's arm, patting it as she looked at him. The creases etched into the skin around her eyes seemed to grow deeper as she whispered, "You saved her, you know, when your boat came to our shores."

The words caught Rune off guard.

"If it hadn't been for you, she would have . . ." She shook her head a little, then reached to trace her fingers around a bruise on his jaw that Rune hadn't realized he had. Her old-woman's touch, light as a cobweb, made tears spring to his eyes. It felt just like Amma's touch.

She caught his eyes again, and he could see how cloudy one of hers had grown. "You gave her a reason to live," she whispered.

As she turned back to her husband, Rune stared after her, blinking furiously. Fulla and Amma had been friends. He remembered the time Fulla had ridden all the way out to the farm to have Amma interpret a dream she'd had, a dream about Gunnar. Amma had chased Rune out of the hut so she and Fulla could talk.

He felt at his bruise, trying to recapture the sensation of Fulla's fingers on his skin, of Amma's, but his rough nails only scraped the skin.

"The king!" somebody called.

People turned, and Rune turned along with them to see

what was happening. Those who were sitting rose, and Rune could see Od, a thin boy a little younger than he was, running to join in, shouting, "Hurry!" to someone behind him.

Just as Od got there, the king stepped into the circle, stopping to acknowledge the crowd as they bowed. Gar escorted him, standing tall, holding his linden spear erect, almost as if to accentuate the slump in the old king's shoulders, the weary plodding of his gait. Behind them came Thora, stiff and proud, her coiled braids gleaming on her head like a crown.

Rune watched the white-haired leader turn to face them, slowly sweeping the crowd with his eyes, stopping to rest on certain faces. As the king's gaze neared him, Rune lowered his head in shame. Twice now he had encountered the dragon, and twice he had been overcome by terror.

When he looked up, the king was staring directly at him, and he stiffened, feeling caught. Then the eyes moved on, and he took a shaky breath.

Finally, the king spoke, his voice cutting through the crowd's murmurs. "Finn is dead."

Rune heard gasps and wondered dully how anyone could not have known. It seemed an age since he had found Finn's body on the mountainside, half an age since Thora had cursed him.

"Now is not the time for mourning," the king said, and the voices quieted. "Now is the time for vengeance!" At the final word, someone—Ketil, Rune thought—clashed a sword on metal, and then a cheer rose through the crowd, followed by more clashing of weapons.

"We will find the dragon and we will kill it!" the king cried.

Beside him, Hemming began the cheering this time. Rune wanted to join in, but his throat constricted and no sound came out.

The bard came forward, holding his rectangular harp. He held up a hand and the noise died. People quieted their movements, a few sitting or crouching on the ground, all of them watching him. For the space of a breath, he glared at the crowd with his single eye, compelling them into a deeper silence. Then, with a quick movement, he pulled the harp into the crook of his arm and struck the strings as he began to chant:

Sigmund by himself sought the hoard guardian;
Under stone he crept, that brave scion of princes,
With Odin's blade grasped tight, the gleaming light
of battle.
The creature in its cave heard its doom draw near.

Rune rearranged his own blade, trying to keep it from poking him, and watched as the poet's fingers attacked his harp strings, accentuating his words. He closed his eyes and listened to the lay, imagining Sigmund creeping into the dragon's barrow, plunging his sword through the iron-hard scales, driving the fire-belching beast against the cave wall. He hardly heard as the bard sang of Sigmund's glory, of the praise heaped on him by men, and of the shipful of treasure he took from the dragon's hoard. Instead, he kept thinking of the way Sigmund had stabbed through those scales, getting within a sword length of the dragon without cowering or running away. How had he done it?

"Courage and honor and praise followed Sigmund," the bard sang, and Rune winced, reminded of his own tumble down the mountainside.

As the song died away, he opened his eyes to the cheers. King Beowulf held up his hands to quiet the crowd. "Sigmund slew the dragon, but his sword was the work of Welund, smith of the gods. What sword do we have that could pierce dragon scales?"

Rune looked down at the hilt of his own sword and shook his head. Even if the sword had been Welund's work, it would take a warrior with strength and daring to wield it if it were to kill a dragon. Hemming agreed; Rune could hear him telling Fulla that they stood no chance of fighting the dragon that way.

Hemming's voice dropped as the bard spoke again. "Sigmund isn't the only warrior who slew a dragon, my lord."

King Beowulf gestured for him to continue, and the bard plucked a single harp string. "Remember Frotho the Dane, whose arrows bounced off the dragon's back."

The king nodded thoughtfully. "He stuck his steel

into the worm's belly, if I remember the story rightly, and killed it."

The king knew it perfectly, Rune thought as a recollection of Amma chanting the "Lay of Frotho" came to him, one of the countless stories she had taught him. He tried to recall how the warrior had gotten so close to the dragon in the first place, but the memory of the story mingled with the memory of its telling, of Amma sitting on her three-legged stool before her loom, firelight flickering on her lined face.

"What about Sigurd?" Gar called out. "That was a belly shot, too, wasn't it?"

The bard nodded and strummed the harp again, then sang lines from a tale Rune didn't know.

In the pit he'd delved the hero hid himself,
That brave battle-leader, before the dragon's barrow.
The worm came crawling from its treasure hoard,
Venom spouting from the creature's monstrous maw;
The poison reached Sigurd, scalding the chief of princes.
Wounded he still wielded his well-made sword,
Thrusting it upward into the dragon's heart . . .

The bard made a discordant sound on his harp and turned to the king. "They say Thorir struck his dragon under the arm. Whatever you do, Ring-Giver, you must come at the dragon from underneath."

Rune couldn't believe it. He'd *been* underneath the

dragon. It had flown right over his head, a mere sword length away. He could have killed it easily. If he'd just thrown away his shield, the way Finn had, he would have had time to pierce the dragon's heart or hit it under its arm. He shook his head in disgust.

Hemming cleared his rheumy throat—age had unloosed his lips. "You have to think of that venom, too. How do you defend against that?"

Dayraven turned toward Hemming, and Rune shifted to avoid being seen. "I've heard ox-hide armor can help."

Someone else, Rune couldn't see who, called out, "If the venom and the poison teeth don't kill you, the fire will."

The king held up his hands for silence. "Fire I am ready for." He looked off to the side, and Hrolf the blacksmith limped forward, carrying a shield in both hands. When he got to the king, he lowered himself on his good knee.

"Rise, Hrolf," the king said, taking the shield from him and examining its boss and its finger guard, running a hand over its surface before he held it up to the crowd. "The dragon may be able to burn wood, but let him test his breath against a metal shield!"

Rune's eyes widened, and he remembered the sound of the blacksmith hammering far into the night. A shield of iron. He gazed at it, astonished. If he'd had it the day before, could he have withstood the dragon's fire?

Rune wasn't the only one who was amazed, to judge from the voices around him.

"They'll tell about this in the stories," Hemming called

out, Fulla holding on to his arm and shushing him. But other people sounded their agreement, and Rune saw Hrolf, his face blackened by soot, edge his mouth into a grim smile.

As the cheering died down, the king spoke again. "Well enough to have a means to fight the dragon." He looked around at the crowd. "But first, we must find it."

At the sound of harp strings, Rune looked back at the bard. "Three hundred winters and more the worm lay hidden on his hoard." It wasn't a poem, but the bard's words came forth in a singsong chant. "From the time of Geat, our people have lived in these lands, with no word of a dragon." He plucked a single string, making a sour sound. "Until now."

"Gar. Ketil." As the king spoke their names, the two hearth companions sprang forward. "Bring forth the cause of our woe."

Rune watched, peering over Fulla's head in an attempt to see. He could hear her asking her husband what was going on, but Hemming looked as confused as Rune felt. The dragon was the enemy. What could the king mean?

Fulla moved again, blocking Rune's view. He stepped forward so he could see around her and found himself looking directly into the face of the stranger he had seen by the mountain.

The man stopped when he saw Rune and grinned, showing his pointed yellow teeth.

Rune sucked in his breath.

Then Gar pulled on the man's arm, forcing him to turn. As he did, something—a thread? A bit of cloth?—dropped from his bedraggled gray cloak and wafted gently downward. Rune stared at the ground where the object settled. It looked like a feather. Before he could see for sure, Gar's foot trod over it. He pulled the man's arm again, leading him to the king. Rune glanced at King Beowulf just in time to see him reach back to where Thora stood in silence, then turn again to face the crowd. Something in his hand gleamed, catching the morning light.

As the stranger approached the king, Gar kneed him from behind to make him kneel. At the same moment, the king raised his arm, revealing a golden goblet.

Rune stared at it, a memory flashing through his mind, an image of the stranger beside the crag shoving something behind his back. Something golden. The goblet?

Suddenly, he understood. The stranger—the slave—was the cause of the kingdom's woe. He must have stolen the goblet from a hoard that had been hidden for over three hundred winters.

The slave had awoken the dragon.

TEN

"YOU WANTED TO BUY A PLACE IN MY KINGDOM," THE KING was saying. Rune watched the scene before him, but his heart was thumping as he tried to recall exactly where he had first seen the slave: at the foot of the path that led up to the crag. He remembered the stranger looking at his pendant. Rune reached for it and fingered the marks engraved in it, the runes the slave had scratched into the dirt. If he had seen the slave at the foot of the crag, the dragon's cave couldn't have been far away.

He looked back at the king. "With gold you tried to buy a place"—the king shook the goblet at the kneeling slave, who stared back at him brazenly—"but you wrought only destruction. No gold will save you here."

Would the king have the slave killed? At a loud cry,

Rune jerked his head, but it was only Elli's baby. The crowd stood silent, awaiting the king's judgment.

"There is only one way for you to regain your honor."

The slave pulled his lips into a sneer. "I have no honor to regain."

"Silence before the king," Gar hissed, his spear's point pressing into the man's neck.

King Beowulf made a slight motion with his hand, and Gar backed away but kept his spear aimed at the slave. Rune saw Ketil's hand tighten on his sword hilt.

"Every man is born with honor. Whether he dies with it"—the king looked from the slave to the crowd—"that depends on the man."

"Well said." The voice was Hemming's, followed by the sound of Fulla hushing him.

"The king is speaking," she whispered ferociously, so loudly that everyone could hear.

King Beowulf smiled. "The king *is* speaking, Fulla, but praise from a proven warrior is always welcome."

Rune saw Fulla's cheeks flush as Hemming straightened his spine and held his head high. Several people in the crowd laughed, and Rune tried to imagine what it would be like to have the king call you a proven warrior. People still told stories about the surprise attack Hemming had led against the Wulfing raiders long before Rune had been born.

The king turned back to the slave. "Gold will not avail

you," he repeated. "You may earn a place here one way only." He paused and the crowd waited.

"You must lead us to the dragon."

The slave said nothing, and the king looked at the crowd again. "This evening, we feast. Tomorrow, at first light, I leave with a handpicked troop, men I will choose tonight. We will find the dragon—and kill it."

Cheers erupted, and the sounds of metal clashing against metal. Hemming yelled, "The king! The king!" and a few feet away from him, Buri and Surt, farmers from a day's journey to the south, took up the cry, sending it around the circle as men rattled their spears and hit sword against shield. On the other side of the circle, Rune could see Ottar's two little boys dancing in excitement, their cousin Gerd frowning at them. Suddenly, he realized that beside him, Hemming was struggling to unsheathe his sword. Rune ducked out of the way just in time as the old warrior swung it uncertainly.

With so many of his hearth companions away, patrolling the borders against a Shylfing attack, the king didn't have many men to choose from. Surely, Rune thought, for all his kind words, King Beowulf wouldn't take Hemming now that age had stolen his strength. Dayraven, of course, who would probably be chosen as the king's successor now that Finn was dead. The people would accept him because of his prowess in battle. Gar and Ketil would go, and Ottar and Brokk. But with Finn gone, and five of the king's best warriors killed during the dragon's attack on the hall, who else was there? Buri? Surt? They knew more of farming and ax-work than sword or spear. Thialfi, with his damaged sword arm? Od, who was even younger than Rune? His mother would never let him go. Rune glanced around the circle of cheering people and saw a pair of furtive green eyes—Ottar's—doing the same. Rune wasn't the only one wondering whom the king would choose— and whether there were enough warriors to mount an attack against the dragon.

Finally, the king raised his hands to quiet the crowd. As the noise died down, the high-pitched wail of Elli's baby rose up and lingered in the new silence.

The king waited. When the infant calmed, he turned back to the slave. "Tell us about the dragon."

The slave grinned mirthlessly and said, "What do you want to know?" Rune could hardly believe the man's inso- lent tone. He, who had caused so many deaths, so much destruction, had just been offered his life, and at what price? Information. He should be happy to give the king what he wanted.

"Everything you can remember." King Beowulf's words sounded mild, but Rune hoped the slave wouldn't test him further.

The bard stepped forward, one hand resting lightly on his harp strings. "Describe the worm—how big? What color? Were his scales ragged? Did you see any wounds?"

The slave cocked his head to the side and squinted at the bard. "Didn't see it, not that you'll believe me. Saw its hoard. Gold, jewels, old swords and drinking horns." He scrolled his fingers through the air, as if to list all the other things he'd seen.

"I believe you," the king said. "It takes more courage than you might possess to remain calm at the sight of a dragon. Battle-hardened warriors have been known to run in terror when such a monster appears."

"You didn't see it, then," the bard said. "But you must have seen something."

"Aye, I saw something." The slave's tone was no less surly when he spoke to the bard. "In the dragon's barrow, I saw piles of treasure—and piles of bones."

The king and the bard exchanged a glance. The poet spoke again. "What kind of bones?"

The slave looked from one man to the other, then sneered. "Human bones." He dragged out the words, shifting his eyes around the crowd as he spoke.

Rune felt a prickling at the back of his neck. Near him, he could hear people murmuring to each other and Fulla hissing something to her husband as she caught him by the arm.

"If you saw the hoard, why couldn't you see the dragon?" the bard asked.

The slave gave another shifty grin. "I reckon it was on the other side of all that gold. Where the smoke was coming from." He gestured at his nose as if to show smoke rising from it.

The king gave his head an impatient shake, making Rune think of a warhorse. "This man might not have seen the dragon, but it's been seen nonetheless." Suddenly, he turned to Rune. "Come forward, son," he said.

Rune's stomach dropped to his knees. He stood rooted to the ground, staring at the king.

"Step forward, he said," a woman whispered fiercely.

"Go on, lad," Hemming said, giving him a push.

The king spoke to the crowd. "Rune was on the crag when the dragon flew over. The fear the monster inspires is so great that he wasn't able to see much."

Someone snorted derisively. Dayraven.

The king ignored it, turning back to Rune. "Ketil tells me you've seen the dragon again."

So Ketil *had* believed him after all. Rune's throat grew dry. He closed his eyes, willing the crowd to disappear, but he could hear them murmuring.

"Tell me what happened," the king said, his voice gentle. Rune opened his eyes and looked into the king's bright blue ones. As he did, it seemed as if the rest of the world had disappeared, taking all the sound and scorn and mockery with it, leaving just Rune and the king.

He gulped in air. "I was on the mountain," he said, "on the trail that leads up from the crag."

The king nodded, encouraging him.

"A mist came up—I couldn't see."

"Ahh, the giant's breath," he heard the bard say, but

Rune didn't take his eyes from the king's. "The giants may be in league with the dragon."

"Go on, Rune."

He swallowed, trying to wet his tongue enough so he could speak.

"It came out of the mist and flew just over my head." He raised his hands as if they held shield and sword, reliving the moment. "It burned my shield—and then I fell, and I lost my sword." Breaking his eyes from the king's in his shame, he looked down at his sheathed weapon and mumbled, "Ketil found it."

A croaking sound made him look up again in time to see a raven settling itself on a thatched roof just beyond the crowd. Finn's roof.

The king saw it, too. He looked back at Rune. "Could you tell how big it was?"

Rune nodded. "Huge, as big as a ship, a longboat. It reared back its head, the way a horse does, before it breathed fire on me."

"You saw that?" the king asked, excitement in his voice.

The bard stepped up to stand beside the king. "You saw its neck, its underside?"

Rune stared at them, trying to remember. It had all happened so fast. "I—" He shook his head.

"Could you see its scales?" the bard asked.

Rune nodded.

"Were they a different color underneath? Lighter?"

Again, he nodded, in his memory looking up again at the dragon as it shot fire toward him. "And when it reared back, there was a light place here"—he brought his hand to his chest—"a white spot."

"A white spot? Are you certain?" The bard fixed him with his single eye, giving him a look that just moments ago would have made him shudder. But now, Rune looked away, nodding, his eyes firmly on the dragon who flew through his memory.

"Yes, I'm certain," he said, and as he spoke, he remembered more. "There was a circle of scales, gold or bronze, maybe, and a spot of white inside them."

The bard looked at the king, who was smiling.

"Do you realize what you've done?" the king asked Rune.

Rune shook his head, not understanding.

The king turned from him and spoke loudly, addressing the crowd. "The dragon's weak spot, the place a sword can enter—Rune has found it!"

Rune kept his eyes on the king while, around him, people began talking. "Every dragon is different," the king said, his voice commanding the crowd to listen. "Each has a vulnerable place on its body—under the arm, in the belly. But now we know about our dragon, our enemy, and with that knowledge, we will defeat it!"

Cheers broke out, and Rune could hear the rattling of spears, the clashing of metal as shields answered them.

Oski, one of Ottar's sons, yelled, "Rune!" and Rune turned to see the little boy waving at him, his brother Omi jumping up and down beside him in excitement.

Rune felt his neck flaming, and he hung his head in embarrassment as a strong arm encircled his shoulder. "Well done," the king said quietly, and Rune looked up to meet his eyes. They looked at each other for a long moment before the king called out, "Ketil! Is there any ale to be spared for this warrior?"

Rune hadn't thought he could flush more deeply.

Ketil gave him a lopsided grin and turned to go, but a voice called out, "I'll get it, Ketil." Wyn. Rune hadn't seen her standing beside her mother, behind the king. Now, her skirts flared behind her as she ran to her house.

As Rune watched her go, the raven on the thatched roof caught his eye. A breeze ruffled the downy feathers around its neck, and it cocked its head, hopped twice along the gables, then spread its wings and wheeled out of sight.

Wyn emerged from the doorway, a drinking horn in her hands. Rune was watching her when he became aware of the slave's voice. "Hear me, O King."

King Beowulf looked at the man, who said, "Where did he get that sword?" and motioned with his head toward Rune.

"It's his—from his father before him."

A sudden silence fell over the circle of people surrounding Rune. Wyn stopped uncertainly, halfway between the doorway and the king, watching.

"Then his father is a traitor and a coward. That sword belonged to Eanmund—and Eanmund was stabbed in the back." The slave's words fell with the weight of an anvil in the hushed crowd.

Rune stared at the slave unseeing and felt the eyes of the people boring into him.

ELEVEN

HE DIDN'T KNOW EXACTLY HOW HE'D ENDED UP IN FINN'S house—it was as if his mind had been stolen from him the moment the slave had spoken. All he could remember was the stricken look on the king's face and someone's hand on his arm, exactly where he had a bruise from falling down the mountain. As men hustled him forward, images and sounds splintered into shards around him, mingling with the sharp pain in his arm.

And now, the dark interior of Finn's house, where the Thor's hammer amulet hung from a peg on the wall, a cup below it, an offering to the god. *Goat's milk? Mead?* Rune wondered distractedly, unable to focus.

"Sit," somebody said, pushing him onto a bench, and he sat, despite the ache in his tailbone.

A body before him resolved itself into Gar, gripping the slave by an arm. Rune looked down.

The bench creaked, and he felt it shift as a man lowered himself onto it. The king.

His mind was clear enough to know that he shouldn't be sitting by the king this way, but as he started to rise, the king put a hand on Rune's leg, guiding him back down.

In front of him, a pair of rich leather shoes worked with decorative stitching, shoes without even a hint of dirt on them—the bard's—paced back and forth, sometimes nearing the slave's stained and ragged shoes. A smaller pair of feet in brown wool slippers peeked out from the bottom of a skirt. They came forward, then backed away. Rune looked up dully to see Thora setting a drinking horn on the sideboard. Dayraven stood beside the door, sword in hand.

"Tell us what you know." The king spoke without ceremony, and Rune turned to him, startled, wondering how to answer. But the king was looking at the slave.

"I know how Eanmund died. And I know who killed him." The slave kept his voice low and steady, with no hint of scorn.

"There are many Eanmunds," the bard said.

"Eanmund, son of Ohthere."

No one spoke.

Rune could hear Gar's whistling breath. Outside, a child called out—or maybe it was a bird—and he pictured the bright bowl of the sky, the clean chill of the air, and wished he were out in it. Anywhere but here, where the thatch of the roof seemed to bear down on him, the wood of the walls tilted in toward him, and his life seemed as if it were being ground into darkness.

His father a traitor and a backstabber! People had been right to treat him with scorn, Maybe cowardice was a family trait.

"So." The king breathed out heavily. He sounded weary. "You are a Swede, then."

"I have been among that tribe."

"And you count yourself loyal to them, although you come here, seeking a place in my kingdom?"

The slave didn't answer.

"Why should we trust his word?" Thora said from the shadows. "He's already told us what he thinks of honor."

From his position guarding the door, Dayraven said, "I want to hear what he has to say about the boy's father."

Out of the corner of his eye, Rune could see the king nodding.

"Go on," he said.

The slave shifted his weight from one foot to the other. Rune looked up at his face, his skin creased and beaten by weather and age and who knew what else. As he watched, the man's face seemed to shift somehow, his skin looking smooth and supple for an instant. Rune blinked. It must have been a trick of the light. The slave flicked his eyes at Rune, then back to the king.

"I was Eanmund's man. I served him well."

When the slave stopped, the bard said, "Where were you when he died?"

"I wasn't there." The sneer returned to his face, the snarl to his voice. "I was a captive. Taken by the filthy Wayamundings to be their slave."

The king made a noise, a cross between a cough and a bark. "So you escaped them and ran straight to me."

The slave raised his chin, giving him a look of such insolence that Gar jerked him by the arm.

"Perhaps you didn't know that my father was a Wayamunding," the king said mildly. "Either way, you haven't told us how Eanmund died."

"Like I said. *His* father"—he jerked a hand toward Rune, who felt it like a blow, as if he'd been hit by elf-shot—"his father stabbed Eanmund in the back. After they'd sworn a truce."

Rune closed his eyes.

"I wonder how you could know that when you weren't there—when you were held captive by the Wayamundings."

"I've heard." The slave's voice dripped with contempt. "They made me a slave; they didn't cut off my ears."

Rune opened his eyes at the sound of a dagger sliding from its sheath and saw Gar pushing its point into the slave's neck just under his ear. "Interesting suggestion," he said.

The king made a tiny gesture, and Gar lowered the blade, giving Ketil a grim smile over the slave's head.

"You have heard." The bard stepped forward. "So have

I. But the story I heard was different. Remember Widsith, the bard who traveled through these parts on his way to visit the Franks." It wasn't a question—Rune was sure that everyone in the room, everyone except the slave, could recall the famous poet's visit. "So great is his knowledge that men say there is no history he cannot sing."

The king nodded.

"Widsith spoke of Eanmund," the bard said. "Of Eanmund the exile, who rebelled against his king. Of Eanmund's death in hard battle." He looked at Rune, who stared back, startled, caught by the bard's single eye glittering under a hedge of brow. "A fair fight with Weohstan."

"Weohstan!" Rune could hear the eagerness in the king's voice. He wanted to listen, but all he could think about were the bard's words: *a fair fight*. So his father wasn't a traitor after all!

"Weohstan the Wayamunding," the king was saying. "I have heard of his honor, his prowess with the sword."

In another part of the room, someone made a noise that sounded like disgust. Dayraven, Rune thought, but his attention was on the king, who turned to Rune, looking him full in the face. "Your father was a good man, Rune."

He swallowed.

"Ketil!" the king called. "Didn't I ask for ale?"

"My lord, you did," Ketil said, grinning at Rune.

Wyn stepped out of a shadowy corner. Rune watched as she murmured something to Ketil, then picked up the drinking horn from the sideboard and brought it to the king.

"My lord," she said, dropping into a graceful curtsy but keeping her eyes on the king's face.

He took the horn and drank a long quaff before he returned it to her. He must have given her some signal, because her mouth moved into the barest hint of a smile before she moved to stand in front of Rune, holding the horn before him in both hands, her eyes on his. They were blue, like the king's. He'd never noticed before.

The bard cleared his throat, and Rune realized everyone was waiting for him. He reached for the horn, hoping it was too dark in the room for anyone to see the blood rushing to his face.

The ale tasted good to his dry tongue and cooled his parched throat.

He handed the horn back to Wyn, then watched as she took it to the bard, to Gar, and finally to Ketil, never taking his eyes from her bright braid, her slender fingers, her solemn face.

Then it struck him. He had been offered the horn first, right after the king, before Gar and Ketil, even before the bard. And he hadn't even realized.

"Come with me," the king said as they left Finn's house. Rune looked back to see Wyn silhouetted in the doorway, leaning down to pick up something from the floor, her movement graceful and assured.

The king saw him looking and glanced back. "That girl is one of the kingdom's treasures. She has her mother's wisdom and her father's cool head."

Just then, Ketil stepped to Wyn's side and the door closed.

"This way." The king touched Rune's shoulder, guiding him down the path that led past the smithy. "Ketil told me about Amma," he said quietly.

The suddenness of the statement caught Rune off guard, and he sucked in his breath, feeling as if he had been punched.

"She is a great loss," the king said, and a choked quality in his voice made Rune look just as the king lowered his head. He thought he saw a tear glinting in the corner of the king's eye. A tear? Why would the king mourn a crotchety old woman who lived on Hwala's farm?

They walked on in silence, stopping beside the blackened ruins of the golden-roofed hall. The dais was gone. So were the long tables that had lined the fire pit in the center of the hall, where the king's warriors had gathered to drink and feast and boast of their deeds. Now, not only was the hall gone, but so were many of the warriors. Only a mead bench remained, a tendril of smoke still twining up from its far end.

Gazing at the destruction, Rune reconstructed the hall in his mind, recognizing where they had held weapons practice; where the alcoves had been in which the women tended to gather; where the bard's high seat had been, on the dais beside the throne. He looked up as the king spoke.

"How much did she tell you about herself?"

Amma? About herself? Rune shook his head. "She told me about you, about the monsters you killed, about—"

The king cut him off with a wave of his hand.

"She was a peaceweaver, a bride whose task was to heal the wounds of two warring peoples, bonding them together."

Rune listened, astonished. He knew about peaceweavers, of course—half of Amma's tales had been about them. But what the king was saying didn't make sense. Not about Amma.

The king sighed, shaking his head. "When the lord is killed, the spear seldom rests, no matter how worthy the bride."

"But I thought peaceweavers were noblewomen," Rune said.

"They are." The king gave him a long look, and finally his meaning began to sink in. Amma had been nobly born?

"She was the daughter of a Frisian earl, sent off to marry a Shylfing lord. The two families had been feuding for generations. When peace couldn't be woven, Amma lost her husband, her brother, and one of her sons. Her husband's clan reviled her, and her own family was destroyed. I offered her refuge."

"But, the way she lived—"

"I know," the king said. "It was her choice. She was sick

and weary of wars and kings and the intrigues of court. She asked to live in Hwala's hut. She made me promise not to reveal who she was." He stared off over the ruins of his hall, thin tears making tracks in the dust on his cheeks.

Rune watched him in awe—it was all too much to take in.

"But there's more," the king said, his jaw clenching. He met Rune's eyes again, not bothering to wipe his tears away. "Amma had two sons. One of them was killed in the feud. The other son died in a different fight." He lowered his head, eyes closed, pausing for so long that Rune wondered if he was going to say anything else.

Finally, the king looked up again, directly at Rune. "When she took you in," he said, "and she *demanded* that I let her, even though I wanted you brought up in the hall . . ."

Rune waited, willing him to go on.

"When she took you in," the king said again, "she must have recognized your sword."

Rune watched him, not comprehending.

"Rune," the king said, reaching out to grip his arm, his fingers digging into a bruise so hard the pain was excruciating. Rune tried to concentrate, to understand what the king was saying.

"Eanmund, the man your father killed—" The king stopped and bowed his head a little, his eyelids closing wearily. Then he met Rune's gaze again.

"Eanmund was Amma's son."

TWELVE

FOOTSTEPS CRUNCHED OVER THE CHARRED TIMBERS OF the king's hall, coming toward him. Rune hunched into his cloak and kept his head down.

When a scout had arrived with news for the king, Rune had stayed behind, sitting on the blackened mead bench, staring at beams that had once held up the hall's golden roof. Dragonfire had almost obscured the stories carved and painted on them. Almost, but not completely. His eyes lingered on an image of Thor wearing his gloves and wielding his hammer, while beside him, Odin listened to the news of the world that his ravens, Huginn and Muninn, whispered into his ears. The interlacing knotwork that surrounded the gods now receded into burned oak. On the other beam, a dragon-prowed ship manned by helmeted swordsmen waited in vain for a wind—its square sail had burned away—while Sleipnir, Odin's eight-legged horse, galloped into ashy darkness, a warrior on his back. A dead warrior on his way to Valhalla.

Gray clouds rolled across the sun, bringing with them a chill wind, making Rune wrap the cloak tightly around himself.

His father might not have been a traitor, but what did it matter? He had killed Amma's son. And Amma had known all along. What else hadn't she told him? She was noble; so was he. Why couldn't she have just said so?

He balled his hand into a fist. *Amma!* he wanted to scream, but he kept the name inside him. Surely it was wrong to feel such anger toward the dead, but he couldn't help it. She hadn't told him *anything*. Why?

The footsteps slowed, then stopped a few paces away. Still Rune didn't look up. He hoped whoever it was would hear his fierce internal command to go away.

"Rune." Wyn's voice.

Not now, he thought. Not ever. His life was over, and he was just starting to realize it. The farm was destroyed—he had no place and no means to live. What family he had was gone. He would never be able to wield a sword well enough to be one of the king's warriors. And his father . . .

Skirts rustled and he felt Wyn sit beside him on the log.

"I want to know about my father," she said. "How he died."

Rune raised his head, startled out of himself. He caught a whiff of rosemary and felt the warmth of her body.

She stared straight ahead, her mouth set in a line. "Tell me."

An image of Finn on the mountainside filled his head, and he swallowed, trying to find his voice. "He died fighting."

She turned to face him, anger darkening her blue eyes. "That's all Ketil would say, too. No one will tell me anything. I'm not a child."

Rune blinked in surprise. "But it's true. He was lying faceup, his sword in his hand. If he had been running away, he would have been facedown."

"Oh." She stared ahead of her again. "Now I see. What else?"

"He was . . . he was badly burned. By the dragon." Rune looked down. "I couldn't tell who it was at first, but then I saw his sword."

Wyn swallowed.

"His shield—he'd cast it aside. He must have known the dragon would burn it." He cringed at the memory of his own stupidity, the way he'd held his shield up as if it could save him. Doing so had cost him the time he would have needed to kill the monster.

They sat in silence until Wyn whispered, "Is it true about Amma?"

Rune bristled, the sharpness of his anger surprising him.

"What do you mean?" Just how much had she heard? Did she know what the king had told him about Amma's son?

"Ketil says she's dead."

His shoulders slumped as the fight went out of him. He nodded.

"And Skyn, too? And Skoll?"

Rune nodded again. "Everybody at Hwala's farm."

"I can't believe Amma's gone." She touched the edge of her cloak, twisting the wool back and forth between her thumb and forefinger.

He looked at her, incredulous. "What do you care about Amma? She's nothing to you, or to anybody else except me." He could hear how surly his voice sounded, but he couldn't stop himself. His jaw stiff with anger, he stared past the fallen beams that marked the far side of the king's hall. Beyond them lay open, rocky ground, stretching to a line of dark firs.

Beside him, Wyn rose. Her skirt brushed against his leg as she whirled on him. "You arrogant fool," she said. "You think you were the only one who knew Amma? What do you think we womenfolk were doing while you were trying to learn how to use a sword? Don't you think we have lives, too?"

Her outburst astonished him. Who did she think she was? Amma had never said anything about her to Rune. And now that Amma was dead, Wyn thought she somehow owned a part of her?

"You know nothing about her." His words came out in

a growl, and he could feel rage billowing in his chest like clouds before a storm.

Wyn's eyes narrowed as she stared at him, and he could see her nostrils flaring. When she finally spoke, her voice was low and measured. "Maybe Dayraven was right about you."

As she turned, a voice called from behind them. "Wyn! I've been looking everywhere for you. Come on, there's a lot to do before tonight." It was her cousin Gerd.

"I'm coming." Her words snapped like breaking sticks.

As the two girls moved away, Rune could hear Gerd saying, "Was that Rune? The bruises on his face look awful. Why is he wearing Uncle Brand's cloak?"

"I thought you were in a hurry," Wyn answered. Then they were gone.

Wyn's uncle's cloak? Rune looked down at the fine stitching on the edge of the wool. Was she the one who had covered him as he slept before the fire? He reached up and tenderly poked at a bruise under his eye. It must have come from his fall down the mountain. Each passing moment made him aware of another bruise or ache, the way he used to feel after a fight with Skyn and Skoll, back in what seemed like another life.

He would give anything to have Skyn and Skoll gang up on him again, as long as it would mean Amma was still alive.

He didn't understand why he felt so angry at Wyn. It seemed as if everything he'd known about himself, about

Amma, had turned out to be a lie. He'd always thought that he was the closest person to her under the wide skies, that the two of them were alone together against the rest of the world. But now it seemed as if everybody else had known Amma better than he had. As if she had chosen other people to share her secrets with, instead of him. As if he hadn't been that important to her at all.

His anger fled as quickly as it had come, and grief filled the space it left behind like black mud sliding down a mountainside to drown a valley below. He slumped against the terrible weight.

His head in his hands, he whispered, "Amma," and as he did, a voice seemed to answer.

"Amma?" He rose, looking toward the fir trees. Had she called him? He stumbled over a fire-blackened bench, righted himself, and began running, his sword slapping against his leg, his shoes hitting the rocky ground beyond the ruined hall.

Just inside the curtain of fir trees, he stopped, listening, but all he could hear was the sound of his own panting. As his heartbeat slowed, he stood in the cold, silent air, breathing in the bright scent of pine, feeling brittle needles breaking under his feet. Far above him, branches swayed in the wind, and when he listened hard enough, he could hear trees groaning. In the distance, some kind of bird beat a rhythm against a hollow trunk. Then it stopped.

Rune felt something, some presence, comforting or malign he couldn't tell. He stiffened.

"Amma?" he whispered, and suddenly a memory flooded through him, one he didn't know he had, of a man with pointed teeth grinning at him—not kindly, either. The slave! But a younger, cleaner version of the slave, clad in rich clothing, a fine sword girt to his belt. A cloak was clasped at his shoulder, its wool stitched with a pattern that looked almost like feathers. He seemed somehow larger, more powerful, than he was now, and his fingers dug into the ruff of the dog that stood beside him. Then the dog turned its head, and as it looked straight at Rune, he saw that it was no dog; it was a wolf, a glint of saliva on its black lips.

As quickly as it had come, the image faded, leaving him with an aching head. Had it been a memory? Had he seen the slave before? He didn't know. Eyes shut to the sharp pain in his temples, he laid his hand against a tree branch to regain his balance. He willed the vision back, trying to recall exactly what he had seen, the pattern on the slave's cloak, the bright golden torque around his neck, and something else, too, if he could only remember—

Something hit against his thigh, making him yelp.

A goat, a white one. It lowered its horns and butted him again, gently.

"What do you want?" Rune said irritably. He'd been so close to understanding the vision; he was sure of it.

The goat bleated, looking at him with strange eyes— one was yellow, the other blue with gold flecks in it. It pranced out of the forest, looking behind as if to see that

Rune was following. When he took his hand off the tree, a wave of dizziness made him stagger.

The goat bleated again.

Rune steadied himself and followed it. As he stepped onto the rocks, a croaking sound made him look back in time to see a raven hopping along a branch, sending a shower of bark to the ground before it lifted into the air.

When he turned around again, the goat was gone. So was the image and all the details he'd been on the verge of remembering. Everything except the splitting headache.

He shook his head and began walking, brushing pine needles off his cloak. Not his cloak—Wyn's uncle's cloak. The uncle who had died in the dragon attack. Anybody could have put it over him while he slept, not just Wyn. It could have been Ketil—he'd found Rune's sword and shared his breakfast with him.

The thought of that breakfast made him realize how hungry he was.

He headed for the stronghold.

The smell of roasting meat wafted from Wyn's house. Maybe she would forgive him. And maybe she would give him something to eat to tide him over until tonight's feast.

He was almost to the door when someone came hurtling around the corner, looking behind him. Rune jumped to the side, but he couldn't get out of the way before a man barreled into him.

"Oh!" the bard said, looking at Rune and then linking an arm into his and pulling him down the narrow street. "You don't want to go in there."

"I don't?"

"Trust me. You don't. Feast preparations." He guided Rune past a bond servant, who hurried by carrying four squawking chickens upside down by their legs.

"You go in there and you're no better off than those hens. They wanted me to chop herbs. Me! A bard!"

Rune thought he saw a glint of humor in the man's single eye, and he hurried along beside him, his arm still caught.

They turned past the stables, and the bard glanced behind him, then slowed. He sighed exaggeratedly, his hand to his chest. "Safe, I think." He looked Rune up and down as if just noticing whom he had waylaid, and suddenly he was the mysterious bard again, his demeanor changed as if he'd donned a new cloak. Close up, the dark space where his missing eye should have been was even more frightening because of the thick eyebrow that outlined it, and in the corner, the eyelashes.

The bard freed Rune's arm, and as he did, he gave Rune an insulted look, as if Rune had been the one who had forced the bard to accompany *him* down the street.

The man shook his head and fixed his single eye on Rune. "I was against it, you know, when our king asked for Amma's hand. It was wrong of me; she would have made a fine queen. That woman's wisdom and her courage . . . well, not that it mattered. She refused him. She'd seen enough of marriage, I suppose."

Rune took a step backward. "King Beowulf?" he said, incredulous. "Asked Amma to marry him?"

The bard's eye skewered his. "Don't you know anything about her?" He stared at Rune for a long moment, the black pit of his missing eye seeming to bore into Rune as if it could see directly into his thoughts. "Didn't you ever ask?"

He turned and walked away, leaving Rune gaping in astonishment.

THIRTEEN

THE STABLES. HE NEEDED A QUIET PLACE TO THINK, TO try to understand. The king had wanted to marry Amma? His own father had killed Amma's son? What else didn't he know about her?

"Rune!" a man called just as he was about to step through the stable door. "We need some help."

He turned to see Buri waving at him. The stocky farmer, his fair skin sunburned from working the harvest, looked harassed. "You're not doing anything—hurry up."

Cautiously, Rune followed him into a barn near the blacksmith's shop. Was this a setup? He'd seen the two young farmers in the king's hall before, but they'd always given him and Amma a wide berth. He didn't think they liked him, and now, having heard the accusations against his father and having seen him hustled into Finn's house, they had even less reason to trust him. They might not have been warriors, but between the two of them, they had enough muscles to bring down an aurochs.

He hung back to let Buri go into the barn first. Then, keeping his hand on his sword hilt, he stepped inside, flicking his eyes around the shadowy space. Surt looked up when Rune came in. His hair was as sun-bleached as the pile of straw he was holding.

"Buri says a dragon has horns like a mountain goat's."

"What?" Rune stared at him.

"You know. Curled." Surt circled a finger beside his ear. "He's wrong, right? Tell him he's wrong."

Rune looked from one farmer to the other. They watched him, waiting. The back of his neck prickled. Suddenly, he knew—he'd walked right into their trap.

Tensing, he looked over one shoulder, then the other, waiting for the attack, but the dark corners were empty except for a cow placidly chewing her cud.

He looked back at Buri's and Surt's faces. They looked eager, not hostile. "What are you talking about?"

"You've seen the monster—what's it look like?" Buri asked. "Doesn't it have horns?"

Surt hefted the pile of straw in his hands. "We have to make a dragon, a straw one for the feast." He gestured with his thumb toward Buri. "He thinks he knows everything."

Rune let out his breath. "Well," he said, "it *does* have horns."

Buri beamed, his sunburned face bright with pleasure. "See? If you'd just listen to me."

"But they're straight horns, not curled," Rune said.

It was Surt's turn to grin. "Ha." He gave the other farmer a friendly punch in the arm, so hard that Rune was sure Buri would fall over. He hoped they wouldn't be that friendly with him.

"Come on, you can help us," Surt said. "We've got wood underneath and then we'll tie straw around it. What about its tail? What does that look like?"

Rune stepped forward, his shoulders relaxing, and grabbed a wisp of straw.

As they worked, constructing a dragon as long as a tall man, the two farmers joked with one another and complained about having to be away from their farms at the height of harvest.

"Your farms weren't burned?" Rune asked them in surprise. He had come to think of the entire kingdom, all its fields and farms, as a smoldering ruin, like the king's hall.

"Wouldn't have believed what they said about this monster if I hadn't seen Wald's farm—the whole thing burned to cinders. Wald, too, and Thorgunna and all their kids." Surt lowered his head for a moment, then shook it. "Shame, that was. They were good people."

"Aye," Buri said. "But if we're going to have any harvest at all, we've got to get back. My wife can't do it—she's got the baby to look after, and the animals, and she's about to have another one."

"What, an animal?" Surt threw him a punch, followed by a grin.

"Hoping for a horse—we sure could use one."

Both men laughed. Then Buri turned serious again. "The king needs to get on with it, get this dragon out of the way so we can get back to work."

Rune stared at him. "It's not like that."

"What's that, now?" Surt asked, looking up from the twine he was winding around the long tail.

"You don't just go out and kill a dragon and have it done with," Rune said, looking from one farmer to the other. "It's not that easy. Finn tried, you know. It got him killed."

"Well, sure, but he went by himself. What a fool."

Rune hardly realized he had moved until he found himself grasping Surt's sleeve and staring directly into his eyes. "Finn was no fool."

Surt gave him a strange look, and Rune stepped back, dropping Surt's tunic. Surt brushed it as if he were dislodging a piece of dirt and then, in the sudden silence, went back to the tail he was constructing. Rune saw the glance he exchanged with Buri.

Finn might have been no fool, but Rune felt like one. Just when he'd gained the men's confidence, he'd thrown it away. "Sorry," he mumbled.

"Hand me that stick, would you?" Buri said, easing the silence.

They continued to work, Surt and Buri speaking in low

voices about their families, their farms, and above all, the harvest, while Rune sank into his own dark thoughts.

As he shaped a dragon's leg with straw, his swordbelt bit into his hip and he shifted it. It would be easier to work if he took it off, but he didn't trust the two farmers—or himself. He'd already lost the sword once.

His father's sword, taken from the man he'd killed—Amma's son. What had it done to her, having the weapon in the back of the hut all those years? He thought of her sitting on her three-legged stool on winter evenings when the wind quested around the walls and sent bursts of cold air through the smoke hole. He remembered the way she would draw the sword from its sheath and hold it up to the dancing firelight, painstakingly checking it for rust before dipping a rag into her pot of whale oil. Carefully, gently, as if it were a ritual, she would smooth the rag over the sharp metal, working oil into the runes etched near the hilt. Now he thought he understood why. It wasn't just his father's sword; it had been her son's, too.

She had had every right to have Rune killed in revenge for her son's death. Most people would even argue that it had been her duty, and in theory, he agreed with them. Instead, she had raised him, nurtured him, treated him like her own child. Once, he remembered, after she had sung a long tale of feuding tribes and failed peace pledges, she had stopped and looked at him. "Men say it's better to avenge your friends and family than to mourn them. That's not how it seems to me." He had argued with her about it, blissfully unaware of his own ignorance. Yet even knowing that she had saved his life, he knew she'd been wrong. Vengeance was the way of the world. All the stories spoke of it, all the wisdom of the tribe taught it. It would have been better for everyone if Amma had demanded his death the moment she saw his father's sword. If she had called for it, the king wouldn't have denied her. Neither would Dayraven.

Rune twisted a strand of straw so hard it snapped.

When he had washed ashore in the boat, people said, Dayraven would have been only too happy to kill him.

"What about that white spot you saw?" Buri said, and Rune looked up. Straw dust hung thick in the air, and he coughed, then swallowed. He could feel the two men watching him.

"The white spot—where does it go?" Buri asked again.

Rune put his hand to his chest. "Here, below the neck."

"How big?" Surt asked.

"Has to be big enough to see at night," Buri said.

Together they painted a target—too large to be realistic, but the idea would be clear to anyone who saw it.

"All right, it's getting dark. We'd better get it down to the Feasting Field," Buri said. "Smell that meat roasting? I'm hungry!"

Rune's stomach growled in answer and Buri laughed. "Come on, ready?" The three of them hefted the dragon to their shoulders and carried it out of the barn.

As they walked down the narrow lane, weaving between

walls to keep from knocking the tail off, a few scattered people watched them. An old woman shrank back against a wall, hiding her face behind one hand. Buri saw her and called out, "Don't worry, Mother. This worm won't bite."

When they stepped onto the path leading to the Feasting Field, more people joined them. Ottar's boys came running, shouting, "Look, look! The dragon!" and jumped up to try to poke it. Two little girls stood hand in hand, eyes wide, as they passed.

"Dragon coming through!" Buri called as they approached two women struggling with an iron cauldron that hung on a beam between them. The women set down their load and cheered as the effigy passed by.

Footsteps behind them told Rune that someone was racing to catch up—Od, a boy he knew from weapons training in the hall. He came alongside and grabbed hold of the creature's sagging back leg. Then Brokk edged in between Rune and Buri, taking part of the dragon on his broad shoulder. "Hey, Thialfi!" he yelled, and the warrior with the damaged sword arm loped up to take a place near the effigy's head.

Rune stepped away, mingling with the crowd, letting Buri, Surt, and the others get in front of him. Ahead in the twilight, torches bobbed in the air as their bearers moved forward, chasing away night-walkers and spirits, preparing the way for the king.

He thought of the king's tears. Had he loved Amma? She had told Rune the king had married once, long ago, but his wife died young and childless. But she'd never told him that the king had asked her to be his wife, his queen. Why had she chosen Hwala's hut over the king's golden hall? Why had she chosen so many of the things she'd done?

A drumming of hooves made him look back. Two horses, tails flying, thundered along beside the path, racing each other to the Feasting Field. Gar and Ketil crouched low over the horses' manes, urging their mounts onward. Gar was slightly ahead, but as Rune watched, Ketil's horse nosed forward. "Come on, Gar!" someone yelled, and a girl cried out, "Go, Ketil!"

As the horses disappeared in a flurry of dirt and grass kicked up by their hooves, Rune turned to see who was cheering Ketil on. Wyn stood watching the race, a heavy pot in each hand. He stopped and waited for her to catch up. When she got close enough, he reached out to take one of the pots. She wrestled it back, never even looking at him, and marched down the path.

FOURTEEN

BY THE TIME RUNE MADE IT TO THOR'S OAK, IT WAS almost fully dark, but lanterns swayed in the tree branches and dozens of torches burned across the field. On the far side, a bonfire illuminated the stone altar with its image of Thor, his beard painted bloody red, his eyes flashing with lightning. In his gloved hand, the god held Mjollnir, his hammer, high in the air. Shadowy silhouettes passed in front of the stone as people scurried by, making preparations, some of them stopping to confer with the group of men huddled near the goat that had been baking in a pit in the ground all afternoon.

Somewhere nearby, fish was frying. The aroma made Rune mad with hunger. He pushed into a group of women, hoping for a handout, but one of them, Elli, recognized him and shooed him away, laughing. "You'll have to wait, just like the rest of us," she said. She looked over his head, her eyes widening, just as Rune heard the clopping of hooves. He turned to see the king riding past on Silvertop, his white stallion, draped in his rich green cloak, a golden torque around his neck and a gleaming circlet on his white head. Rune dropped to his knees, while Elli and the other women knelt alongside him, pulling their children down with them.

They rose as the king passed, and a new smell— chickens roasting on a spit—filled Rune's nostrils, tormenting him further. He wove his way toward the fire, where he could see the sizzling meat. But it was too late. The ceremony had begun. He'd have to wait for the feast before he could quell the grumbling of his belly.

In front of the bonfire, King Beowulf sat high on Silvertop's back, his golden torque catching the firelight as the bard chanted words Rune couldn't hear. The bard held a spear stretched out like an offering in both hands. The king took it from him.

Rune heard the intake of the crowd's breath as the old king pulled his arm back. Then, as he let the spear fly, a strong, sure shot over the wind-whipped flames and into the black night beyond, people cheered.

Dayraven yelled, "For Odin!" and several voices answered, "Odin!"

"Well, I suppose they have to appease him," an old woman near Rune said.

"Hush! We may be Thor's people, but you don't want to anger the raven god," a man replied.

Rune edged closer to the bonfire, stepping past couples, dodging children who scampered between grown-up legs, excited to be out in the night. Now he could see the goat's head, skewered on its long pole, dancing a ring around the bonfire. Too many bodies pressed in front of him for Rune to see who carried it.

A sound like thunder started low from near the oak tree. As it built, growing louder and louder, rolling and booming like a storm, the crowd hushed.

Suddenly, it stopped. In the silence, the king called out, "Thor, our beloved friend, hear us! May the Hammer-Wielder receive our sacrifice."

The goat's head dove into the fire, and as sparks flew into the night sky, the crowd erupted in cheers, men raising their fists and slapping each other on the back, a woman swinging her child around in her arms, friends laughing and calling, "The Thunderer!" and "The Hammerer!" and "Thor!"

Rune ducked past Hemming, who had his arm around Fulla, and sidestepped a group of chattering girls. Everyone had someone, everyone except him. Even if Skyn and Skoll had tormented him, even if Hwala never allowed him a moment's rest, he and Amma had still been a part of their farm.

Firelight glinted off teeth in grinning faces and

gleamed in eyes as people smiled at each other. In the dark, Rune pushed past them, moving toward the fire, hungry and sore from his fall down the mountain. His tailbone ached. So did his shoulder and the bruise on his hip that his swordbelt kept rubbing against.

As he found a place where he could see better, the king held up both hands for silence. Ottar raised a finger to warn his boys, and Elli patted her baby on the back to calm him. Now people moved forward, forming a half-circle around King Beowulf. When all was quiet except for a crying toddler, he dismounted and handed his reins to Gerd, who proudly led the white stallion away.

Rune glanced back at the bonfire and caught a glimpse of Wyn, firelight shining off her face as she looked up at Ketil. He leaned down as if he was whispering to her. Rune felt a sudden pang. Ketil? And Wyn? How long had that been going on? A long time, he realized, thinking of the times he'd seen them together, of their easy familiarity with each other. How had he never noticed before?

The bard stepped forward to stand beside the king, who gave him a nod. The king faced the crowd again, the glow of the bonfire catching his circlet, turning it into a fiery crown above his dark face. He looked around the gathering, meeting people's eyes. Finally, he spoke. "Many are those the dragon has taken. We honor them tonight."

"Finn," the bard called out in a commanding voice.

"Finn," the crowd answered, and Rune shut his eyes to the image of the warrior dead on the mountainside.

"Brand," the bard said. Again the people answered, calling back the name of the king's hearth companion, committing him to the care of the gods.

Modi, Thorgrim, Beorc the Red. On and on rolled the litany of the people killed by the dragon. Rune stared into the fire, repeating each name along with the crowd. When the bard came to Amma, Rune formed the word with his lips, but no sound came out. Nor could he say the names that came after: Hwala, Skyn, Skoll, Ula.

Not until the bard had moved on to Wald and Thorgunna and their children did the constriction in his throat loosen, unlocking his voice.

The bard finally fell silent, and Thora stepped forward, a flagon in her hands. She stopped in front of the bonfire, and Rune could see her lips moving, saying some ritual words he didn't know. Then she poured a stream of golden mead into the fire.

"May the gods receive them all!" the king called out, and the crowd repeated his words, adding their own. Names floated into the black sky as voices called them out. A woman wailed, "Thorgunna!" Her mother, Rune thought, or maybe her sister.

He bowed his head. "Hwala," he said in a low voice. "Skyn. Skoll. Ula." He swallowed and took a shaky breath. "Amma." He looked up, staring into the flames. They blurred and he blinked, then spoke again. This time his voice was clear and strong. "Amma."

After a few moments, the king held up his hands again,

asking for attention. "The dragon killed them. For that crime, with Thor's help, we will kill the dragon!"

Thundering erupted from behind the oak tree, and Rune looked toward it. He could just make out the shapes of men and boys drumming on hollow logs.

Now a path began to open in the crowd as people stepped backward. He watched, trying to understand what was happening. Then he saw Buri and Surt stepping into the light, each with a straw dragon arm on his shoulder— the effigy he had helped them build. People's tears turned to laughter as the dragon wove through the crowd, diving at a group of women and children, who screamed and ducked. As it came closer, Rune could see Brokk and Thialfi balancing the back legs on their shoulders and, behind them, Od holding up the tail.

Buri glanced his way and called out over the noise, "Rune, come help!" but Rune didn't move.

They veered away from him, the crowd parting before the dragon, Oski and Omi leaping up to touch its tail while Gerd ran after her cousins, trying to catch them and smiling at the laughing crowd as the little boys kept just out of her reach.

When the dragon neared the fire, the drumming intensified. The men carrying it held the effigy high in the air, twisting it like a dragon in flight. Then the drumming stopped and so did the dragon. The king raised his sword. Into the silence, he shouted, "You who battled the Midgard

Serpent, help us slay the serpent who torments us. As it has burned our kingdom, so let it become ashes. The dragon will die!"

His sword flashed down, and as it did, the men threw the straw creature into the fire. Flames consumed it, sending sparks flying, and the drumming began again, the sound competing with the cheering of the crowd.

Rune's face felt too stiff to cheer. On the other side of the bonfire, he could see Wyn, standing by herself now, tears still glinting on her cheeks as she smiled and clapped. As he studied her, a memory came to him, a winter memory from the hall, where her father had been teaching spear-work. He remembered setting down his heavy linden spear and looking into a corner to see Amma, firelight illuminating her hands as she wove them through the air, the way she did when she told stories. He could almost hear her bracelets clinking as they danced up and down her wrists. Sitting before her, a group of girls and women nodded their heads appreciatively as she spoke. Nearby, leaning against a beam, Wyn stood transfixed, her eyes on Amma's face.

It wasn't the only time he'd seen them together, he realized now. Memories flickered through his mind like light through oak branches on a summer day: Amma and Wyn walking together, arms linked, talking; the two of them bending over a bowl, Amma explaining something about cooking or healing—Rune wasn't sure what.

Wyn turned in his direction, and he looked away, ashamed of the rudeness he'd shown her, embarrassed to have thought she might have favored him.

The noise began to lessen, and he looked up to see the king holding his arm out to Thora. She advanced toward him slowly, the great, curved drinking horn in both hands. Its polished silver fittings gleamed, and Rune could see the honey-colored mead spilling over and running down the horn's sides.

The king spoke. "Tomorrow, the dragon dies. I will take with me ten warriors, the best of those here tonight. Thora!"

Thora held out the horn to the king. He took it from her, drank, and handed it back as people murmured their approval.

Then she walked toward Dayraven. As cold as the night air was, the warrior wore no cloak and his arm muscles bulged from his sleeveless tunic, exposing his gold armbands—all the rings he'd earned from the king for his prowess in battle. He accepted the horn and held it high. Rune could hear the sounds of approval from the crowd. Dayraven might have lost three fingers on his shield hand, but it hadn't lessened the power of his sword arm. He was a proven warrior, the one people were saying the king would choose as his successor now that Finn was gone. Dayraven turned to the crowd. "The wild ox who gave us this horn tried his best to kill me." He brandished the horn like a weapon, and mead sloshed from its mouth. "But just as I slew the great aurochs, so will I kill the dragon!" He took a long quaff, then handed the horn back to Thora.

"Dayraven!" someone yelled, and people clapped and whistled as the warrior stepped forward to stand beside the king.

Silence fell again as Thora walked around the circle. She stopped in front of Gar and stretched up to give him the horn; he had to lean down to take it. After drinking, he glanced around the crowd and gave a sudden grim smile. "The Wendel tribesmen are missing a warrior because of my sword." He unsheathed it with a ringing sound and held it in the air, where it caught the light from the bonfire. "And because of my sword, the dragon will be missing his life." He sheathed it again. As he strode up to join the king, people in the crowd slapped his back and called his name.

Ketil was next. Rune watched his friend accept the horn. Ketil had always been good with spear and sword. His father had been a warrior; he'd grown up in the stronghold. Nobody had been surprised when he'd been made one of the king's hearth companions. Rune could hear people murmuring words of favor as Ketil drank. He gave the horn back to Thora, his gray eyes wide in his solemn face. A movement made Rune turn just as Ketil began to speak his oath. It was Wyn, clasping her hands to her breast. He gazed at her shining eyes, the look of eagerness on her face. When he turned back, Ketil was already standing beside the king, and Thora was moving toward the next man.

Ottar took the cup and drank. Rune squinted at him—

the blond warrior's beard looked as if it were dripping with blood. He must have just dyed it in honor of Thor, Rune realized, and looked around to see if anyone else had done the same, but it was hard to tell in the wavering firelight. Ottar asked the god to stand with him in the fight, then shook his spear before he took his place. As he did, he wobbled and came so close to tripping that Ketil had to reach out to steady him; clearly, this wasn't the first mead Ottar had swallowed tonight. As he regained his balance and shook his spear again, the crowd cheered.

Brokk stepped forward next, firelight gleaming off his bald pate. He swung his cloak back to expose his armbands, but he didn't need to. Everyone knew Brokk was an obvious choice to fight beside the king. "You know what Thor did to the frost giants?" he called out.

"Hit 'em with his hammer!" somebody yelled.

"That's right—he cracked their skulls, just like I'll do with the dragon!" Brokk said, and people clapped and cried out, "Brokk!"

The cheers died down after Brokk joined the group of chosen warriors, and a muttering went through the crowd. Rune looked to see Thora heading toward Thialfi. "But his arm!" a woman near Rune whispered, and another hushed her, saying, "It's his warcraft the king wants." Scattered encouragement followed Thialfi as he joined the king, his sword arm hanging useless. Rune knew he wasn't the only one thinking about Finn and the five dead members of the king's hearth companions, or wondering when the border patrols would return home. Still, he could barely believe it when Thora approached Hemming. Age had robbed him of his strength—could his experience make up for it?

Hemming handed the horn back to Thora and cleared his throat. "The Wulfings," he started before he had to cough and clear his throat again. "The Wulfing raiders, they had us outnumbered," he said, and Rune heard someone near him groan lightly. Was Hemming going to tell the whole story, the way he did every chance he got?

Fulla laid her hand on her husband's arm and said something so quietly that only he could hear.

Hemming jerked his arm free and then looked back at Fulla. "My wife thinks I'll just talk the dragon to death," he said, and then glared at the crowd. "Maybe I will."

Dayraven roared with laughter, breaking the tension, and others joined in. Rune looked to see the king smiling at Hemming, who was now smiling himself.

"I'll tell it how we surprised the Wulfing raiders, how we came around from behind—"

Fulla gave him a push forward, and he turned back to her. "Old woman, you listen to how I'll kill that dragon."

She smiled. "Save your breath for the monster. Go join the king."

Hemming looked around at the crowd, gave a little shrug, and walked forward.

"Hemming!" someone yelled, and the crowd erupted into cheers.

When the noise finally settled, Thora offered the

horn to Buri. He took a step back, his sunburned face reddening further, glanced at Surt, and then accepted it. Rune could see his Adam's apple bobbing as he swallowed. "For Wald and Thorgunna," he said, and then quickly joined the king. Ketil reached out and clapped Buri on the arm as he got near, and Rune saw Buri ducking his head in embarrassment.

Surt was even more abashed than Buri. Whatever vow he made was lost—he mumbled it so low that no one could hear, and he kept his head down as he went to stand beside Buri.

Warriors were scarce if Buri and Surt were needed to make up the ten. The two men did know the southern approach to the mountain, Rune thought, and they could wield an ax. They'd trained with spear and ax like everybody else, even if neither of them owned a sword. But they were farmers who just wanted to get back to their fields. He shook his head.

He counted the men standing by the king. Nine.

People shifted, looking around to see who was left. Behind him, Rune saw Od, who was younger than he was, shaking his mother's hand off his shoulder.

Then he turned. Thora was walking directly toward him, her face solemn, the drinking horn in her hands. His mouth went dry. What vow would he make?

He had no spear, no helmet, he realized. Maybe he could ask Wyn to let him borrow her uncle Brand's.

He could feel his heart pounding with nervousness and

excitement as the horn got nearer and nearer, and now he could see the faces of the crowd reflected in its silver fittings.

He reached out his hands to take it.

Thora brushed past him, her eyes on someone else.

FIFTEEN

"OD!" A WOMAN CRIED, BUT RUNE DIDN'T SEE THE BOY beyond him taking the horn. His pulse pounded in his ears, and his breath came fast and shallow.

He'd been on the mountain. He'd seen the dragon—twice. He'd even seen the spot on the dragon's chest. And he had to avenge Amma.

None of that mattered. He hadn't been chosen.

He looked back at the men standing by the king. Could there be a mistake? He counted them again. No, no mistake.

The king didn't want him. It was that simple. Of course he didn't—Rune had already told him exactly how he had fallen, trembling, to the ground when the dragon flew over. The king needed warriors, not boys afraid of their own shadows.

He stared straight ahead, unseeing, barely noticing as Od moved past him to join the king, not listening to the king's words to the men, their vows to him, the crowd's cheers.

The circle broke as people headed for food. As hungry as he had been, his appetite was gone. He felt sick with shame—for thinking the horn had been coming to him, for thinking he had been worthy of it. For not being worthy.

To the king, Buri and Surt seemed like better warriors than he was. Od, too, even though he was at least a winter younger than Rune, maybe two. Hemming, whose sword hand wavered with age, and Thialfi, who couldn't even bear a sword. All of them were better to have beside you in a dragon fight than Rune.

People moved past, brushing against him, but he stood rooted like a tree.

"You ought to get some of this—it's good," a voice said. He blinked and saw Ketil standing near him, chewing on a hunk of meat. Goat meat, from the buck that had been sacrificed to Thor. The heart went to the god, the liver to the king, and the choicest parts of the meat to his warriors. People like Rune got what was left.

"Thought you'd be going with us." Ketil shook his head ruefully as a dribble of juice made its way down his chin.

"What, someone who can't even hold on to his own sword?" Rune spat the words, then turned and walked out of the fire's light.

What a fool he'd been to think the king liked him,

trusted him. Look at what he'd just found out—King Beowulf had loved Amma, whose son Rune's father had killed. He thought of the way the king had looked at him earlier, just before the messenger had called him away, his eyes conveying something that Rune hadn't recognized at the time. Contempt? For what his father had done?

He walked farther into the dark, stumbling over a clod of earth, and stood watching his breath condense into white clouds in the cold night. He wrapped Wyn's uncle's cloak tightly around him. Wyn. He couldn't even think about how stupid he'd been, how his unfortunate mouth had ruined everything when she was trying to be nice to him.

And Ketil. Of course Wyn would want a man like Ketil, a warrior, not a spineless rabbit like Rune. Had Ketil known anything about Rune's feelings for Wyn? Rune hoped not, even if Ketil would never have said anything about it.

Behind him, the sounds of the crowd wove together like a comforting blanket warming all those who stood inside the circle of firelight. He stepped farther into the cold shadows.

The bard plucked his harp and called out, signaling the start of a song. Rune recognized the opening words—it was the tale of King Beowulf fighting Grendel, defeating the horrifying monster bare-handed, without so much as a sword.

He looked back at the bonfire. The bard was a dark

figure in front of it. Around him people clustered, eating and drinking as he chanted his lay. Then Rune saw someone walking through the crowd, stopping to talk with people, firelight catching his golden crown. The king leaned in close to speak to a woman, and when she turned her head, Rune saw that it was Var, Brand's widow. When the king stooped down to Var's little girl, she hid her face in her mother's skirts. The king didn't move, but before long, Var's daughter did, taking a tentative step toward the king while still holding on to her mother's protective skirt. He waited, unmoving, allowing the child to come to him. When she dropped the skirt and reached out, he folded her into his arms for a moment before she scurried back to her mother.

"Rune? Is that you?" a woman called, making him jump.

He turned to see Elli not far from him, reaching for a basket.

"Did you get anything to eat? Come, there's plenty."

Reluctantly, he walked toward her while she waited.

She held out the basket. "Carry this for me, will you?" When he took it, she turned back to the light, and Rune followed her to the fire, where she still had fish frying. A group of women and children bunched on a log near it moved over to make room for him. As Rune sat down and took the fish Elli handed him, a little boy he didn't know ambled over to him. Standing, the boy was just tall enough to look into Rune's face.

"You saw the dragon."

Rune nodded, chewing.

The boy watched him with wide eyes.

Rune took another bite. His hunger had returned with a vengeance, and he finished the fish, crunching the bones and licking the grease off his fingers.

"Were you scared?" the boy whispered.

Rune looked back at him, then nodded.

"Is he bothering you? Here, have some more," Elli said.

Rune took the fish and bread she offered, nodding his thanks. "It's all right; he's not bothering me." Turning his attention to the boy again, he said, "I've never been that afraid in my life."

The boy nodded solemnly and watched him finish his second helping. "I would have been scared, too," he said, then ran to join his mother. She was speaking quietly to someone beside her, and Rune wondered if she was one of the widows the dragon had made or if she was one of the lucky ones, whose husbands were still out on patrol.

His belly finally satisfied, he sat silently as quiet conversations ebbed and flowed around him, women talking about who had died, who had survived, when their men would return. Across the fire from him, a girl crooned a lullaby to a baby—Elli's, he thought—while toddlers, growing sleepy, leaned into their mothers' skirts.

When he turned his attention to the bonfire, he saw that the bard was still singing, now about Sigmund the dragon-slayer. Brief snatches of the lay penetrated the women's talk. Rune watched the bard's expression as

Sigmund crept past gray stone to enter the dragon's cave alone, courage his only companion. Beyond the poet, the flames leapt and danced fiercely, fearlessly.

It was no mere adventure the king and his warriors would be seeking in the morning when they rode out to find the dragon, Rune thought. They would be fighting to save these women and children, as well as the rest of the kingdom, with its farms and fields and families. The king needed men beside him he could count on, men who wouldn't be overcome by their cowardice.

He lowered his head, wishing he were one of those men, knowing why he wasn't. The truth of it bit into him, galling him—he was no warrior.

The king had been right not to choose him.

SIXTEEN

THE WARRIORS LEFT BEFORE DAWN.

It had been a short night. After the mead-drinking and tale-singing, the bonfire had finally died out and Rune had joined the long line of people making their way back to the stronghold, smoking torches lighting their way and fending off the spirits of the dead. He carried a basket for Elli in one hand and over his shoulder, a sleeping child, the boy who had spoken to him while he had eaten. He followed the boy's mother to a house, and as she held up a light for him, he laid the child in his bed.

Finally, bone-tired, he found himself a spot in the campsite where he didn't think he'd be trampled, took off his mail shirt and his sword, wrapped himself in his borrowed cloak, and—despite his bruised body and his wounded pride—fell into a deep sleep.

It seemed as if he'd barely lain down when the sounds of footsteps and hushed voices woke him. Groggily, he listened to a dog barking and the clink of chain mail being pulled over someone's head. It was already morning. As he roused himself, he could hear women farewelling their men while children whimpered at being up so early. Torches lit the dark, and Rune stood to watch, pulling the cloak around himself against the cold air as bond servants led horses from the stable and warriors mounted them.

One horseman kept himself away from the others, and with a shock of recognition, Rune realized it was the slave. Over the flickering light of a campfire, he looked straight at Rune and bared his sharp teeth in a mirthless grin.

Rune recoiled. The malevolence in the slave's expression struck him like a physical blow.

Then the slave pulled his horse's reins hard, making it whinny and wheel toward the king, who turned Silvertop just in time to avoid hitting the slave's horse.

With the slave in front beside the king, the warriors rode out of the stronghold, some singly, some in pairs, the sounds of hooves and jingling mail fading into the darkness. When they were out of earshot, the crowd dispersed, people returning to their huts and houses, leaving Rune alone in the open.

He lay back down, knowing he'd never be able to go back to sleep. Burrowing under the cloak, trying to ignore the cold, he regarded the lopsided moon hanging in the western sky. It looked no bigger than a shield.

There was no point in his staying in the stronghold, he decided. He wasn't needed here. When it got light enough, he might as well go back to the farm to harvest the single remaining field and to see what he could salvage. He tried not to think of the men going to find the dragon, of not being one of them. Shame wove together with regret in a pattern that lulled him into uneasy dreams.

He woke suddenly. The sound of a hundred heartbeats filled his ears, and he sat upright, blinking in confusion before a wave of dizziness hit him, making him roll to his side, holding his head against the sudden throbbing in his temples. Everything went black.

"Survivor of war," a voice said. Amma's voice.

Rune caught his breath.

The slave's face looked directly into his own, eyes glinting with malice. Then it disappeared and Rune saw a misty cliff. What was it? It didn't make sense.

Amma's voice sounded inside his head again. "He leads men astray." The words triggered something in him, some knowledge, but exactly what floated just beyond his grasp.

He stared at the cliff, trying to understand. A third time came the voice: "You know where to go." Where? What did she mean?

"Now! Go!" The voice was harsh, startling him to attention.

"Amma?" he said, but the vision was gone.

Rune blinked. He felt as if he'd been taken far away, to another place and time, but here he was, still on the ground in the stronghold, his head feeling like it would split apart with pain, his heart pounding, his breath coming in gasps. He blinked again and swallowed the bile in his throat, steadying himself against the dizziness that still made him feel as if he weren't entirely solid.

Carefully, he looked around him, at the sun's rays just starting to filter through the birch trees, at the smoking remains of campfires the warriors had left behind them, at the mist that lay thick on the ground. As he gulped in the cold morning air and tried to understand what he'd seen, the answer came rushing into his head. The cliff—it was the place where he'd almost gone over the edge when he'd hunted the dragon. And the stranger. Rune didn't know who he was, but he was sure of one thing: the man was no slave. Was he even human? Whoever—*what*ever—he was, he would be taking the king and his men to the dragon by now.

No, not to the dragon. He'd be leading them astray— over the cliff?

He remembered the look in the slave's eyes and sucked in his breath.

The king—he had to warn the king!

Adrenaline rushed through his veins. He threw off his cloak and grabbed at his mail shirt, pulling it over his head and cinching it as fast as he could; then he strapped on his sword, fingers fumbling in his hurry. He raced for the stable, calling out, "Hairy-Hoof!" as he ran. She whinnied and pranced in her stall, excited by his mood. Once her saddle was on, he swung himself onto her back, whispered, "May the Hammerer give you strength," into her ear, and kicked his heels into her sides.

Like a warhorse, she thundered out of the stable and past a servant, who scrambled to get out of the way. As they rode out of the stronghold and into the morning light, Rune looked toward the mountain, hoping to see riders in the distance. But no, he realized, too much time had passed—they would be far ahead of him.

His tailbone ached, his swordbelt bit into his bruises, his head pounded, but he ignored the pain. None of that mattered now. The only thing that mattered was finding the king in time.

Down the path that led to the Feasting Field he rode, and through the stand of birch trees, green and red-gold leaves flashing past, chittering sparrows rising from the branches, disturbed by the noise. As he left the trees, the mountain came into view and Hairy-Hoof broke into a gallop. Rune leaned forward to ease his aching body and closed his eyes against rising nausea from the pain in his head. "Just hold on," he told himself, "just hold on."

They rode through shadowy fir trees, then emerged into the light again. As they passed the marshes, the dank smell of rotting vegetation reached Rune's nostrils. Up one rise and then another, through thickets of ash and elm, branches grabbing at them like claws and making Hairy-Hoof shy. Always, the mountain drew them forward. But it was still so far—they would never make it in time.

Hours seemed to pass, or maybe it was only minutes; he couldn't tell. They seemed no closer at all until they emerged from a stand of trees and Rune looked up to see the mountain's steep sides. As they approached, a whinny told them other horses were nearby. Hairy-Hoof tossed her head, and Rune let her have her way—she wanted to join them.

The horses greeted each other as Rune slid from Hairy-Hoof's back.

He leaned his head against her flank for a last moment of warmth, then straightened his sword and looked up at the crag path. No footprints disturbed the dirt. Where were they?

Hurrying past the horses, he scanned the ground and the mountainside, following the trail of disturbed earth. Just past the place where he'd come down the mountain when he'd found Finn's body, footprints led upward. He hesitated. He didn't know the way to the cliff from here, and if he tried to follow the footprints, he might lose them on the rocks.

Besides, he thought, maybe he'd been wrong. Maybe he'd misunderstood the vision.

A sound made him look back, past the horses, to the bottom of the crag. A white goat stood there. He watched as it eyed him, then bounded up the path to the crag.

Swallowing hard, he broke into a run. The horses, seeing him coming, whinnied and scattered out of his way. But at the bottom of the crag path, he stopped, overwhelmed by indecision. He looked at the trail of footprints the king and his men had left, then back at the crag path. What if the other way was a shortcut?

Go. Now. Amma's voice pounded at the insides of his skull, making him blink at the pain. He started climbing.

Twice he slipped in the loose dirt; twice he fell to his knees. There was nothing to do but haul himself back up and keep going. His sword slapped against his leg, threatening to trip him as he bent double to climb the steep path. Wind whipped his hair into his eyes.

Finally, he made it to the top of the crag and stood breathing heavily, looking at the path he'd taken before, the one that had led him to the sheer drop-off, the hidden cliff edge. "Don't let me be too late. Oh, gods, please, don't let me be too late," he whispered, wishing he'd taken the time to dedicate something on Thor's altar in the Feasting Field. He started forward again, scrambling up the rocky slope, keeping his body low and grabbing at bushes to pull himself along.

At first, he kept his eye out for signs to remind himself of the path he'd taken when he'd come this way before, but soon he realized he had no need to. Without understanding how, he knew exactly where to go. If only he could get there faster. He needed Freyja's falcon-skin cloak to fly high and fast above these rocks and trees. He needed Thor's goat-drawn chariot that flew through the air.

He slipped on loose pebbles, hitting his knee on a rock and righting himself before the pain had time to reach his brain. Up and up, around a boulder, over a grassy dip, past a stand of fir trees, his breath coming in sharp gasps.

When his foot crunched on the same skeleton he'd seen before, he stopped to get his bearings, straining his ears for the sounds of the troop. Instead, he heard the whistling wind and, far away, the shriek of an eagle.

An eagle! He'd seen one below him before, when he'd almost fallen over the hidden cliff edge. It shrieked again, a fierce hunting cry, and Rune looked up to see a line of fir trees. Directly beyond it was the cliff. He raced forward, pushing through prickly fir branches, emerging into the light again.

Nobody was there.

He was too late.

SEVENTEEN

HE SLUMPED TO HIS KNEES, SICK WITH DESPAIR. IF ONLY he'd been faster, if only he hadn't fallen asleep again after the warriors had left. How much time had he wasted at the bottom of the mountain, trying to decide which way to go? The other way must have been faster; he should have taken it.

He crouched in the dirt, letting the cold wind batter him, not bothering to pull his cloak around his shoulders. Nothing mattered now.

Another gust of air brought with it a sound. A voice.

He stiffened, listening.

Again, a voice. The slave?

Rune stood. Moving stealthily, he stepped into the fir trees. Did the slave have an accomplice? Was he a Shylfing spy, preparing for an attack on the kingdom?

Rune stood silent as snow, listening. Now he heard feet and the jingling of armor.

"This way," the slave said.

"You're sure?" someone asked.

Rune gasped with relief. It was the king's voice. He wasn't too late after all.

Through the branches, the slave emerged into view, the king less than a step behind him, his boar-crested helmet covering his forehead and cheeks. Crowding close came another warrior, chain mail hanging from his helmet, obscuring his face. Dayraven, Rune realized when the wind blew back his cloak, revealing his shining armbands. Behind him, two more helmeted warriors stepped heavily, their mail clinking.

"Of course I'm sure. Hurry—it's that way." The slave pointed toward the cliff, and Rune saw him hesitate a moment, letting the king get ahead of him. From that angle, the king wouldn't realize it was a cliff until he was already over it. No wonder the slave had chosen a different route.

"My lord!" Rune called, stepping out from behind the trees. "King Beowulf, stop!"

Two steps away from falling, the king turned to look at Rune. As he did, a sudden movement caught Rune's eye. The slave rushed forward, shoving the king.

Rune screamed a warning and lunged at the two men as Dayraven and the other warriors surged forward, not realizing their peril, pushing the king closer to the cliff. In the tussle of bodies and helmets, Rune grabbed an arm. Somebody backed into him, stepping on his foot. An iron helmet smacked against his cheek. Where was the king?

A flash of gold, the king's golden torque, fell forward, and he grabbed again, closing his arms around someone's chest, the two of them falling together. A scream rent the air, a long trailing cry that turned into a shriek like a falcon's.

Someone had gone over the cliff.

In the sudden stillness, Rune felt the heartbeat of the man under him and the wool of a cloak pressing against his cheek.

Cold iron jabbed into the back of his neck.

"Unhand the king," a harsh voice said.

Below him on the ground, encircled in Rune's arms, King Beowulf twisted his head to look up through the eyeholes in his helmet's mask.

"He could unhand me more easily if you weren't skewering him with your spear," the king said mildly.

The iron came away from his neck and Rune sat up. The king reached out a hand, and Rune pulled him up as they both stood.

"Who went over?" the king asked, looking from one warrior to another.

"The slave, my lord," someone said. Gar.

The king nodded. "Dayraven, lower your weapon."

Rune shifted his eyes to the right and saw the warrior's

spear pointed directly at him. The other men crowded close, circling as if to keep Rune from escaping.

"But, my lord—" Dayraven said.

The king raised a hand, palm up, to stop him. "The slave was our enemy, not Rune." He adjusted the gleaming torque at his neck and shook his chain mail into place, brushing dirt from his cloak. Then he looked at Rune and spoke in a low voice. "How did you know?"

Rune opened his mouth and then closed it. How could he explain? The king watched him, waiting. He swallowed and met the king's eyes. "Amma," he said.

"A vision?" He looked toward the cliff, not waiting for an answer. "Did she tell you who he was?"

Rune licked his dry lips. "I don't think he was a slave."

The king looked back at him. "Go on."

"His clothes were . . . In the visions, he was wearing rich clothes." He searched his memory for details. "There was, well, a wolf, standing right beside him. His cloak was like feathers. And he had a sword." He looked down at his own sword hilt, careful not to touch it while Dayraven's spear still hovered, ready to strike.

King Beowulf followed his gaze. "You've seen all this? Visions from Amma?"

Rune nodded.

The king watched him with a thoughtful expression.

"My lord," Gar said. "There could be others—the slave might have had accomplices."

"I think not," the king said, turning to his troop. "But you're right—we should be wary. And we should get away from this cliff."

As they began moving back the way they had come, Rune heard angry whispering. Buri and Surt, looking less like warriors in their borrowed helmets than they would have with no helmets at all, were arguing in muted tones. Buri carried the king's iron shield for him, holding it as if it weighed no more than a stalk of oats. "You *have* to tell the king," he said loudly enough that the others fell silent. The two men looked around to see everyone else staring at them.

"Tell me what?" the king asked, his voice light.

Surt gave Buri an angry look, then whipped his helmet off and stepped forward. "It was nothing, I'm sure."

"What was nothing?"

"My lord, I can barely see out of this thing." Surt held up the helmet.

"Then, Surt, I'll keep that in mind when you tell me what you may or may not have seen."

Surt looked back at the other farmer, who whispered, "Go on, tell him."

"Oh, all right. When that slave went over the cliff," Surt said, and looked at the ground. "He fell a long way, and then, it was like—" He stopped and looked at the king. "My lord, I couldn't see with this helmet on."

"I understand," the king said.

Surt turned his face back at the ground and breathed out heavily. "It was like he was falling and then he wasn't even there, but there was a bird—it looked like a falcon—flying away." He shook his head helplessly. "But this helmet, I can't even see."

"Thank you, Surt," the king said, and touched him on the shoulder.

Surt stepped back beside Buri, giving him an angry glance.

The men looked at each other, but no one spoke.

Finally, the king said, "Only the gods can shift their shapes." He glanced around. "Let's go."

With a jingling of mail, the men began walking back down the path they had come up.

Rune joined them. What did the king mean, *only the gods can shift their shapes*? he wondered as he walked, trying to keep his headache at bay. He remembered the image from Amma's wall hanging, of the goddess Freyja holding her falcon-skin cloak out to Loki, the Sly One, who used it to fly from world to world.

He wished he could put it all together, but his head hurt too much.

A hand slapped his back, startling him out of his thoughts. Ketil, his flat nose obscured by the ornate metal nasal on his helmet, fell into step beside him. Ketil gestured with his head, his cheek guards swinging from their hinges, and Rune glanced back to see Dayraven keeping pace a little behind him, like a guard, his spear at the ready.

Ketil grinned and rolled his eyes, giving the tiniest shake of his head.

Rune smiled back. He turned his attention to the trail—he thought he remembered this part. In fact, he was sure he did. He was equally sure that it was the wrong way to the dragon.

Ahead of him, he could see Ottar leading the way, his red-dyed beard protruding from under his masked helmet. Instead of giving him a menacing look, as he intended, to Rune the dye made him look slightly comical, like a little boy who'd gotten into a bucket of berries. Directly behind Ottar came Thialfi, his damaged sword arm dangling useless under his cloak. The two of them turned at a spruce tree, heading left.

"That's the wrong way," Rune said, his voice low, and then, looking at Ketil, he spoke again, loudly. "We're going the wrong way."

"Halt!" Dayraven cried. Relieved that the older man believed him, Rune turned toward him.

Eyes narrowed to slits behind the holes in his mask, Dayraven raised his spear and pointed it directly at Rune's heart.

EIGHTEEN

SWORDS SLID FROM SHEATHS. RUNE HEARD THEM AS HE stood without moving, his eyes on the spear at his chest, his hands held away from his weapons.

"We should have sent this cursed wretch over the cliff with the slave," Dayraven snarled.

The king stepped in front of Rune, pushing Dayraven's spear to the side. "Put your weapons away," he said, looking around at the other warriors.

Rune watched the king's face, barely daring to breathe. Nobody moved.

"I said, put your weapons away." The king's voice was a threat.

This time, Rune could hear the ringing of metal as swords met sheaths. Dayraven lowered his spear, driving the butt into the ground, and sneered at Rune.

"Do you have an argument to settle with Rune?" the king asked.

Rune held his breath. Did Dayraven still believe that not killing him when he was a baby had put a curse on the kingdom?

The warrior stared at him but spoke to the king. "He was waiting for us beside the cliff. He tried to push you over."

The king pulled off his helmet and tucked it under his arm. He gazed at Dayraven. "Did he? Try to kill me?"

Rune opened his mouth to protest, but no words came out. How could the king think that?

"He knew exactly where to find us. And now he says he knows the way—into another trap, if you ask me." Dayraven pounded the butt of his spear on the ground.

"Rune saved the king's life!" Ketil said, and Rune shot him a grateful look.

As he did, the king caught his eye. "That's what it seemed like to me." He smiled.

Relief flooded through Rune's muscles, making his knees feel weak, and he let out the breath he hadn't realized he was holding. He started to smile at the king, but as he did, a wave of pain and nausea swept over him. He staggered, hand to his head.

The king grabbed his arm, steadying him. "Sit," he said.

"I'm all right," Rune said, but the king guided him down.

His backside had barely touched the ground before the

next wave hit him, blinding him to everything except the blackness that engulfed him—and to Amma's voice.

"Go now! You must not delay!"

A face swam in and out of focus. Rune swallowed the bile in his throat, waiting for the nausea to pass. When he opened his eyes again, he realized he was lying on the rocky ground with the king crouched over him.

"She says we have to hurry," he croaked.

King Beowulf nodded, his brow creased with concern. "You know the way?"

"Yes."

"Come, then." Carefully, the king pulled him to his feet. Rune swayed as he stood and found Ketil at his side, grasping his sword arm to steady him.

He could barely focus on the king's commands and the men snapping to attention around him. Instead, his head was filled with images he knew weren't his own. He saw the three boulders, the ones he'd seen before. He'd been right— the dragon's barrow lay beyond them, but not exactly the way he'd thought. There was a stream first, and then a flat place, strewn with rocks.

"Rune?"

He blinked. Ketil was looking at him cautiously, his hand still on Rune's arm.

"Three boulders. On the sword-hand side," he said.

Ketil nodded. "My lord!" he called, and repeated Rune's words so the whole troop could hear.

They moved out, Rune stumbling along with them,

barely able to keep his eyes open. He didn't understand the pain, just that the visions caused it.

"No, I want him in the middle," he heard the king saying, and he felt himself being propelled behind Gar and Ottar. Ketil stayed beside him. Vaguely, he wondered what had happened to Dayraven—and the point of his spear—before another wave hit him.

"Close your eyes if it helps," Ketil said in a low voice, and Rune closed them as Ketil led him up and around stones and bushes. This time he saw the black mouth of a barrow, a burial mound, and knew the dragon was inside it, stirring, unfurling its wings, readying itself to set forth.

He opened his eyes again and looked up the mountain slope. "There," he said, pointing at a group of boulders high above them.

"The dragon?" Od said. His voice, not yet finished changing, squeaked.

"No, the three boulders," Gar answered.

"There's another cliff," Rune said, his voice strong now. "Just beyond a rock face. Stay to the right."

"You heard," the king said. "Let's go."

The troop moved out, and Rune felt his head clear. "I'm all right," he told Ketil, shaking his arm loose.

Ketil gave him a nod, but Rune could feel his friend watching him.

He kept his eyes on the path as they rounded a fir tree. "This is where I was when the mist came down."

"The giant's breath," a voice said to his left. The king.

Despite his age and the steepness of the slope, he wasn't out of breath. "The bard thinks the giants are in league with the dragon, that they protected it all these years, and here we are, walking through their domain." He paused, looking up the slope. "Of course, the bard also thought I shouldn't bring you along," he added. "The bard and Thora. I shouldn't have listened to them."

Rune turned, staring at him in surprise.

"They had their reasons, but I didn't agree."

Rune's heart leapt. The king *had* wanted him in the troop after all.

"A king should hear his advisors, but the final decision must be his own. Remember that." King Beowulf shook his head ruefully, smiling at Rune, who smiled back, eyes shining.

They came to a narrow place in the rocks, and the king motioned him to go first. When the rock formation widened, he saw Gar at the opening, reaching his hand to pull Rune forward but looking anxiously behind him. For the king, Rune realized.

As he stepped into an open space, he could see Brokk and Ottar surveying the landscape ahead, their swords out.

The king came through the passage, followed by Ketil and then Dayraven. All of them stopped, waiting for the rest of the troop.

"Where are those three boulders?" Dayraven said.

Rune gazed up the slope. They had disappeared from view. He could feel the men looking at him, but he spoke only to the king. "As straight up as we can. We'll come to a rock face. There's a cliff beyond it, but we stay to the sword-hand side and keep climbing."

Dayraven breathed out a *huh* of disgust, but when Rune turned, Ketil was beside him. "Ignore him," he said quietly.

"Brokk, Ottar?" the king called, and the two warriors set out again, leading the troop.

As Rune began to climb, he heard heavy breathing coming from behind. It turned into a wracking cough. Hemming stood bent over, hands on his knees, trying to get his breath. Ahead of the others, Brokk and Ottar hesitated, looking back.

Rune wasn't sure the old warrior would make it the rest of the way up the mountain.

"This passageway is treacherous. An enemy could ambush us here," the king called out. "I need someone to guard it. Ketil—no, wait, I need you to stay with Rune," he said. "Hemming, you fought the Wulfing raiders. You'll know what to do."

Hemming straightened. "My lord," he said, bowing briefly.

"The rest of you, move out," the king called.

As they did, Rune heard Hemming breaking into another gasping cough that went on and on until they were beyond the reach of its sound.

No one commented, but Rune was sure that everyone, including Hemming, understood what the king had just done.

Beyond a stand of spruce trees, they met the rock face. Without the mist, it looked different, less of an obstacle, but the route was still obscured.

"There's a goat trail to the right," Rune called. "And up ahead, there's a sheer drop-off."

No one answered, but he saw Ottar's stance shift.

Then the red-bearded warrior said, "I see the trail."

"A goat trail," Gar said. "That's a good sign."

"Aye, the Hammerer is with us," Ottar answered.

They climbed the trail, loose dirt and rocks skittering under their shoes, showering down from the men above to those below. Rune slipped, staggering as he tried to catch his balance. Ketil reached out to steady him. Then it was Ketil's turn to slip. "Watching you and not the trail," he said, grinning ruefully as Rune grabbed his arm.

"Whoa!" Gar said from above them. "There *is* a cliff—careful!"

As Rune passed it, he saw the curl of tree root that had caught his foot, keeping him from going over the edge. He looked back to see Od staring over the cliff, his eyes wide, his face white. "No more drop-offs, we're all right now," he called down to the younger boy, keeping his voice low.

Od met his gaze, took a breath, and began climbing again.

The slope flattened and broadened as they rounded a bend, and the three boulders came into view. Now that they were so near, they loomed as huge as the king's hall.

"Look! What's this?" someone hissed.

As Rune climbed over a rock, he saw Gar and Ottar kneeling down, examining something on the ground, Brokk guarding them, his sword in his hands.

Rune peered between them. A round black eye stared up at him.

The remains of his shield, the metal rim and boss blackened by the dragon's fire.

Ketil came up beside him. "That's your shield. You fell from here?" His voice rang with awe. "My lord," he said, turning to the king, "I found him at the bottom of the mountain. He fell from here and survived."

"I didn't fall all the way," Rune said, anger that he knew wasn't reasonable rising in him. "Only about halfway."

"My lord, I take it back. He only fell halfway down the mountain and survived." Ketil grinned.

Rune looked away. He didn't understand his anger, but he felt as if this was no time to joke. They shouldn't even be talking—they should be listening with every fiber of their beings.

A nameless panic rose in him, making it hard to catch his breath. He closed his eyes, trying to understand the feeling, trying to keep it from overwhelming him. Then he saw it: the dragon, inside its barrow, its body glowing red with fire. It was ready to set forth. They had to stop it— now, before it destroyed the rest of the kingdom.

He opened his eyes. The king watched him, waiting.

"My lord," he whispered. "It's here. The dragon is here."

NINETEEN

A CRY CAME FROM ABOVE. RUNE LOOKED UP TO SEE A raven circling, and then another meeting it, as if they were holding a conversation midflight. He watched as first one and then the other settled on the tallest boulder.

The king was watching them, too. Rune saw him bow his head a little, his lips moving as he mouthed a silent something—a vow? A prayer?

Then he straightened, turning his attention to the troop. "Men at arms!" he called, his voice clear and strong.

Rune's breath quickened and he stepped forward. So did Ketil and Brokk. Gar and Ottar rose from the remains of Rune's shield and looked toward the king. Thialfi raised his head, and Rune saw Buri cast a glance at Surt. Someone brushed against his cloak—Od, trying to get closer to the king.

"Our enemy is here, the foe who ravaged my kingdom with his flames. No more will he do so. Today he dies." The words rang out in a voice Rune had never heard before.

He gazed at the king, awestruck. The gentle old man he had known since childhood gave way to a different figure altogether, a powerful prince, a hero. The king looked taller, his stooped shoulders broad and square now. The cloak of old age seemed to fall away from him, revealing a menacing warrior in his mail coat and masked helmet. Around his neck, his golden torque gleamed and the garnets in his cloak clasp shone like new-spilled blood.

Rune stood taller, too, and moved along with the others as the troop came closer, encircling the king like a shield rim.

"My shoulder companions," the king said, looking from face to face, stopping to rest on each one. When the king's eyes met his, Rune knew he would follow the man anywhere, into the very shadows of Hel's underworld, if the king asked it. He tightened his hand around his sword hilt and gazed back at the king.

"Long ago I fought Grendel single-handed, with no weapon but my bare hands," the king said, gesturing as if he were strangling the monster. "I wish I could do so now, but against the dragon's fire I will take my sword and iron shield."

Gar nodded and Rune and Ketil exchanged glances.

"You have come with me here on a dire journey, as

I asked. Now you must stay here, hidden behind the boulders—this task is mine alone, for glory and for my kingdom."

"My lord!" Ottar said.

The king held up a hand for silence. "This is not your fight. As king, it falls to me to test my strength against the enemy, to win or to let the battle bear me away."

Rune shook his head in disbelief. He glanced across the circle at Ketil, who had a stricken look on his face.

"Shield-bearer!" the king called. Buri stepped forward and, bowing, handed him the heavy iron shield. The king hefted it in his left hand, then held it aloft as if it were a toy. His sword rang out as he pulled it from its sheath.

"The Nailer," Od breathed in awe.

The patterned blade glinted in the light as the king held it high. "The time for words is over. Now for the sword's hard edge. Come!"

He whipped off his cloak, letting it fall to the ground, and strode toward the boulders. When he reached them, he stopped and raised his sword in salute to the troop. Then he turned and took the path between the rocks, crying out, "Come forth, vile worm! No more will you harry my people!"

With the others, Rune hurried to the boulders and peered between them, jostling for a better view.

"Out of my way, witch's whelp," Dayraven growled, shouldering Rune aside.

Rune ignored the provocation, backing away and finding another spot. Nothing mattered now except the king. Did the old man really have the strength to fight alone?

"Come forth, I say!" the king cried out again.

From between the boulders, Rune could see him, sword raised high, striding through the stream that lay before the barrow's black mouth. Then Gar shifted, moving into Rune's line of sight.

Suddenly, a rumbling filled the air and an acrid, burned-leather smell. "There it is!" Ottar hissed.

Rune peered around Gar just as a monstrous triangular head emerged from the barrow. He heard a whimper and saw Surt, standing by him, staring slack-jawed at the dragon.

"Courage," Rune said, but the farmer looked at him wild-eyed and then broke into a run, making for a distant stand of firs.

The ground trembled. Rune looked back to see the dragon hauling itself from the barrow, first its long neck and then its front legs. Each curved claw was as long as the king's forearm.

The king brandished his famous sword and shouted something, but Rune couldn't hear the words over the ground's rumbling. The familiar terror rose up in him, but he fought to push it away, grinding his teeth with the effort, and kept his eyes on the scene before him.

The dragon crouched, wings furled, its long, curved fangs dripping with venom, smoke rising from its nostrils.

It moved its head from side to side to side, scrawling smoky messages in the air as it regarded King Beowulf first with one eye and then the other.

The king stood his ground.

Then the dragon uncoiled its neck, rising up as the king raised his iron shield.

The white spot—Rune could see it. Could the king? *Now, before it strikes,* he thought.

"Thor help us!" someone said, and Rune felt a warrior running, joining Surt in the trees, but he couldn't take his eyes from the king to see who.

"Watch out!" someone shouted to the king as the dragon pulled back its head. It seemed to be filling its lungs.

"Now! Strike now!" Rune yelled, hardly realizing the words came from his mouth.

But it was too late. Fire spewed forth from the fanged jaws.

The king turned his body to the side. The shield held against the flame.

"Let me by!" Od squeaked, and pushed past Rune, running for safety. Rune stepped forward to take his place. His hands were clenched so tight he'd never be able to hold his sword if he needed it. He forced them to relax. Around him he could hear the ragged breathing of the other men.

The dragon reared again. This time its red eye seemed to pierce the boulders, as if it was searching for something.

"It's coming this way!" Ottar yelled. He cowered,

hiding his face. Buri ran past him, and Gar inched around the boulder away from the fight, hands up as if to ward off a blow.

Rune couldn't blame them. They'd never seen the dragon before. He remembered what the king had said about dragons terrifying even seasoned warriors. His own breathing was fast and shallow, and cold sweat ran from his armpits. He felt sick with dread.

The dragon writhed, turning toward the king again, preparing for another blast. As it did, King Beowulf pulled back his sword. The Nailer flashed, slashing through the air, landing such a blow on the creature's neck that its head should have been severed. Instead, the blade bounced off the hard scales.

The dragon screamed, its red eye narrowed in rage, and belched forth more fire.

Rune's hand went to his lips as he watched the king dodge under the shield just in time. His sword flashed again, but again, it missed the white spot. For a third time, the dragon shot flames at the king and for the third time, the shield did its work. Red-hot it glowed, but the king's hold on it didn't waver.

Rune clutched a rock outcropping beside him, his eyes never leaving the king. He felt as if he were out there with his lord, burning from the searing heat of the flames, watching, waiting for the moment to strike.

The dragon seemed to be waiting, too, or resting, and Rune saw the king bow his head in pain or fatigue. "Ring-giver," Rune said. "The gods are with you." The rock he clenched bit into his fist.

Suddenly, the dragon reared to the side, sending a stream of flames under the shield.

"My lord!" Rune screamed as the king leapt aside.

Fury seemed to take the king. He swung his blade again and again, but each time it bounced off the dragon's hide.

Then, as Rune watched in disbelief, the king fell to his knees.

"We have to help him!" he cried. "He needs us—we have to help him!" He looked around at his companions. Only Ketil and Dayraven were there, staring at him with stricken faces. Rune ran around the side of the boulder, where Gar crouched, face hidden. "Gar!"

The tall warrior hunched his shoulders as if warding off a blow.

Rune shook his arm. "Gar! He needs us! Have you forgotten your vows when you drank the mead?" He looked toward the woods. "Come back!" he yelled. "He needs us!"

No one stirred. Desperate, he ran past Gar, screaming, "You made a vow!" He leapt around the boulder again.

Ketil looked at him, his eyes filled with anguish. His mouth worked, but no words came out before he collapsed to his knees, hiding his face.

"Come on!" Rune shouted to Dayraven. He pulled his sword from its sheath and raced through the boulders, the other warrior a step behind him.

Then the terror took him, and his steps slowed as if he were running through mud. *I can't, I can't, I can't,* he told himself, squeezing his eyes shut to the sight of the dragon, falling to his knees as he reached the stream.

The splash of cold water surprised his eyes open again, and he saw the dragon coiling back for another blast of fire as the king staggered to his feet.

"My lord!" Rune cried. He scrambled up again and raced through the water.

The red eye turned. The dragon shifted its aim, bringing its jaws toward Rune. The head drew back a little as if the creature was taking a breath—and then it came forward, a torrent of fire hurling from its jaws.

"To me!" the king shouted. Rune threw himself under the metal shield as King Beowulf held it high.

He lay on the rocks, stunned, waiting to see if he was still alive, shuddering with horror, coughing and gasping for breath in the sulfurous fumes. The heat was unbearable.

Wildness overtook the beast. It flung flame after flame as the king tried to shield them both. Rune screwed his eyes shut in terror.

"Rune," the king said sharply, and he looked up, taking a shaky breath. "Help me. Hold the shield."

Rune rose, fighting off the horror that threatened to overtake him. He was no use here. He shouldn't have come.

The king pulled him close, and Rune could see the sweat pouring from under his helmet. "You can do this," the king said fiercely, looking into his eyes.

Rune stared at him, then nodded.

"Here," the king said, handing him the shield.

Rune took the leather handle, staggering under the shield's weight and the heat radiating from its iron skin.

King Beowulf met his eyes again, waiting, and then mouthed, "Now." He ducked out from under the shield, his mighty sword held in both hands. As Rune watched, the dragon looped its neck back, bringing its head low to guard the white spot on its chest. As the head came near, the king raised the sword, yelling a battle cry as he brought it down with all his weight on the creature's skull.

The sword snapped in two.

Rune watched in horror as the top half bounced on the rocks, the metal blade shining with reflected dragonfire.

TWENTY

THE DRAGON HISSED IN FURY, STEAM POURING FROM ITS nostrils, its eye blazing with red hatred. It whipped its head toward the king as he staggered back.

"My lord!" Rune screamed, scrambling to place the shield between the king and the dragon.

He was too late. The creature found an exposed place on the king's neck and clamped down its fangs.

Blood spurted, running down the king's arm and chest. The dragon bit down harder.

Rune dropped the shield and ducked under the creature's neck. The white spot! He could see the circle of bronze scales surrounding it, and just inside of them, the dirty-white scales. He pulled his sword back, gripping it with both hands, and held his breath to help keep his aim true. Then he rammed it at the white spot. The dragon skin seemed to push back at the sword. Teeth gritted, putting his entire weight behind the sword, Rune shoved again. The blade went in.

The dragon let go its hold on the king, rearing back in pain and anger. A thin ribbon of fire streamed from its jaws, searing Rune's sword hand. He screamed and dropped his sword.

The king rushed in beside him, whipping his dagger from his belt and thrusting it hard into the creature's chest beside Rune's weapon.

Rune reached for his sword, ignoring the fire in his hand. He raised the blade to strike again, but the king grabbed him, pulling him to the ground, rolling with him out of the way as the dragon's monstrous head came crashing down.

They lay unmoving, waiting, the king on top of Rune, shielding him with his body.

Moments passed and nothing happened.

Stillness thundered in Rune's ears.

He edged his eyes open and saw blood seeping from the king's neck. A rivulet snaked over the exposed skin, and then, reaching a link of chain mail, it ran in a circle around it. A drop hung for a long moment before it fell, splashing onto Rune's cheek.

The king grunted and rolled off him. "Careful," he said. "Venom."

Rune raised himself onto his elbows and looked to the right. Its eyes closed, a trickle of smoke rising from its nostrils, its neck curved in an unnatural shape, the dragon lay beside them. It was dead.

His senses returning to him, Rune turned to the king, who lay on his other side. Breathing heavily, the king struggled to sit up.

"My lord," Rune said, trying to help him.

"Let me see your hand." The king took Rune's burned fingers in his own. He probed them and Rune hissed in pain. "It may heal, given time."

Then he closed his eyes. "Rune," he said, his breath still labored. "I have taken my death wound."

"No," Rune said. "It's not that deep. You'll be all right." On his knees now, he peered at the king's wound and believed his own words.

"Help me to the rocks," the king said. He draped an arm over Rune's neck, and together the two of them stood.

It took all of Rune's strength to get the king to the rocks by the barrow's mouth. "Here, my lord," he said, helping King Beowulf to sit and loosening his helmet. Gently, trying to work with only one hand, he pulled it off, then, making sure the king was steady enough to sit by himself, he ran to the stream, skirting the dragon's head. Kneeling, he filled the helmet with water and raced back to the king.

"Here, my lord, drink," he said, holding the helmet to the king's lips, gritting his teeth against the agony that pulsed through his hand as the helmet touched it. King Beowulf leaned forward, his eyes closed, and took a long swallow.

Rune ripped a piece of cloth from his shirt sleeve and dipped it in the water. Carefully, with his good hand, he worked at the wound on the king's neck, dabbing the blood away, cleaning the torn skin. Even as he washed it, he could see the pink flesh taking on a greenish tinge. The blood grew dark and began to bubble.

"The venom," the king said. "It's working its way through my body."

"But you'll be all right," Rune insisted, dabbing away the blood, keeping his eyes on the wound.

The king reached for his arm, stopping him. "Rune," he said, and as Rune looked at him, he saw that the whites of the king's eyes were yellow and bloodshot. His brows and hair seemed whiter, brighter, next to his sweaty, soot-blackened face.

"Go, look at the dragon's treasure; bring it to me."

Rune shook his head. "I can't leave you."

"I'm commanding you to. Hurry."

Rune rose, his face a mask of concern, and walked fearfully toward the barrow's mouth. When he reached it, he looked back at his lord.

A hint of a smile came to the king's face and he nodded. "Go."

Rune turned and ran down the dark passageway into the barrow, the clinking of his chain mail echoing off the rock walls. The place reeked of dragon, of smoke and venomous breath and rotting meat.

The passageway opened suddenly into a wide room.

A stream of light filtered through the dust from an opening in the roof, and Rune stopped to stare. What he took at first for a pile of pebbles transformed into jewels as he gazed at it. A golden goblet lay at his feet, some story of the gods inscribed into its side. Piles of treasure lay scattered across the dirt floor—gold coins, rusted armor, rings and necklaces and armbands decorated with interlacing patterns. He tried to take it all in, the glittering tapestry hanging from the wall, the helmets, their leather sides eaten away by time, leaving only their crests and brow guards and nasals like the faces of long-forgotten warriors, but there was too much to comprehend. When he stepped forward, his foot crunched on something. A human skull. He took a shaky breath and looked up at a golden banner, a battle standard woven of shining threads that caught the light and illuminated a green gemstone below it.

For a long moment he stared. Then, in a sudden panic, he remembered the king, alone and wounded. He grabbed a gold cup and a gleaming bowl, stuffing them full of gemstones and jewelry, trying not to cry out as they touched his throbbing hand. He took a sword and a helmet and slipped three armbands over his wrist before he reached for the golden standard and fled, tripping over the treasures, down the dark passageway and into the light.

The king lay slumped against the stone wall, his eyes closed.

"My lord!" Rune cried, running to him, dropping the

treasure with a clatter. "King Beowulf!" He leaned over the king, shaking his arm.

The king opened his eyes. They looked dim, rheumy. Dark blood flowed freely from his neck wound now, staining the tunic below his mail shirt.

"Here, my lord, here's treasure, see?" He held a cup up desperately, and the king looked at it vaguely. "And here, armbands." Rune slipped them off his wrist and piled them in the king's lap.

"Rune," the king said, his voice weary. "Sit here." His hand fell to the rock beside him.

Rune sat, trying not to stare at the yellow liquid bubbling at the edges of the wound, willing the king to be strong. "My lord, you'll be all right. I know you will."

The king shook his head and gazed up at Rune from beneath his white brows. "I have no son to pass on my armor to, my helmet, my kingdom." He raised his hands to the back of his neck, struggling with something. Then he lifted the golden torque from his neck. "Put this on," he said.

"My lord, no," Rune said, tears welling in his eyes.

"You are a Wayamunding, Rune, the same as I am, the same as my father was. My father killed a man, you know, just as yours did. Hrothgar paid the wergild, putting me in his debt." A grim smile lit his face. "I paid that debt off—I killed Grendel and his mother."

"You did, my lord, and you survived. Just like you will now."

"No, Rune." He leaned his head back against the wall, closing his eyes, working hard for every breath.

Suddenly, Rune's head pounded and nausea took hold. He clutched at his temple, cupping his hand over his eye. *Not now,* he told himself, *not now.* But over the vision he had no control. He hung his head over his knees, trying to keep from passing out as the world went dark.

Amma whispered in a voice so gentle he thought at first it couldn't be hers. "Survivor of war." Rune caught his breath as a sudden unbearable sadness twisted his heart. Then she was gone.

When he sat up again, breathing shakily, the king was watching him. "What did she say?"

Rune shook his head, swallowing. "It doesn't make any sense." He blinked, accustoming his eyes to the light again. "She's said it before. It was the last thing she said before she died."

The king leaned forward, his eyes on Rune's. "Tell me."

"She said, 'Survivor of war.'"

King Beowulf gave a hint of a smile. "Don't you know? It's your name. It's what's written in the runes on the pendant around your neck. Wiglaf. That's what it means. What remains after battle, what survives a war."

He sat up a little straighter, and as he did, fresh blood welled from his neck.

"Here, my lord," Rune said, dipping the cloth into the water in the king's helmet and pressing it against the wound. "Let me clean it."

The king put his hand on Rune's arm. "Stop. Listen to me. Your father was Weohstan, a Wayamunding. He was my kinsman." He looked into Rune's eyes, holding them with his own. "Rune." His eyes fluttered and then opened again. "You are the last of my kin."

Rune stared at him, not comprehending.

"Wiglaf, son of Weohstan," the king repeated, "I name you my heir."

He closed his eyes, and slowly, as if he were falling asleep, the king's head fell forward.

TWENTY·ONE

"MY LORD!" RUNE CRIED. "KING BEOWULF!" HE SHOOK THE king's shoulder, but the old warrior slumped farther forward.

Rune hauled him upright, leaning the king's head against the rocks. "Here, drink, my lord," he said, dipping water from the helmet into a golden cup from the barrow. He held it to the king's lips, and they parted, his lower jaw falling open. The water dribbled down his chin.

Rune dropped the cup and dipped the cloth into the helmet again. "You'll be all right; you'll be fine," he said, his words thick with tears. They coursed down his cheeks, mingling with his sweat, running into his nose and mouth and dripping onto his neck. Gently, he swabbed the king's face, wiping away soot and battle grime. "My lord?"

Rune laid his ear to the king's heart, but his own breathing kept him from hearing the sound he was listening for.

The king didn't move.

"God of thunder, help him," he said. "Please help him." Scooping water into his burned hand, he held it to the king's lips. "Here's water, my lord. Drink." Again, the liquid ran down his chin.

"No, my lord!" Rune cried, his voice a ragged sob. A second time he shook the king's shoulders. A second time it did no good. He lowered his head against his lord's chest, overcome by grief and exhaustion, and wept.

A light hand touched Rune's shoulder.

He raised his face to the king's, but the eyes were still closed, the mouth still hanging open. He lowered his head again, his cheek pressed against the hard iron rings of the king's chain mail.

"Rune?" someone said, and again he felt the hand.

Eyes swollen with tears, his own hand still resting on the king's shoulder, he slowly twisted his head.

"I was standing just over there. I heard what he said." Ketil spoke softly, as if to keep from disturbing the king, who was beyond disturbance now.

Rune looked at him, unable to speak, then lowered his face back to his lord's chest.

He heard movement behind him, the tread of feet, but he didn't look up. Someone knelt on the rocks on the other side of the king's body. Rune opened his eyes to Ketil's face.

"Come," Ketil said gently, reaching his hand out to help Rune to his feet.

Rune stared at him for a long moment, then extended his hand. When Ketil took it, Rune pulled it back, hissing in pain.

"Sorry," Ketil whispered, his eyes widening when he saw the blackened flesh. He put his hands under Rune's armpits and pulled him to his feet.

As Rune turned, he saw men standing in a circle around the king. Around him. Shame shadowed their faces. Gar's head was bowed. So were Thialfi's and Ottar's. Surt scuffed the ground with his boot, and Buri stared at the king, tears wetting his cheeks. Od stood a little behind Buri, sobbing.

Brokk met Rune's eyes and gave him a soldier's nod.

"Where's Dayraven?" Rune asked, his voice a croak. "Is he all right?" He didn't remember seeing the warrior after they had crossed the stream together.

No one spoke.

Beside him, Ketil made a movement and Rune turned. "He . . . he ran," Ketil said in a choked voice.

Rune's eyes fell on the dragon's carcass stretched across the rocks, its fire extinguished, its red eyes closed. "The king said there's something about a dragon, some magic maybe, that freezes even a hardened warrior's blood. He said there's no shame in it."

Still, nobody else said anything. Ottar shuffled his feet. What were they waiting for? Rune felt frustration rising in him, competing with his grief. Why didn't somebody *do* something?

Finally, unable to stand it any longer, he spoke. "Our ring-giver is dead. We need to take him down the mountain. We'll build his pyre in the Feasting Field by Thor's Oak."

Gar raised his head. Thialfi looked at Rune expectantly.

"We need spears and a cloak." He saw Od, his face wet with tears, standing a little to the side. "Od, see if you can find the king's cloak. We'll make a litter to carry him."

Od nodded without looking up and ran to the boulders. The rest of the men watched Rune, but still no one moved. "The dragon—we should push it over the cliff into the sea." When no one spoke, Rune went on. "Can we? Buri? Surt? Brokk? Do we have the strength, if we do it together?"

Buri looked at Surt and the two of them moved cautiously toward the dragon.

"Be careful of the venom—don't touch it," Rune called as Brokk and Ottar joined them, pushing at the creature, testing its weight.

Rune turned to Gar. "There's treasure in there." He pointed at the barrow. "A treasure hoard beyond belief. We should carry as much of it with us as we can for the king's pyre. See if there's something we can put it in, will you?" Gar nodded and went into the barrow.

Rune turned. The king still sat propped against the rock wall, his eyes closed, his mouth open.

Rune felt his whole body crumple, and he staggered, falling to his knees, dropping his face into his hands as a sob overtook him.

"Here," Ketil said. "Drink this." He held his helmet forward. It was filled with water.

Rune took a shaky breath, then another, before he looked at his friend.

Ketil gave him the helmet, and Rune drank long and deep. When he finished, he handed it back.

Ketil met his eyes. "That was well done," he said. "The king would have been proud. My lord." There was no hint of a smile on his face as he added the last words.

Rune shook his head. "No, Ketil."

"It's not your choice." Ketil watched him for a long moment until Rune finally dropped his eyes. "How's your hand?"

Rune held it out, palm up.

Ketil examined it, carefully keeping his fingers from the burned part. Then, using his dagger, he cut a long strip from his cloak and gently wrapped it around Rune's hand. "There," he said. "Maybe that will help."

At a sound behind them, they both turned to see Brokk, Buri, and Surt leaning into the dragon's side, their muscles straining.

Rune and Ketil rose to join them, but as Rune stepped toward the dragon, Od stopped him. Keeping his face down, he held the king's cloak up to Rune as if it were an offering. "Thanks, Od," Rune said. "Put it by the king and let's help with the dragon."

Od nodded, still looking down.

"Od," Rune said, putting his good hand on the younger boy's shoulder. "The first time I saw it, I lay there sniveling in the dirt. I thought I was dead. The second time wasn't much better."

Od raised his face just enough to meet Rune's eye before stepping toward the king's body.

It took their combined strength to move the dragon.

"It's a good fifty footmarks long," Surt said. He'd walked from head to tail, measuring.

In the end, they had to roll it to the cliff edge. "Let the tide take it, and good riddance," Brokk said as the carcass fell, thundering over the mountainside to the sea far below.

They rested for a moment and then returned to the king, whose body they had laid on his cloak, the hilt of his broken sword on his chest. The cloak they tied to two strong linden spears, making a litter. Beside the king lay treasure from the barrow, filling a bag Gar had made from his own cloak.

The men stood in a huddled group near the king. Rune looked at them, wondering what they were waiting for.

"My lord?" Ketil asked him.

Rune glared at him, but the other men raised their faces, listening for his response. He sighed and gave in.

"Brokk, Ottar, Buri, Surt," he said, pointing to a different corner of the litter as he said each name. They moved to their places. "Gar? The treasure."

Gar picked up the bulky sack, and a helmet slid out.

"Od, help him, will you?" Rune said. "And, Thialfi, will you bear the king's shield?"

Thialfi bowed his head in acquiescence.

Then, taking one last look around the ground where he and the king had killed the dragon, Rune said, "Let's go."

The king's litter carriers went first, handing the body to each other through the passage in the boulders. Rune followed them, Ketil just behind him, and finally Thialfi with the shield and Gar and Od managing the treasure. As he stepped through the boulders, Rune saw his cloak lying where he'd left it when he'd run toward the king. He reached out his sword hand, then pulled it back, wincing.

"Let me," Ketil said.

Rune was too tired to protest. He wasn't sure he had enough strength to make it down the mountain, let alone all the way back to the stronghold. As they crossed the flat space before the trail narrowed, a loud bleating came from nearby and a large white goat trotted into view.

"We should sacrifice it to the Hammerer," Thialfi said. "For the king." He laid down the iron shield and pulled out his dagger.

"No!" Rune said, anger rising in him. "Leave it alone!"

Thialfi exchanged a glance with Gar.

The goat sprang onto a rock and gazed directly at Rune

with its strange eyes, one yellow, the other blue. He gave the goat a half-bow. It bleated again, hit the rock with its hoof, sprang high into the air, and vanished.

"Did you see that?" Gar said. "It just disappeared!"

"It went behind the rocks," Thialfi said.

"No, it didn't; Gar's right," Brokk said. "That goat disappeared. The Hammerer!" He clutched at his Thor's hammer amulet.

So did Ketil, and Rune heard several men muttering quick prayers to Thor.

The procession started up again. Rune's head throbbed and his hand was on fire. Exhaustion spread over him like a blanket, and he stumbled on a rock.

Ketil was beside him instantly, catching his arm.

"I'm all right," Rune said.

Trying not to think about what he had just seen, one more unreal thing in a day full of unreality, he followed the king's body down the mountain.

TWENTY·TWO

LIGHT SLID UNDER HIS LASHES AS RUNE OPENED HIS EYES
a fraction. He didn't know where he was. He lay still, listening. Somewhere nearby, a man and a woman were speaking
quietly, and he could smell porridge cooking. His stomach
grumbled, and he looked down to see a fine woolen blanket
covering him. He raised his head a little and blinked at the
wooden horse heads at the foot of the bed.

He'd never slept in a bed before in his life, not that he
could remember, anyway. Where was he? His head ached,
and he laid it back on the pillow. He'd never had a pillow
before, either. It was astonishingly soft and smelled of
herbs.

His sword hand throbbed, but bearably. When he lifted
it, he saw that it had been neatly bandaged. Suddenly,
memory and grief came crashing down on him.

The king was dead.

When he could catch his breath again, he opened his eyes and gazed at the tidy thatch of the roof, the wooden walls, the light seeping through the cracks. On one wall there was an altar to Odin, two ravens etched into metal. A cup sat below them—mead for the god, he supposed. He looked to the other wall and saw a second altar, this one to Thor, with a carved figure of the god riding in his goat-drawn cart.

The goat—had Thor sent it? Had it really vanished?

He shut his eyes, remembering the goat and the way Hemming had met them halfway down the mountain, his sword held hilt-up, his head bowed in King Beowulf's honor. He had seen them coming, bearing the king's body, and as they drew close to him, he fell into step beside them without speaking.

When they finally reached the bottom, Rune told Surt and Buri to go home to their farms. "Your wife needs you," he remembered saying to Buri, adding, "and the kingdom needs your grain." Or at least he thought he remembered. Maybe he had dreamed it.

The ride back had passed in a haze of sorrow and pain. He had wanted to leave the others and go to the hut on Hwala's farm.

Ketil had stopped him. "Not yet," he'd said. "First we have to take the king home."

They had tied his body to Silvertop, his white stallion, who had pranced and neighed nervously before settling into a stately pace. Four warriors, spears raised, had taken their places as the king's honor guard. Rune hadn't been one of them—it had taken everything he had to keep from falling off Hairy-Hoof as they rode through the evening and into the night.

After that, his memory failed.

A breeze wafted the scent of porridge past his nose, and his stomach growled violently. He pushed the covers away and sat up. Immediately, he regretted it. He had to lean his head to his knees to stave off the pain and dizziness that threatened to overtake him.

When he looked up again, Thora stood in the doorway, a bowl in her hands. "Get back under the covers," she said.

Obediently, he did. She reached to plump a pillow behind his back, helping him to sit up, and handed him the bowl.

He thanked her and plunged the spoon into the porridge. It was thick with butter and honey and so smooth that not a single piece of grit crunched between his teeth. He didn't think he'd ever tasted anything so good.

Thora stood watching him, her arms folded across her chest. When he finished, she took the bowl from him. "No more just yet," she said. "Let's make sure this stays down." Then she slipped out of the house.

Rune leaned back on the headboard. He must have fallen asleep again, because when he opened his eyes, Thora was back, a cup in her hands, and the bard was standing beside her, holding a leather bag. Both of them were watching him.

"Here," Thora said, stepping forward with the cup.

He took it and drank, welcoming the cool feel of the ale on his throat.

The bard pulled up a stool and sat beside the bed. He cocked his head at an angle and narrowed his single eye as if he were judging Rune and finding him wanting. Finally, he spoke, his voice sharp. "Wiglaf, son of Weohstan."

Rune flinched and looked away. The last thing he wanted was to be reminded of what the king had said.

"A sword-age awaits us if the Shylfings attack, a wolf-age. And attack they will if we lack a strong leader. We may not survive."

"What about Dayraven?" Rune asked.

The bard shook his head. "He hasn't been seen since . . ." His voice trailed off.

Dayraven was still gone? Rune remembered running to the king's aid, Dayraven just behind him—and after that, the terrible fight with the dragon. At the time, he hadn't spared a thought for the warrior. Other men had run from the creature, but they'd returned. *He'll come back*, Rune thought, *and so will the men out guarding the kingdom against the Shylfings.* Surely one of them would make a good leader— Wyn's brother Wulf, perhaps. He looked back at the bard.

The single eye pierced his, holding him in its gaze. "The men will follow you."

"No," Rune said.

From beside the bed, Thora spoke. "They already have."

Rune looked at her, his eyes pleading. She hadn't been there; she didn't know what had happened. The others hadn't followed him. Once the king had fallen, every man had worked together to bring their leader down the mountain.

Another thought occurred to him. "What about the men out on patrol? They would never accept me," he said.

"Who are any of us to refuse our king's final command?" the bard said, his voice harsh. He pulled the king's golden torque from the bag, the neck ring King Beowulf had given to Rune before he died. "This is yours."

Tears filled Rune's eyes, and he blinked furiously, rejecting them. "I don't want it," he whispered.

"It's not your choice," Thora said.

"Rune," the bard said, and this time his voice was gentle. He laid his hand on Rune's arm. "I will help you. So will Thora." He glanced over his shoulder and she nodded.

"I think Amma knew your fate," the bard added. "Everything she taught you, every decision she made—it was all for this."

Rune stared at him dully.

"She was a far-minded woman, one who saw beyond herself. The things she did in life didn't always make sense to me, but now they do. Finn was the king's heir"—he bowed his head briefly toward Thora, who gave him a sharp nod in return—"yet somehow she knew you would be needed."

"She could see the war clouds on the horizon, the Shylfings waiting for our king to die before they attacked, just like the rest of us could," Thora said.

"She saw that, yes. But also much more. More than any of us could have seen." The bard turned back to Rune. "She raised you to be king."

The room fell silent, the only sounds the scritch of the bard stroking his close-cropped beard and a twig snapping on the fire.

Then he stood. "The funeral pyre is being prepared at the Feasting Field for tonight." He walked to a chest, opened it, and pulled something out. His harp. Rune realized he must be in the bard's house. Of course. Who else sacrificed both to Odin, who had drunk the mead of poetry, and to Thor? "You should sleep now," the bard said. "We'll wake you in time." He gave Rune a last look, then walked through the door.

Thora watched him for a moment before coming to sit on the bed. She reached out to smooth the hair from his forehead, making a sharp noise with her tongue as she peered at the bruise under his eye. "How do you feel?" she asked.

"I'm all right," he said. He wished she would leave.

"More porridge?"

He shook his head.

"Try to sleep." She leaned forward and kissed him on the cheek, then got up and left the room.

Rune lay back down, knowing he would never be able to sleep now, no matter how much his body hurt, no matter how tired he still felt. The idea that Amma had taught him anything about kingship was laughable. She hadn't even wanted him to learn how to use a sword. He knew nothing about how to be a king. He didn't *want* to be a king.

Bitter tears slid down his cheeks, wetting the pillow.

The sound of the door creaking woke him. His eyes were crusted from sleep and dried tears. He reached up to rub them until he could see.

Ketil stood in the dim light. Someone moved behind him.

Wyn stepped forward, a bowl in her hands. "Are you hungry?" she asked.

Rune blinked, befuddled from the nightmare images that still ghosted through his mind. He sat up and took the bowl from her. It was some kind of meat stew. He took a bite.

"It's good," he said, taking another and then another, trying unsuccessfully to slow down. His stomach still felt empty.

She smiled at him. Hadn't she been angry at him? He dimly recalled that she had, but he was too tired to remember why. Whatever the reason, she seemed to have forgiven him.

When he finished, she took the bowl from him and backed up to stand beside Ketil. She gazed up at him, and he leaned down to kiss the top of her head.

Another thing Rune had forgotten—Wyn and Ketil. Framed in the low doorway, they looked as if the gods had made them for each other. He should have known about the two of them long ago. He thought he should be happy for them, but at the moment, he couldn't feel anything at all. Eating had wearied him again. He laid his head back on the pillow and shut his eyes. As he did, he heard someone leave the room.

After a moment, Ketil spoke, waking him again. "My mother sent clothes for you."

Clothes to wear to the king's funeral pyre. Nothing had changed. The king was still dead.

"How's your hand?" Ketil asked.

Rune held it up for his friend to see.

"You didn't like *my* bandage, then?" Ketil said in mock distress.

Rune made a noise through his nose that might have sounded like a laugh. Then, gathering his strength, he swung his legs out of the bed, groaning at the stiffness in his muscles. When he looked down, he was surprised to see how clean he was. Somebody must have wiped away the blood and dirt before they put him in the bard's bed. The bard had probably insisted on it.

Ketil handed him a tunic and a pair of breeches—not Rune's, but they fit well enough. He concentrated on putting them on, then sat on the mattress to pull on his shoes. With an effort, he looked up and said, "I could get used to sleeping in a bed like this."

Ketil smiled. "You probably will."

It took Rune a moment to understand.

"Here," Ketil said, reaching behind him for Rune's mail shirt. It, too, had been cleaned. Next, he passed him his swordbelt. Rune buckled it on and looked up to see Ketil holding his sword out. As Rune took it, Ketil gave him a slight bow.

He knew Ketil wasn't trying to irritate him, but he was annoyed all the same. Using his shield hand, he slammed the sword into its hilt.

Ketil didn't seem to notice. "You're not going to like this, but the bard says you have to wear it." He pulled the golden torque from its leather bag.

Rune stared at it and scowled. Ketil was right—he didn't like it. The torque belonged to the king, not to him. He had no right to wear such a thing.

"The bard will have my head if you don't put it on," Ketil said. "So will Thora." He raised an eyebrow, and Rune realized what he meant: Thora, his future mother-in-law.

He gave in, giving Ketil a wry smile. "Can't have her angry with you, I suppose."

"Not yet, anyway." Ketil moved behind him to fasten the torque around Rune's neck.

The metal was cold against his skin, and the catch pulled at his hair. Awkwardly, his bandaged hand slowing him, Rune retied the thong that held it back. Twist his neck as he would, he couldn't make the torque feel more comfortable.

"It's time," Ketil said. He walked to the door and held it open, looking back at Rune.

Rune stared through the open doorway. How could he possibly walk through it? It seemed to him that before the pyre was lit, Beowulf was still king. But once his body was gone, turned to ashes . . .

With his left hand, he took hold of the pendant hanging below the torque, running his fingers over the runic inscription: *Wiglaf*, it read. "Amma," he pleaded silently. He didn't know what he was asking for—except for nothing to be the way it was now, for the dragon never to have woken.

A sudden flash of warmth flooded his gut, and he shut his eyes to see an image of Amma looking into his face. "Amma," he whispered again, this time in thanks, not supplication.

He took a deep breath and straightened his spine. Then, throwing his cloak over his shoulders, he crossed the threshold.

TWENTY·THREE

THE PYRE HAD ALREADY BEEN BUILT BY THE TIME RUNE
and Ketil rode up to the Feasting Field. Hung with shields
and helmets, drinking cups and bowls that Gar had collected from the dragon's hoard, the wooden bier stood just
far enough from Thor's Oak that the flames wouldn't ignite
the tree branches or threaten the Thor effigy with its red-
painted beard. Oil-soaked logs wound round with holly
crisscrossed the bottom. On top lay the king's body, richly
dressed, his hands on the hilt of his broken sword, his
wooden shield at his feet.

People milled around the pyre. Some wept openly,
some stared despairingly at the king's body. Somewhere a
woman wailed, her cry resounding in the twilight. A baby
joined her wailing, and then another baby began to scream,
as if giving voice to the Geatish nation.

Rune and Ketil dismounted and handed their reins to Ottar's son Oski, who bowed to them both, his eyes wide with admiration. When Rune thanked him, the boy blushed, unable to speak.

The bard raised a hand from the far side of the crowd, signaling Rune to the pyre.

Rune glanced at Ketil. The older youth gave Rune the smallest of nods, then moved to stay by his shoulder as they wove through the crowd.

A woman touched Rune's arm. "Dragon-slayer," she said, and dropped into a curtsy.

Rune winced and kept walking. Hrolf, the blacksmith, saw him and turned to bow.

Rune looked at Ketil, his eyes bleak.

"You can do this," Ketil said, his voice low enough that only Rune could hear.

The bard beckoned as they approached, hurrying Rune along. "You'll need to call everyone together before you light the pyre," he said. "They need to hear their lord's voice."

Rune resisted the urge to tell the bard he wasn't anybody's lord. "What am I supposed to say?"

"You'll know." The bard glanced around the crowd, then at Thora, who stood beside the pyre in a cloak of fine wool, her hair bound up in dark bands. She lowered her head to signal that she was ready. At each corner of the pyre, a warrior stood, spear in hand: Thialfi, Brokk, Ottar, Gar. As the bard looked at them, they stood at attention, squaring their shoulders.

"Now," the bard said.

Ketil shot Rune a look of encouragement.

Rune drew in his breath. "People of the Geats," he said.

Fulla, standing nearby, turned, and so did Gerd. They shushed those beside them, but the rest of the crowd kept up their weeping and their quiet talk.

"Louder," the bard said.

"People of the Geats!" Rune called out. This time the crowd's noise dropped, and they turned to him.

"Our ring-giver is dead, slain by the dragon," Rune said, his voice growing stronger as he spoke. "We ask the Thunderer to guard his spirit."

Voices murmured in agreement.

"Go on," the bard whispered, nudging Rune.

"The dragon will harry us no more—it died at the hands of our lord." He looked up at the king. "We light this pyre to send Beowulf, son of Ecgtheow, to feast with his fathers."

He knew he should say something else, but the bard was wrong—he didn't know what. Fumbling for words, thinking of the way the king had always treated him, he added, "Of the kings of this world, he was the mildest of men, the most gentle, the kindest to his people, and . . ." He paused, remembering the king standing outside the dragon's barrow, telling his warriors the fight was his alone. He thought of the way the king had seemed to grow in stature, how he had flung off the cloak of old age and taken on the mantle of a hero. He recalled the king's words to the circle of warriors. *For glory and for my kingdom,* he had said. Finally, a phrase came to him: "And the most eager for fame."

The bard grimaced, shaking his head. "That will have to do," he said as a boy handed him a flaming torch. "Here." He gave it to Rune, who held it high.

Then, in the half-light before the fall of dark, he lowered the torch to the oil-soaked logs. For a moment, nothing happened. Then the first log caught, and rivulets of fire raced the length of it, igniting the wood above it.

Smoke rose, swirling skyward. Flames lapped at the logs, then climbed the pyre, embracing the dark holly leaves woven into them, making the berries sizzle and pop. The pyre blazed up, committing the king to the flames.

Thora stepped forward, her proud head held high. Eyes unseeing, she began the song of mourning, her voice a keening wail.

As her song beseeched the gods, Rune stared into the red-gold flames, seeing in them an image of Finn and the king standing shoulder to shoulder, their swords drawn. He saw Amma's face and Hwala's. The words of Thora's lament washed over him, and now other voices joined hers, crying out in grief. In their wordless sorrow, Rune caught echoes of the trouble to come, and in the flames he saw the torches of Shylfing raiders as they swept onto Geatish shores to plunder the land and enslave the people, seeking vengeance for wrongs long past, finding a nation weakened by the loss of its king.

Thora's voice rose higher than the others, carrying with

it the anguish of a woman who has lost not only her king, but her husband as well. Rune glanced at Elli, her baby drooling on her shoulder, warm in his wool cap, unmindful of the future, while his mother's face contorted with grief. Beyond Elli, Fulla stood with Hemming. The old warrior's body convulsed as he sobbed, and Fulla reached out to encircle him with her arms. It wasn't just the king they mourned tonight, Rune thought, but their sons as well, all three of them sacrificed to Shylfing spears. Never while they lived would their sorrow cease.

He scanned the crowd, firelight playing on faces bright with tears: Gerd, her blond curls illuminated by the flames, leaning back against her mother; Hrolf standing with his wife, bouncing his daughter in his arms to comfort her. Their little boy stood between them, gazing up at the tears making flesh-colored tracks on his father's soot-blackened face.

No, Rune told himself. *We can't let the Shylfings attack.* These people didn't deserve to be enslaved, to die. He didn't think he could bear the anguish of another widow, the loneliness of another orphan. *Why should we Geats cower in fear, waiting for the enemy to appear on the horizon?*

The fire snapped and a shower of sparks lit the night sky. As they wafted earthward, Rune stood taller. He wouldn't let the Shylfings overtake them. How, he didn't know. His bandaged hand strayed to his sword hilt, but he snatched his fingers away—the lightest touch brought searing pain.

The feud with the Shylfings—Amma had taught him the poem about its beginnings, all those long years ago in the days of King Hygelac. Hygelac's son had carried on the fight after him and had been killed because of it. Three generations after the feud started, King Beowulf still nursed the desire for vengeance in his heart, Amma had said. But who now, besides the bard, even remembered the feud's origins? *We have no argument with the Shylfings,* Rune thought.

He looked back at the pyre as the flames climbed higher. They licked at the king's body and then enveloped it, swallowing it like a greedy spirit, melting the flesh and sending greasy black smoke spiraling upward into the night. The wind sent a shower of ashes over the crowd, and Rune felt them settling in his hair, on his shoulders, his cheeks—the last earthly remnants of the king.

The tears he'd thought were spent coursed down his face. The king was truly gone.

When the pyre burned to embers, harp strings sounded in the night. The bard stepped forward, his face reddened by the glowing coals. "Listen!" he called out, and the crowd shuffled toward him, raising their heads.

"We have heard of the deeds of our king in days gone by, the exploits of our mighty leader," the bard chanted, keeping the beat with his harp strings.

People gathered round, and on the other side of Thor's Oak from the pyre, someone kindled a bonfire, its flames friendly and comforting after the ravenous blaze that had consumed the king.

A hand on his shoulder made Rune look up to see the blacksmith gesturing toward the ground with his head—he'd hefted a log to serve as a stool. Rune sank gratefully onto it and turned his attention back to the bard's words.

A youth men doubted, he made known his merit,
Nine sea monsters he slew in his swimming feat,
He saved the Spear-Danes from their monstrous
  night-stalker.

A rustle of skirts made Rune turn to see Wyn crouching beside him, holding a goblet. He was relieved to see that it wasn't the ceremonial drinking horn but an ordinary cup.

"I thought you might be thirsty," she said.

He took it, thanking her, and drank the rich mead. "I was thinking of your father," he whispered as he handed the cup back. "Next to the king, he was the best of men."

She lowered her head. Rune could barely hear her words. "Someone will have to tell my brothers when they come home." She took a shuddering breath, then looked back up, her eyes fierce with the tears she held at bay.

He touched her hand with his good one. "I was the one who found him. I'll tell them, if you want me to."

She hesitated, then nodded and slipped back into the

crowd. As she did, he wondered if the task should fall to Ketil, not him. Ketil would be a part of their family now. He'd been standing beside Rune earlier. Where had he gone?

The bard struck the wooden side of his harp and made a guttural sound. Rune turned his attention back to the story just as the monster Grendel, eyes aflame, grabbed one of Beowulf's warriors who lay asleep in the mead hall and gorged on the body, eating it all, even the hands and feet.

Everyone knew the tale, but the telling of it still elicited gasps. Skyn and Skoll had loved this part of the story, Rune remembered. As boys, they had played it often enough, fighting over who got to be King Beowulf and tear Grendel's arm off. They always made Rune be Hondshio, the warrior Grendel ate. The game had been far from gentle, especially for Hondshio. He smiled wryly, shaking his head at the memory.

The bard skipped over the feasting scenes, the celebration in Hrothgar's mead hall, and went directly to Beowulf's battle with Grendel's mother, his daylong plunge to the depths of her mountain lake, the failure of his sword.

Rune thought of the Nailer, snapped in two when the king had swung it double-handed onto the dragon's skull. Swords had been of little use to King Beowulf in his battles, Rune realized; his hand had always been too strong, no matter how hard the blade.

On and on the chanting went, each of the king's

exploits turned to song. Rune's burned hand began to throb, and he held it protectively to his chest. Now that his part in the ceremony was finished, weariness crept over him, making his limbs and eyelids heavy. He blinked, then blinked again, finally allowing his eyes to close, his head to droop. Memories swam like dreams as images of his lord's final acts played through his mind: how he had stood fearless and alone before the hoard guardian, warding off the dragon's fiery blasts with his iron shield. The events shaped themselves into words, as if the king's final battle were already a song: *The fierce fire-dragon seized him by the neck— blood gushed forth. Then I have heard, in the king's hour of need, the spirit rose up in the heart of his kinsman Wiglaf, son of Weohstan.*

Rune blinked awake, confused. The events *were* a song; the bard was singing them. As Rune looked up, firelight caught the gleaming harp strings, and the bard looked directly at him.

*That brave man's hand was burned; when he plunged
    his sword
Into the creature's chest, his courage did not fail.
The gold-giver of the Geats drew his dagger, his battle-
    sharp blade;
Together the two noble kinsmen felled their foe.*

Rune listened in wonder. How could the bard know all this?

A movement beside him made him turn, and suddenly he understood. Ketil was back, crouching beside him—his shoulder companion.

Rune caught his eye and Ketil grinned, just like the old days, back when they were boys in the hall.

TWENTY·FOUR

HE WAS LOST IN A DREAM OF FIRE AND DARKNESS WHEN the drumming of hoofbeats startled him awake. He lay taut, listening. Horses neighed. Men shouted. Shylfings? An attack? He flung off the blanket and, grabbing his sword, opened the door a finger's breadth to peer out.

It wasn't Shylfings—a border patrol had returned.

By the time Rune had dressed and rushed outside, the eight members of the patrol knew all the news from Gar, who had been on guard. They stood clustered together, their clothes stained by days in the saddle, their horses behind them, stamping impatiently. As he neared them, Rune could feel the men eyeing him, taking his measure. They had returned expecting to speak to King Beowulf in his golden hall. Instead, they found blackened timbers, a smoking funeral pyre—and an untried youth masquerading as king.

"My lord." Gar stepped forward so that all the members of the patrol could see him bowing, and Rune appreciated his support. "My lord," he said again, "Horsa and his men have just returned from the northern borders."

There was probably some formulaic way to respond, Rune thought, but it wasn't something he'd ever learned.

"Horsa, what have you seen?" the bard asked, hurrying toward them.

Everyone turned to the poet, and Rune was relieved of the need to speak for the moment.

"Horse trails through the forest—trails we didn't make," a solid man in a mud-spattered cloak said. He handed his reins to one of his companions and held up an arrow shaft, its tip broken off. "Shylfings. See the feathers?"

The bard took the arrow from him. He looked at it closely and nodded before handing it to Rune. Rune stared at the feathers, wondering what Horsa saw in them that identified them as Shylfing work. He was sure the warriors gathered behind Horsa could sense his ignorance.

Before he could speak, a man in the back of the group called out.

"Mother!" He and another man detached themselves from the other warriors and moved toward Thora, who hurried from her house with a shawl hastily thrown over her shoulders, still knotting her braids behind her head.

· 243 ·

Wyn's brothers. Gar must have already told them about their father. Thora reached out, silent, and placed her palm first against one son's cheek and then against the other's. As she did, each man closed his eyes and tightened his jaw, as if he was drawing strength from her. Then all three walked to Thora's house and disappeared inside.

Rune watched them go, feeling in his heart the bleakness that would overtake them. He jumped as Ketil whispered in his ear, "Welcome them home and thank them for their service." When had he gotten there?

Then, as if the exchange had never taken place, Ketil moved to stand beside the bard and bowed to Rune.

Rune turned back to the remaining members of Horsa's troop. "You are welcome home." The words sounded false, as if he were playacting with his foster brothers the way they had when they were children. "Many thanks for your service to the kingdom."

The men regarded him, unmoving.

"The hall may have been burned, but there is meat and ale for hungry warriors," he added. He gestured at a bond servant who hovered close by. The man scurried off to bring food. "Rest now, and eat."

Nothing happened for a moment, and Rune stood rigid, waiting. Then Horsa inclined his head. As he did, the others bowed briefly before they dispersed, the jingling of their horses' bridles and the clopping of hooves filling the dreadful silence.

Rune watched them go. The king might have named

him his heir, but the words meant nothing if the warriors didn't accept him as their leader.

One of the men looked back over his shoulder, staring a challenge at Rune. He straightened his spine and met the man's eyes. The warrior turned away again, following his companions.

"We'll need to rebuild the hall, first thing," the bard said, rubbing his hands against the morning chill. "We can't have meetings out here like this."

Rune nodded. The hall did need to be rebuilt. Winter was coming and people would need a place to gather.

He gazed around him. Morning mist hovered near the ground. Autumn mist. He looked toward a line of birches at the edge of the stronghold. Their leaves had almost all turned. A sense of urgency filled him. If people were to survive the winter, the harvest had to be brought in. It was too late for many fields—the dragon had seen to that—but not all of them. Yet, with so many farms burned, every bit of grain they saved would count.

He looked back at the bard. "The hall will have to wait."

The bard fixed his single eye on Rune. The dark, empty socket seemed to stare at him, as if it could see right through him.

He struggled not to shudder. "The fields have to be harvested."

Ketil stepped closer, his hand on his sword hilt. "We've never been more vulnerable to attack. You heard what

Horsa said. If everyone's out in the fields, we'll be in even more danger."

"The hall has to come first," the bard said. "It's a symbol of the kingdom's strength. We'll need it for your coronation, too."

Rune felt his shoulders sag. His stomach growled. Didn't these two have any idea where the kingdom's grain came from, or the hay for the horses?

At that moment, the bond servant he had sent to get food for the patrol returned, a huge tray in his arms. He looked around, expecting to find Horsa and his men.

"We'll take that," the bard said. He grabbed a drumstick off the tray and bit into it.

Rune shook his head in exasperation. For the bard, he thought wryly, food probably always came from trays, served up to him hot, anytime he wanted it.

By the time the sun had burned off the mist, Rune ached to be home, harvesting Hwala's single unscathed field. A small group had gathered to plan their next move, but to Rune, all the talk seemed pointless. He'd already explained himself, and more than once, but the discussion went round and round.

Horsa still wore his travel-stained cloak. "The signs we saw weren't fresh, but they were definitely Shylfing," he said. "Three patrols are still on the borders; we don't know what they've seen." He took a bite of the bread he was holding and spoke through a full mouth. "It's not just the

Shylfings we should fear, either. Other tribes will hear about King Beowulf's death, too, and know we're weak."

At the word *weak,* Rune felt Horsa's eyes on him, but he didn't respond.

"If they see the golden roof on our hall, they won't think us weak," the bard said. "It gives the people the symbol of hope they need in these times."

How had King Beowulf stood it? If the bard said one more word about the hall, Rune thought he would scream. He could almost feel his sinews moving in time to the scythe, cutting the grain that would help feed the kingdom. What would it take to make the others understand that hunger was just as deadly an enemy as Shylfings?

Unexpectedly, Thora came to his aid. She had left her sons sleeping, Wyn attending them. Her eyes still bore a haunted look from their bitter homecoming. Now, she looked at the bard and spoke dryly. "Hope is easier to come by on a full stomach." She turned toward Horsa. "If the people starve to death over the winter, they'll hardly need your sword."

At her words, Rune felt a flush of warmth. Emboldened, he stepped forward, a new idea forming in his mind as he spoke. "Long ago, there was a feud between our people and the Danes." He thought about something Amma had taught him, a part of the "Lay of Beowulf" the bard never sang. "That feud came to an end when King Beowulf offered his strength to the Danish king—when he killed the monster Grendel," he said, and looked around. Horsa was scowling, but at least he was listening. The bard was examining his fingernails, not looking at Rune, but he was sure he had the man's attention.

"Go on," Ketil said.

"King Beowulf's feud with the Shylfings—it's not my feud. It wasn't his feud, either. Do any of you even know how it started, what we're avenging? Anyone besides the bard, I mean," he added quickly.

Thora looked at him sharply.

He stiffened at her expression, then plunged ahead. "Why should we wait for them to attack us? If they were our allies, the way the Danes are now, think how strong we would be."

Nobody spoke. Rune kept his head up, but he trained his gaze on the blank space between Horsa and the bard, unwilling to meet anyone's eyes.

Thora cleared her throat.

Before she had a chance to argue with him, he went on. "We could end the feud. We could send envoys to the Shylfing court."

"Envoys to the Shylfings? You mean dead men," Horsa said. "They'd be killed before they delivered their message. If we send anyone to the Shylfings, it should be an army to finish them off."

"We barely have enough men to make an army," Ketil said, sweeping his arm toward the burned timbers of King Beowulf's hall, as if to remind Horsa of all the warriors who used to gather there and how many of them had been killed. "Even if we did attack the Shylfings, we'd be leaving the kingdom vulnerable to Wulfing raiders, not to mention half a dozen other tribes."

"Send my sons," Thora said.

Everyone looked at her.

"My lord, you're right," she said to Rune. "The time for this feud is long past." As she stepped forward, Horsa backed up, making room for her in the circle. "Thialfi's mother was a Shylfing," she said. "He's skilled with words. He could speak for us. My sons will go with him as guards."

Rune realized his jaw was hanging open. He clamped it shut. Thora's husband was dead, yet she was willing to send her sons into such danger? It didn't matter, Rune realized. They were in just as much danger if they didn't send an envoy. Without peace, every day was another chance for death from a Shylfing spear.

"I'll find Thialfi," Ketil said.

Rune watched him go, mindful of how lucky he was to have Ketil's support.

"We'll still need border patrols," Horsa said.

"Yes, of course we will," Rune said. "You and Gar will be in charge of them. And we'll need a seasoned warrior at each harvest site, and a fresh horse for a messenger, in case there's an attack. Do we have enough men?"

Horsa thought for a moment. "Not yet, but we will as soon as another patrol returns." Then he looked at Rune, inclined his head, and added, "My lord."

.   .   .

Rune planned to ride to Hwala's farm that day, but he hadn't anticipated how long all the preparations, all the talk, would take. There was so much to be decided: which warriors would stay on patrol; which would guard the stronghold and which the harvesters; what they should do in case of attack; and, most important, the instructions for the envoys and the gifts they would take with them. Thialfi had been easy to convince, and Wyn's brothers readily agreed with their mother. Rune met with them privately; Wyn had asked him if he would. They listened gravely, courteously, as he described finding Finn on the mountainside, and then asked him questions about the dragon and about their father. When Rune suggested putting a memorial runestone at the place where Finn had died, the brothers agreed, thanking him. They seemed eager to go with Thialfi, and Rune thought he understood their desire to embark on a dangerous task, to leave the stronghold and the mourning behind them.

The bard spent most of the day scowling, angry that the hall and the coronation would have to wait. "He'll come around," Wyn whispered to Rune. "He just wants his seat of honor in the hall again, where he's the center of attention."

It was evening before all the plans were settled. Rune and Ketil sat by themselves, cross-legged in front of a campfire, eating. "Did you know about Finn's argument with King Beowulf?" Ketil asked.

Rune shook his head.

"Having you say we should send envoys to the Shylfings—it was like having Finn there again. He always said the feud should be forgotten. But the king . . ." Ketil looked over at him. "You've made allies out of Thora and her sons, that's for sure."

Allies? Rune gazed across the campsite that now served as a gathering place. He could see Gar and Ottar talking to two of the men who had returned with Horsa's patrol. Gar, Ottar, and the other men who had been at the dragon fight he could count on, he thought. And now, Thora's sons and perhaps Horsa. But the rest of the warriors, the ones who would be returning from patrolling the borders, he knew all too well what they would think of a mere boy succeeding the king, a boy who wanted to give up the feud with the Shylfings.

He stared into the blue flames that danced at the bottom of the fire. Even if the Shylfings agreed to a truce, what right did he have to end a generations-long feud? Feuds had to be avenged; that was the way of things. Not a single living Geat was old enough to remember a time before this fight. Who was he to try to stop it?

TWENTY·FIVE

THE SKY HAD YET TO LIGHTEN AS RUNE AND KETIL SET out for Hwala's farm the next morning. Hairy-Hoof seemed as eager as Rune to leave the settlement. Rune wondered if she had felt as stifled by the crowd of horses in the stable as he had by all the people—and all their *opinions.*

They rode quickly, their senses alert, their weapons at the ready. Rune flexed his burned hand, trying to accustom himself to the feel of the padded glove that protected his palm. Accompanied by her cousin Wyn, curly-haired Gerd had brought it to him the previous day, presenting it to him shyly. Once Wyn pushed her forward, though, Gerd forgot her timidity. "I made it to protect your hand," she said. "Here, do you want help putting it on?"

He had declined the help but was grateful for the glove.

It allowed him to touch things, even to hold Hairy-Hoof's reins, without flinching in pain. Wielding a sword was still beyond him, though, and he wasn't sure what he'd do if they were attacked.

As it rose, the sun's rays brought not light to Rune's eyes, but visions of enemy spears glinting on the horizon. There had been so much talk of the kingdom's danger that a sense of dread weighed on his heart. It seemed as if each stand of firs, each rise in the terrain hid a band of enemy warriors.

Shylfing warriors were hardly the only danger. Every patrol that returned would find out what Rune had done, that he was trying to end the feud. He knew that his supporters would do their best to convince those men that he was right. But what if it wasn't enough? If the kingdom turned in upon itself, splitting into factions, that would be far worse than a Shylfing attack. And it would be all his fault.

He shifted in his saddle. Beside him, Ketil rode in silence. Rune could see his eyes flicking from side to side, alert to his surroundings. He wondered whether Ketil thought he'd made the right choice, but he didn't want to ask.

By midmorning, as they skirted the mountain's slopes, Ketil began whistling, and Rune's spirits lifted at the sound. He searched in his saddlebag and tossed his friend half an oatcake, crunching into the other half himself.

They made good time, reaching the runestone that

marked the edge of Hwala's farm by midday. Hairy-Hoof perked up her ears and took the lead along the path through the scorched fields, down through the trees that bordered the stream, and up again to the farm.

As they rode past the blackened homefield and dismounted outside the ruined farmhouse, Ketil ceased his whistling. The place seemed very still. Even the chatter of birds in the ash tree was muted as Rune knelt by Amma's grave. When he walked through the farmhouse and the stable, he felt as if he were trespassing. He hoped that Hwala, his sons, and his servant had accepted their hasty burial in a common grave with no one to sing them out or perform the rituals. Although he could sense no angry spirits haunting the place, he moved cautiously just in case.

In the drying shed, ghostly strips of herring hung flapping in the breeze, and in the corner, Rune found bags of groats from already harvested grain. He set some to soak for their supper before he led Ketil to the single unburned field, their swords never out of arm's reach. The oats had waited so long to be harvested that they were already dry on their stalks. There would be no need to tie them into shocks; instead, they would be able to thresh them the next day.

Even with his hurt hand, Rune was more skilled than Ketil, who struggled to manage Hwala's scythe. After watching for a moment, Rune shook his head and repositioned the tool in his friend's hand. "It's a scythe, not a sword," he said. "Watch." He swung the blade through the stalks, then stepped aside as Ketil tried. It took him three attempts before Rune was satisfied enough to return to his own row. As he moved down it, he began to feel at home in the harvest rhythm. Insects buzzed in the oats, and the smell of sun-warmed soil overpowered the lingering odor of smoke. Over and over, he reached to grab the golden stalks, swung his blade, then stepped forward to reach again. The sun beat down on his shoulders, and the familiar movements loosened the dread that knotted his muscles.

Behind him, he could feel Ketil watching him, trying to imitate his movements and muttering angry oaths when he failed. Rune smiled and kept going.

As he toiled, he began to gain an appreciation for all the work Skyn and Skoll had done when they hadn't been busy tormenting him, for how quickly they could move down a row of oats, goading each other to go faster. Skyn hadn't been so bad when Skoll hadn't been around. Rune wondered if they could have found their way to being friends—if he'd ever tried. He wished he had. And that he hadn't always been so quick to react to Skoll's taunts. He could see Amma's angry face and hear her words: *Always your fists, never your head.* How many times had she said that to him? Now, thinking of the ways feuds got started and how an argument between two men could lead to the destruction of families and even all-out war between kingdoms, he understood her impatience.

They finished the field as the sun was setting and

hurried to put their tools away before half-light, when it would be too dangerous to be out. While Ketil cared for the horses, Rune brought the fish and groats into the hut he'd shared with Amma. Stooping to keep from hitting his head on the lintel, he stopped, struck by how small the place seemed, how silent. Outside, he could hear Ketil whistling. The sound accentuated the hut's stillness. As his eyes adjusted to the gloom, he looked at the loom leaning against the wall, the three-legged stool in front of it, the blackened fire pit, the pot still hanging from its tripod— the comforting elements of his childhood.

A noise startled him. He froze, heart pounding. The sound came again, a rustling from the corner of the hut— from under the goatskin that had covered his weapons. He'd left it lying on the ground.

Stepping cautiously, he moved toward it, just as a head poked out from under it, making him yelp.

"Everything all right in there?" Ketil called.

"It's fine—I'm fine," Rune said, trying to calm his breath. It was just a squirrel. The little creature crouched, unmoving, looking from Rune to the doorway, as if calculating its odds.

"Go on, I won't hurt you," Rune said. He stepped aside to allow the squirrel passage. It eyed him a moment longer, then raced out of the hut. Rune crossed to the goatskin and pulled it up, revealing Amma's nut crock lying on its side, its contents spilled out. Only a handful of last year's withered harvest remained. He righted the crock, and as he did, he saw something underneath it in the shadows, half buried in the hut's dirt floor. Gently, he worked it loose, revealing a whalebone box no longer than an outstretched hand. He didn't remember ever seeing it before. Was it Amma's? He shook it gently and heard something rattle inside it.

"I'm hungry," Ketil said, coming through the doorway. "What's to eat?"

Rune brushed dirt from the box's sides and felt for the latch, his fingers twitching with anticipation to find out what was inside.

"What have you got?" Ketil asked.

"I can't tell. It's too dark in here to see." He started for the door.

"You shouldn't be out there now. I'll build a fire."

Rune nodded, his attention focused on the box. The metal latch was rusted shut, and he had to work to pry it loose without breaking it. It came open just as the fire blazed up. Rune crouched down and held the box to the light. As he opened its lid, he gave a low cry of dismay.

"What's wrong?" Ketil asked.

"There's nothing in it, just a piece of wood," he said. Disappointment flooded through him. He wasn't sure what he'd been expecting, but something more than this.

Ketil took the wood and squinted at it in the firelight. "There's something carved on it." He scowled and handed it back. "Not very good carving, though."

Rune agreed. Figures were scratched into it with no

artistry, no skill, as if they'd been made by a child or in a hurry. He shook his head and tossed it onto the woodpile.

As Rune cooked their supper, Ketil poked around the hut, keeping his head down to avoid hitting it on the roof beams. "Do you remember when my father and I came to help with the harvest? The time Hwala was sick?"

Rune nodded, trying to remember. Ketil's father had been killed in a hunting accident not very long after that.

"I was as bad with a scythe then as I am now. Amma finally took me with her down to the sea to collect birds' eggs and seaweed."

"She did?" Rune didn't remember that, but it sounded like something Amma would do. Rune had spent many childhood days climbing cliffs up to seabirds' nests and carefully handing the eggs down to Amma, or raking up seaweed for her to boil into sand-filled soups he had hated.

Ketil nodded. "I was in the way." He peered at the wall hanging that Amma had woven with stories of the gods. "I was a little afraid of her because of, you know, the sorts of things people sometimes said about her."

Rune looked up from the pot. "You mean, what Dayraven said about her."

Ketil didn't answer.

"I still can't believe he ran from the dragon."

"I can," Ketil said.

Rune looked at him, surprised by the vehemence in his voice.

"You didn't see him running from the king's hall when

the dragon attacked it." He frowned as he sat down by the fire. "I did."

"But dragons—they do that to people; even the king said so."

Ketil shook his head as he took the bowl Rune handed him. "There were men sleeping in the hall, and he knew it. He could have shouted something, given them a chance to save themselves. He didn't." He took a bite of porridge. "Hey, this is good!"

"Of course it's good," Rune said. "I made it."

They ate in silence for a moment, chewing the meaty oats, stopping every now and then to spit out husks and grit.

"I used to really admire him," Ketil said. "I used to want to be just like him."

Rune stared into the fire.

"Do you know how many arm rings Finn had?" Ketil asked.

Rune thought for a moment, remembering Finn standing beside him in the hall, helping him to get a better grip on his sword hilt, watching his swing with a practiced eye. Had Finn even worn any arm rings? He had been the king's shoulder companion—he must have won plenty of rings over the years, but Rune couldn't recall seeing them. He shook his head.

"Of course you don't. He only wore one of them. And he never spent any time polishing it, either, the way Dayraven did." He scraped porridge from the bottom of his bowl, then took a bite of dried herring, working it with his teeth to make it soft enough to swallow. "When it was time for weapons training, did you ever notice how he disappeared instead of helping teach the boys in the hall?"

There was no need for Rune to answer.

"Like I said, I used to really admire him. But after I got made a hearth companion and got to know him better . . ." His voice trailed off. "Finn never talked about all the things he did. He just did them, putting himself in danger with hardly a thought. Wyn's brothers are like that, too."

Rune didn't know what to think. He remembered standing behind a beam in the hall, listening to Dayraven tell a group of boys about how he'd killed the aurochs. The warrior's armbands had flickered in the light from the roaring hall fire—as if they'd been polished. "Warriors always boast," he said tentatively.

"But not just about themselves," Ketil said. "And not at the expense of others."

Others like Amma, Rune thought. He stirred the fire and picked up a piece of kindling to add to it—the wood he'd found in the box. Instead of putting it on the flames, though, he turned it over in his hands, looking at it closely. Dirt was packed into the crude carvings, making them hard to decipher. Had he made them when he was a child?

A log rolled over, making the fire flare. As it did, a pattern jumped out at him: runes. The same runes that were cut into his pendant. His name was carved into the wood.

He sat up, holding it as close to the fire as he could

without it being burned. There was his name, along with more runes that he didn't recognize, marching in a line across the wood.

ᚹᛁᚷᛚᚨᚠᛋᚢᚾᛟᚠᚹᛖᛟᚺᛋᛏᚨᚾᛋᚨᚦᛁᛏᚷᚨᛏᛁᛁᚱᛗ

Under them, he could see what looked like human figures. One of them, wearing a long skirt, stood beside what looked like a boat. He caught his breath.

Ketil came around the fire and crouched beside him, staring at the wood. "She's putting a baby into a boat," he said. "Isn't she."

It wasn't a question.

"Men fighting—see the spear?" Ketil pointed. "And something else. Flames? Is that a hall on fire?"

Rune shook his head, trying to comprehend what he was seeing. "Can you read it?" Unlike farmers, boys who were raised in the hall, the way Ketil had been, were taught to read runes.

Ketil took the wood and studied it. "'Wiglaf, son of Weohstan,' that's how it starts," he said. "Then something else: 'and Inga Til,' Inga the Good." He handed the wood back. "Your mother. The one putting you into the boat."

That's why he'd been in the boat all those years ago. He was no sacrifice to the gods, as Dayraven had believed. The failure to kill him hadn't brought a curse on the kingdom. Instead, his mother had simply been trying to save his life.

Clenching the piece of wood in his good hand, he

closed his eyes, probing his memory for any hint of his mother. "Inga Til," he repeated to himself as the cookfire snapped. His nostrils filled with the smell of smoke, harsh and biting. Against the backs of his eyelids, a scene formed, and he tightened his grip on the wood. Flames, he saw flames in the night as a hall burned, as people ran to save themselves. Horses whinnied in terror, and he smelled not just smoke but also burning flesh. He heard children screaming and the clash of sword against sword. A young woman with a baby in her arms ran toward dark water, a servant beside her carrying weapons and armor that clinked together as she ran. Ahead in the shallows, a boat rocked. The woman turned to look behind her. A man, silhouetted by flames, brandished his spear and began running toward them. He heard a cry of anguish—"My child! Wiglaf!"— and felt the warmth of a body pressing to his cheek, a heart beating in time to his. Then: darkness. Darkness and cold and the slap of waves against the sides of the boat.

He opened his eyes. The ground was beneath him. He was sitting in front of the cookfire in Amma's hut. He unclenched his hand from the piece of wood that was cutting into it. Cautiously, he raised his head. Over the tops of the friendly flames, Ketil was watching him.

He swallowed and looked away. "Let's get some sleep."

The next day, Rune felt hollow and drained. He was relieved by the speed with which Ketil learned how to work a flail, bringing the heavy, jointed sticks down on the stalks to separate the oats from the chaff. As they worked, he could tell Ketil was keeping a close eye on him. It was hard to keep his focus on the threshing, to lose himself in the work. The rhythm he had found in the previous day's reaping eluded him, and twice Ketil had to leap out of the way to avoid being hit by his flail.

He hadn't slept well. All night long, disturbing images and sounds and smells had woken him. He didn't know what he'd seen as he sat in front of the fire—a vision? Or had he just imagined it? He didn't want to think about it, but he couldn't stop himself.

Before they left Hwala's farm, Rune returned to Amma's grave. He took the carved piece of wood out of the pouch at his belt and turned it over in his hands. He thought he might understand some of Amma's reasons, her choices. It would have been a terrible burden for him to grow up knowing his father had killed her son. But one secret was connected to another like a long chain of dark beads, and revealing one might have led to others. In the end, she must have chosen to keep all of them wound up inside herself until it was almost too late. *Survivor of war,* she'd said. It wasn't just his name. She'd been trying to tell him what he was: the flotsam bobbing on the waves after the wreck of war. Like Amma herself.

They rode out, bags of groats tied to their saddles, straw drying in the shed. They could send someone for it later if it was needed for the settlement's horses. Amma's woven hanging that had covered one wall of the hut for as long as he could remember was rolled up and tied to Rune's saddle, where he could see it as he rode.

They stopped at farms, looking to see who needed help, taking a hand with a scythe or rake, driving a cart full of hay, always keeping watch for raiders. Despite his burned hand, Rune welcomed the work. Harvesting made sense: you grew grain, you cut the stalks and allowed them to dry, and you threshed them when it was time—all so you could feed yourself and your livestock. He wished the rest of his life were equally straightforward.

At every farm, Ketil chatted amiably with the farmers as he worked, telling them about Thialfi and Wyn's brothers, about Rune's idea to put an end to the feud. The first time he realized what Ketil was doing, Rune shot him a warning look, but it was too late; the words were already out.

Then it was Ketil's turn to signal for Rune to listen as the farmers talked among themselves. "It's what a good king does," one of them said as Ketil held Rune's eyes. "Brings about peace so we can get on with farming."

"Not just farming—living," another man answered, and an older woman agreed with him.

"Bringing up children you don't have to send off to war," she said.

Rune wondered how many sons she had lost to the Shylfings.

But not everyone thought the truce was a good idea. At the next farm, a young farmer exploded with anger at

Ketil's words. Ketil kept working alongside him, and Rune heard him asking who the man had lost to the enemy.

"Nobody in my family," he answered as he swung a bale of hay onto a cart.

"Friends of yours, then," Ketil said sympathetically.

"No, nobody I know," the man said. "But you can't just stop a feud with words. Those Shylfings, they'll say they want peace, but when we let our guard down . . ."

"No matter what happens," Rune said, "we'll never let our guard down."

The farmer stared at him for a moment, then leaned over to pick up another bale. The man was right, Rune thought. King Beowulf had known it. What did Rune think he was doing, acting against the king's wishes, against all of the wisdom age and experience had conferred on him?

Then he remembered what Amma had taught him about the king ending the feud between the Danes and the Geats. Some feuds could be ended, some couldn't, but how was he to know which was which? He shook his head in bewilderment.

After that, Rune kept his mouth shut and let Ketil do the talking. More often than not, the people on the farms they visited supported the truce. Sometimes Ketil asked them if they knew how it had started. Only once did someone say she did, a wizened old woman who wore a hat that looked like a sack. But the version of the story she told was different from the one Rune knew. He wondered if either of them was right.

As they left Surt's farm, Rune pictured Thialfi and Wyn's brothers on their horses, riding through hostile lands. Could they have reached the Shylfings yet? Ketil said no, that it would take many days to get there, then time to negotiate and travel home again—if nothing went wrong. Rune couldn't stop worrying that Horsa had been right: any envoys to the Shylfings would be killed before they delivered their message.

What was I thinking? Rune wondered. When Thora had backed him, sending the men had seemed like the right thing to do. Now it seemed like a fool's errand, or worse. Had he sent them to their deaths?

He looked down at the pouch on his belt where he'd tucked the piece of wood and once again saw the vision of terror and destruction his mother had saved him from. Could that happen to the Geats? Had it already happened at the settlement, while he and Ketil had been away? He imagined Wyn and her mother cowering in their house; Elli holding her baby, terror and grief on her face as a sword came down.

The sound of Ketil whistling broke into his dark thoughts. He looked up at the bright autumn sky, at a group of birches in the distance, their leaves flickering red and gold. A breeze ruffled through his hair and across his eyelashes. Ahead, he could hear the sounds of men in the fields, laughing as they worked. He nudged Hairy-Hoof's sides, and as she broke into a canter, Ketil kept pace beside him.

They stopped at Buri's place last. The young farmer needed no help, but he was glad to see them all the same and to show off his new son. "I wanted to call him Beowulf, but the wife said no," he said. "Too high for the likes of us, she said, so we're still trying to decide."

Rune held out his shield hand. The baby grabbed his little finger, twisting it hard. He gritted his teeth, letting the infant have its way. "Quite a grip on this one."

Buri laughed.

"Finn was a good man," Rune said. "What about Finn for a name?"

Buri nodded. "Fair but firm he was, wasn't he?" He turned around to look at his wife, who peered shyly at them from the doorway. She nodded and Buri looked down at his son. "How does Finn suit you?" he asked.

The baby gurgled happily.

From Buri's, Rune and Ketil made their way back to the settlement, their path leading them through a wide swath of land the dragon hadn't burned. They passed field after newly harvested field, and Rune thought there might be just enough grain and hay to get the kingdom through the winter, at least if spring didn't come too late.

As long as the Shylfings didn't attack.

And as long as the warriors hadn't already splintered into factions while he and Ketil had been gone. What would they find when they returned?

TWENTY·SIX

RUNE STOOD UNMOVING, HIS ARMS HELD OUT LIKE WINGS, flinching at pricks of pain. There was no escape.

In front of him, Wyn looked him up and down, frowning, hands on her hips. She pulled a pin from between her lips and took hold of his shirt.

"Ow," Rune said, and looked at Thora, who stood beside him, pinning on a sleeve. Gerd worked on the other one, on his sword-hand side, giggling occasionally as she warned him not to move. She was the best seamstress of the three women, and Rune trusted her not to touch his burned hand. He was still wearing the padded glove she'd made him.

If only the tunic would fit as well as the glove did. It had been Finn's best, embroidered down the front, and

Thora had cut it down for Rune. Nobody said it, but Rune was sure the task would have been simpler if Thora had allowed Gerd to do the initial cutting. Now, no matter what they did, the three women couldn't get it to fit Rune properly, with the embroidery in the right place.

He endured their ministrations. There was no point in protesting—they were doing their best, and they didn't have much time. The coronation was tomorrow, and the cloak still wasn't ready, either. Fulla had been working feverishly on it, and now several other women were helping her. Or so Rune had been told.

It wasn't as if they had waited until the last minute. They had worked as hard as Rune and Ketil had. So had everyone else—men, women, and children. Carts of grain had rumbled into the stronghold—not as full as in previous years, Thora had told him, but perhaps enough to see them through the winter. Rune had been gratified to hear people remarking on them, and more than one warrior had given him a nod of approval at the sight of a cart laden with hay.

There had been no word from the envoys when Rune and Ketil got back to the settlement. Even though he knew it was too early, Rune couldn't quell his anxiety. They increased the number of border patrols, and finally Rune agreed with the bard that it was time to rebuild the hall. It wouldn't be anything grand the way King Beowulf's golden-roofed hall had been, let alone shingled with shields the way Odin's hall was said to be. For now, plain thatch would have to do, despite the bard's disappointment. If they were to finish before the snows set in, they didn't have time for luxuries. What they needed now was a place for the people to assemble, especially in case of attack, a place where the men and boys could practice their weapons during the winter. Rune thought the women needed to meet there, too, even if he wasn't sure what it was they did.

The last of the border patrols that had left before King Beowulf died came riding in when they were just finishing the roof. The men watched Rune, their eyes expressionless, as the troop leader gave his report. Later, Rune saw them looking with disdain at the new hall's dirt floor, not a wooden one like in King Beowulf's hall; at its wooden beams as yet undecorated with the elaborate carvings they were accustomed to; at its simple thatched roof that made it look like a farmhouse. Seeing the hall through their eyes, he understood how it fared in contrast with the great mead hall they had left behind them when they went out to patrol the borders. Their entire world had collapsed while they had been gone, and the new hall was a symbol of just how diminished things had become. Well, Rune told himself, it would have to serve. At least it had long benches lining its interior, surrounding the fire pit, like King Beowulf's hall had had. And at least there would be enough food to survive the winter, if the hunting was good.

As the patrol dispersed, Rune could hear murmuring among the men. It wasn't just the hall they were objecting to, he was sure. He set his jaw and turned back to helping Gar with the thatch they had been working on.

That night, they consecrated the hall to Thor, sacrificing a goat in his honor and cooking it over a roaring fire in the middle of the structure as warriors gathered on the benches. Outside, the wind whistled, nosing around the eaves, inspecting the walls and finding no entry. Sawdust still littered the ground, but the joints were solid.

The bard took charge of the ceremony, and Rune was content to watch until a servant bowed low in front of him, holding out a platter. Unsure of what to do, Rune sought out the bard with his eyes, but the poet was looking elsewhere. He was the only one—everyone else in the hall seemed to be staring at Rune. Then he remembered the last goat sacrifice he'd seen, at the Feasting Field, when King Beowulf had chosen the men who would help him fight the dragon. The king had eaten the goat's liver first, before the warriors ate the choicest cuts of meat. He took a deep breath, then grabbed the liver from the platter, held it up for the people to see, and took a bite as the juices dripped down his wrist and chin.

After the meal, people made themselves comfortable on the benches, firelight and torches illuminating the pale wooden walls, while shadows lurked in the corners. Bond servants moved around the hall, refilling cups and drinking horns and adding wood to the fire. Rune directed them to make sure the newly returned patrol had everything they needed. He watched the men from that troop watching him and pretended not to notice. When they whispered to each other, he told himself they were just catching up on the news. The other patrols seemed to have accepted him. This one just needed time.

The bard strode forward and struck his harp. "Listen!" he called.

Conversations quieted and people turned toward him. Rune watched the firelight gleaming on their teeth when they smiled. It shone in the whites of their eyes and reflected off gold arm rings as warriors shifted on the benches.

"We have heard of the deeds of the kings," the bard began, signaling the start of the "Lay of Beowulf." People nodded their heads in recognition; it was an appropriate tale to soak into the timbers of the newly consecrated hall, reminding men of the deeds of a hero from days long past.

But as Rune listened, he realized the bard was skipping over the familiar parts of the story and beginning instead with the dragon fight. Winding his words into sinuous patterns, the bard sang the dragon—and the king—back to life. Warriors leaned forward, listening. Not all of them had heard this tale.

The harp strings thrummed as the bard plucked them. "Then I have heard, in the king's hour of need, the spirit rose up in the heart of his kinsman Wiglaf, son of Weohstan," he sang.

Sitting up front where everyone could see him, Rune

felt alone and exposed. He wished Ketil hadn't drawn guard duty for tonight. He closed his eyes to the crowd and listened, allowing the song to flow over him, the past to flood back into his head. Knowing what was coming, he cringed at the memory of the dragon's fangs biting into the king's neck, the poisonous venom bubbling green on the king's skin. But the words didn't come. Instead, the bard took a new turn.

Who among men knew when the boat came to Geatish
*   shores*
That its cargo would be a king.
The son of a princess, raised by a princess,
The young hero who rushed to his ring-giver's side.
Heedless of danger the two fought the dragon,
Saving the kingdom, revealing the new king.

The back of his neck grew hot. Rune knew the bard was doing his best to help the warriors accept him as their leader, but knowing so didn't make him feel any less awkward.

When he'd shown the bard the piece of wood from Amma's hut and asked him if he knew anything about his mother, he hadn't expected her to become part of a song. He should have, he realized. Especially when the bard had nodded gravely and said, "Inga Til. I know the name. Her father was the king of the Brondings. What became of her

I have never heard." He had stared at Rune with his piercing eye and said, "From your father, you are kin to King Beowulf; from your mother, to the lord of the Brondings. And brought up by a noblewoman, too." He fell silent, but he kept up his fierce gaze until Rune had to look away.

Later, when there was time, Rune thought, he might tell the bard the vision he'd had, of his mother racing from terror and destruction to save her child's life, certain of her own death. For a moment, he could feel the rough wool of her clothes against his cheek, the beating of her heart as she placed him in the boat. If anyone deserved a song of her own, she did.

He looked out into the firelit hall and again saw men watching him, appraising him, their expressions unreadable.

As the song ended, there was a roar of approval. Rune signaled the bond servants to refill the drinking horns. They would have to be more careful with their resources later, in order to get through the long winter, but he didn't think now was the time. Tonight, at least, the people needed to celebrate.

"Let's have the part where the dragon comes out of the barrow again," someone called, and the bard rang his fingers across the harp strings, happy to oblige.

Rune slipped out the side door of the hall and took a deep breath of the cold night air. He heard someone coming out behind him and turned to see Wyn pulling her cloak tightly around her.

"While you and Ketil were gone, he sang the dragon

fight every time a new patrol came back," she said. "But the part about your mother—that's new."

He nodded.

"I'm glad he added it."

"So am I," Rune said. Something cold landed on his cheek, and he looked up to see white flakes spiraling down through the dark.

The first snow. They had finished the hall just in time.

Now, a day later, they rushed to prepare for the coronation.

"Ow!" Rune said again, and Gerd laughed.

"If you'd hold still, you wouldn't get pinned." Her face turned serious as she concentrated on his sleeve.

"I *was* holding still," he said.

A knock sounded at the door, and Ketil stuck his head in, shaking snow from his hair. "Thialfi and your brothers are back," he hissed, looking at Wyn. "With a bunch of Shylfings."

Shylfings? Rune looked sharply at Ketil.

"Shylfing envoys," Ketil said.

Rune dropped his arms, and the women quickly stripped him of the new shirt and tunic. Gerd stuffed his old clothes into his arms, and he dressed fast. "Here," Gerd said, fastening the garnet clasp on his cloak. His sword and mail coat were in the chest by his bed—King Beowulf's old bed in his house just beyond the hall. He looked at Ketil, spreading his hands to indicate that he didn't have them here.

Ketil nodded his understanding. "I'll take them the long way to the hall," he said. "You can come in the side door."

Rune glanced at Thora. "Would you—?" he started to ask, but she was already moving, her cloak over her shoulders, a basket on her arm.

"Wyn," she said. "Find the bard. Gerd, make sure there are no chickens in the hall."

They ran.

Rune got to the hall a half-step before Ketil. As he straightened his cloak, he could hear him speaking to the Shylfings, who were stamping snow from their boots in the alcove that kept the wind from howling through whenever the door was opened.

Someone had already lit the hall fire. Rune mouthed a silent thanks to whoever it had been. He moved toward it as the bard came hurrying, Thora just behind him. They stood on either side of Rune, all of them listening to the sounds of swords being pulled from sheaths. Ketil would be directing the Shylfings to leave their weapons at the door.

Ottar and Gar stepped to the sides of the hall, helmets down, spears up, and Rune felt rather than saw Wyn and Gerd falling into place near the side door, ready to help if he needed them.

Ketil strode into view and then Thialfi, the pair of them flanking two Shylfing warriors. Behind them, Rune could see another figure hidden by a furred cloak—not a fighter, perhaps an emissary—and another Shylfing warrior, followed by Wyn's brothers. He heard their mail clinking as they approached, and before he could speak, one of the Shylfings stepped forward.

"Hail, Wiglaf, son of Weohstan," the man called out.

He watched the warrior carefully, the mustached face, the dark brown beard, the powerful shoulders.

"Our king sends you greeting," the warrior said in a strong voice. Rune saw him glance around the hall, his eyes taking in everything in an instant before he looked back at Rune. What was his expression? Contempt? Rune wasn't sure.

He stepped forward. "You are welcome to the land of the Geats. You have journeyed far and returned our valued thanes, free from harm. We thank you." At least he hoped they were free from harm, but he didn't want to take his eyes from the Shylfing's to check. Much as his fingers itched to clutch his sword, he clamped his gloved palm to his side.

"Past hostilities have divided our people," the Shylfing said. "My king asks that they be forgotten." His tone suggested that he didn't agree with his king.

Rune almost bowed, catching himself just in time. *Never show submission to an emissary, no matter how high his status,* the bard had told him as they had waited for the envoys' return.

"Your lord speaks wisely," Rune said.

The emissary regarded him coldly. "We thought we would find a king," he said.

Rune nodded, enlightened. "The coronation takes place tomorrow," he said, inwardly cursing himself. The bard had wanted to have Rune crowned as early as possible, but Rune had postponed the coronation until after the harvest, and then again until after the hall was built. He hadn't thought about what it would mean to the Shylfings. "You will be our honored guests," he added.

Without moving his head, the Shylfing warrior glanced at the man beside him, who gave him a curt nod. They both looked back at Rune. The first man spoke again. "Our king sends a peace pledge between our two nations." He stepped back, and the figure behind him came forward, pushing back the furred hood of a cloak.

Rune's eyes widened. A profound silence filled the hall. Only the fire dared dance and snap.

"Hild, our king's sister-daughter," the warrior said.

A grave-faced girl, her dark hair pulled back, sank into a low curtsy.

"Be welcome, Hild," Rune said, stepping forward to raise her by the hand.

She matched him for height and met his eyes with her own dark ones. One eye looked directly at him, while the other seemed to see beyond him, making it hard for him to know where to focus. Just like Amma's eyes, the girl's seemed to see right through him, challenging him, taking his measure.

He struggled to find his voice in a mouth gone dry as stone. "Be welcome, all of you," he managed to say, then added, "Sit and rest after your journey." He guided Hild to Thora, and the two curtsied to each other before Thora led the girl to a bench near the fire.

Suddenly, the hall was a flurry of activity as the Shylfings took their seats on the mead benches, as Geats brought them food, as a bond servant dumped a load of logs by the fire and built it to a roar.

Ketil came alongside Rune and looked him a question.

"That," Rune said, his knees weak, "was more terrifying than any dragon."

TWENTY·SEVEN

IN THE KING'S HOUSE IN THE KING'S BED, RUNE LAY AWAKE, staring into the midnight air, the day's events replaying in his mind. The Shylfings' arrival had taken them all by surprise, and he'd been too busy to digest everything that had happened. Thialfi had been a good choice for emissary, Rune could see; the Shylfing warriors respected him, treating him like a member of their troop. He ate with them, introducing Geatish warriors who joined them at the mead bench. They seemed to like Wyn's brothers, too.

Wyn and Gerd had circled Hild warily, casting suspicious glances at her as she sat before the fire. But it didn't take long for compassion to melt their hearts, and Rune watched as they escorted her out of the hall, taking her off to Thora's house to bathe in front of a fire. Later, Gerd whispered to him, "I don't think she's very pretty. And she doesn't say much."

He'd been thinking about the warriors more than about the girl, knowing that they saw in him an untested youth too green to rule. Would they take that report back to their king? And would their king attack, despite the presence of a peaceweaver?

Rune screwed his eyes shut so hard he saw stars, then stared into the dark again. That was what Hild was: a peaceweaver, just as Amma had been. It hadn't worked with Amma—hostilities broke out again, leaving her bereft. Why did anyone think it would work now? King Beowulf had thought peaceweaving was a foolish idea. *The spear seldom rests,* he had said, *no matter how worthy the bride.*

Bride? Rune froze under the blanket. He knew what peaceweavers were; he knew what the Shylfings intended, but he'd been too preoccupied to recognize the implications. Hild was to be his bride, a pledge of peace between their lands.

He was supposed to *marry* her.

Did he have a choice in the matter? Did she? The bard had said there would be time for negotiations after the coronation. Was he talking about a wedding?

And the coronation. A shudder ran through his body. Tomorrow, like it or not, he would be king. Up until now, he'd been busy enough to avoid thinking about it. Now it would be real. He hoped Amma would still be with him in some way.

And what of the gods? It had been a long time since he'd been butted by a goat or seen a raven watching him from the eaves. Were Thor and Odin still toying with him? And Loki—was he lurking in the shadows, watching? Maybe the gods were finished with their games. He wondered what the stakes had been—and who had won.

Groaning, he rolled over, trying not to think of tomorrow, knowing he'd never be able to sleep.

The scent of fresh-cut lumber filled Rune's nostrils, and he tried to focus on it, tried to remember to breathe as he stood before the dais, the golden torque biting into his neck, a forgotten pin sticking him under his arm.

The bard had explained the ceremony, which was simple enough. Or would be if his mind would work, if he didn't keep blanking in terror.

He'd sacrificed a goat to Thor at dawn. Hadn't he? Yes, he knew he had. He remembered riding Hairy-Hoof to the Feasting Field. The bard had been there.

Then he'd come back, washed the blood off, and eaten something—bread, yes, and some kind of meat, but he couldn't remember what.

Ketil had come looking for him and hurried him to Thora's house, where Wyn and Gerd were still working on his clothes.

Ketil flopped down on the three-legged stool in the corner, folded his arms behind his head, stretched out his legs, and watched.

Rune reached up to scratch at an itch.

"Don't move!" Gerd said, but it was too late—his shirt made a tearing sound as a seam ripped open. "Now look what you've done."

Ketil laughed.

"Sorry," Rune mumbled. He didn't see why the clothes were so important; it was the crown that mattered. The crown and the not insignificant fact that the warriors trusted him. But the bard disagreed. So did Thora. On the matter of clothes, Rune had been overruled.

Gerd was growing frantic. "Look at what he did!" she wailed, and Wyn crossed behind Rune to examine something that he strained over his shoulder to see. "Turn back around," Gerd snapped, and when he did, Ketil grinned at him.

"You could just sew him into them for the day," Ketil said.

"Sew him into his clothes?" Gerd was aghast.

"You're not helping, Ketil," Wyn said.

"No, I'm serious," Ketil said, sitting up. Rune watched his expression change as his joke transformed into a suggestion.

"Sew him into his coronation clothes?" Gerd said again, but this time she giggled.

"He *will* be wearing a cloak—a long one," Wyn said, considering. "No mail, but his swordbelt would help hold the tunic together."

"It might look funny," Gerd said.

"No, Gerd," Ketil said, leaning back again. "It *won't* look funny; it will look fine and we'll be the only ones who know."

"All right," Wyn said. "Let's try it. Hold this for me, Gerd."

"Watch out for that bit there," Ketil said.

"It's a sleeve, Ketil, not 'that bit,'" Gerd said.

Rune looked up. "Where's Hild?"

"With my mother in the guest quarters," Wyn told him.

"What about the Shylfings? Who's escorting them?"

Ketil's eyes widened. Without a word, he grabbed his cloak and rushed from the room.

They watched him go, Wyn shaking her head in amusement. Then she stepped back to look at Rune appraisingly. When she pointed at a seam, Gerd took her needle to it.

"That's too tight," Rune said.

"Don't worry, it's just for today," Gerd told him. She finished the seam and attacked something else he couldn't see. "Stop wiggling."

Rune sighed. They were going to sew him in so tightly he would barely be able to breathe.

Finally, Wyn said, "Finished."

"Are you sure?" Gerd asked.

"Look at him," Wyn said. The two of them walked all the way around him, narrowing their eyes as they evaluated the tunic.

"I'm sure," Wyn said. She put down her needle and thread, then stepped up to Rune, tucked her hand into his elbow, and led him out the door.

"This really is too tight," Rune said as they made their way down the narrow lane. It was hard to move his torso, and he had to keep his breathing shallow, which made his lungs yearn for a deep breath of air. When he finally took one, he could hear little ripping sounds in the seams.

Wyn rolled her eyes. "You'll survive."

As they approached the king's house, Rune heard a sound—cawing?—and thought he saw something dark flitting through the air. He turned to look, but Wyn pulled him forward. "I know Ketil's supposed to arm you," she said, "but just this once, I'll do it."

As they crossed the threshold, he said, "You and Ketil—"

She smiled at him. Her face looked so bright that he wondered how he could ever have not known where her heart lay.

Then she grew serious. "Did you know that his mother and my parents made the agreement the night the dragon attacked?"

He shook his head.

"We never had a chance to get King Beowulf's

permission." She looked away for a moment, and Rune knew she must be thinking of her father.

"Oh, Rune, you'll be such a good king," she said.

It was his turn to look away, but she threw her arms around his neck. "You already are," she whispered into his ear.

He started to hug her back, but she said, "Don't you dare! You'll ruin your clothes!" and stepped across the room to the bed.

Rune followed her with his eyes and saw the magnificent cloak of finely wrought wool.

Wyn held it up. It was longer than an ordinary cloak, a ceremonial mantle fit for royalty. "Fulla has been working on it ever since King Beowulf's funeral. Look." She showed him the border with its exquisite interlacing pattern embroidered in gold thread.

He peered at it more closely. "Are those hammers? For Thor?"

She nodded. "And look." She pointed at a sinuous dragon woven into the pattern. "You are the dragon-slayer, after all," she said. "Put your sword on."

He reached for the weapon. He'd worn it, but he hadn't used it since the dragon fight, and it came as a surprise that the hilt fit his hand much more easily than it had before. It must be the glove, he thought.

He buckled on the belt and adjusted the sheath. He felt Wyn's eyes on him, and he looked at her. Did she know the sword's history?

He took a deep breath, cringing at the sound of ripping seams, and slid the blade into the sheath.

Without speaking, she moved behind him to fasten King Beowulf's torque around his neck. Then she gathered up his hair and tied it neatly back, her fingers touching his skin. There was a time, he realized, when her touch would have sent a shiver tingling through him. Today, it felt warm, the touch of a friend he could always count on.

Satisfied with the torque and his hair, Wyn settled the cloak over his shoulders, standing on tiptoe to reach, and arranged it around him. It fell all the way to his feet.

"Now," she said, "I know you already have a clasp for your cloak, but I thought you might like this one." She reached into the folds of her gown and held out her hand. On her palm lay a gold brooch. Inside it, worked in blue cloisonné, was a falcon, wings spread.

Rune glanced at the tapestry Amma had woven, with its image of Freyja's falcon-skin cloak; when he'd brought it from the farm, he'd hung it on the wall opposite the bed. He looked back at the brooch. It was the same falcon pattern.

"Amma gave it to me years ago," Wyn said.

"I can't take it—it's yours."

"Borrow it, then. You need something of hers with you for the coronation." She reached up and pinned it to his shoulder to hold the cloak together. Then she stepped back to look him over. "Turn," she said, and he did, the cloak swirling around his legs.

"You'll do," she said, smiling. "Now, stay here and I'll go find out if it's time."

As she slipped out the door, Rune wanted to sit down—he couldn't remember the last time he had done so—but was afraid he might ruin something. Instead, he reached up to touch the brooch. As his fingers met the patterned gold, a memory came to him, one he didn't know he had, a remembrance of a time long ago, when he must have been very young. He'd sat on Amma's lap, running his fingers over this very brooch, while she crooned a song to him. It wouldn't have been a lullaby; that wasn't her way. Instead, it would have been a lay of heroes and giants and gods, of kings of old and feuds between tribes. He closed his eyes, remembering the feel of her chest rumbling as he leaned into it, the warmth of her body, the comforting scent of smoke and sweat and herbs. He remembered the way she stirred a pot with one hand, encircling him with her other arm. When had she stopped wearing the brooch? He didn't know. What he did know was that always she had been there for him. And that always she had been preparing him to be king. He'd just never realized it before.

Slowly, his nervousness calmed.

Now, as he stood before the dais, his trepidation returned. His tongue was so dry that he'd never be able to say the words the bard had taught him, and he felt sick to his stomach. He reached up to tug at the torque around his neck, trying to settle it more comfortably against his skin, and watched the blur of brown cloaks as people filed into the hall. Not just those who lived in the stronghold, but people from all over the kingdom had made the journey to see their new king crowned—and to join the feasting that would follow.

The fresh scent of new lumber had given way to the odor of wet fur and unwashed bodies as more people crowded inside. Babies cried and children shrieked as they chased each other around the mead benches.

He closed his eyes, trying to remember the words he was supposed to say, but they were gone. He'd have to ask the bard again. Where was he?

Rune saw him to his right, just coming in the side door.

Then the drumming started. It was too late. The ceremony had begun. Rune felt people falling into place, Thora stepping to his left side, Ketil to his right, Gar and Hemming at either end of the dais, Brokk standing at attention by the fire, holding shield and spear, Horsa just behind him.

The thundering of the drums grew louder, calling to the Hammer-Wielder, and the crowd stilled, turning to face front.

Desperate, Rune fought to find the words. What was he going to do? Out of the corner of his eye, he saw the Shylfings, Hild standing amid the warriors. Her black hair rippled like water down her back, and she wore a deep red gown of some rich-looking material. Gerd had said she wasn't pretty, Rune remembered. She'd been right—Hild wasn't pretty. She was beautiful, like a queen from the legends. He stared at her face, letting his eyes linger on her dark brows, her straight nose, her slightly parted lips. Then she moved her head, and Rune realized she was looking directly at him. He dropped his eyes, wincing at the thought of forgetting the words while she was watching.

He willed himself to relax, silently calling on Amma, but it didn't help. The bard was coming toward him, the golden circlet in his hands. Closer he came, and closer still. A wave of dizziness hit him and Rune swayed.

The bard stopped directly in front of him, and suddenly the drumming ceased. In the silence, the bard's words were clear and loud.

And as Rune heard them, his response came flooding back. Weak-kneed with relief, he spoke the required phrases, his voice ringing through the hall.

The bard lifted the circlet, and Rune began to lower his head.

"Stop!" A commanding voice spoke from the back of the hall. The crowd turned. A figure in a torn and dirty tunic, metal bands shining on his bare arms, eyes glinting behind his masked helmet, strode forward.

"Dayraven!" a glad voice cried out.

Ottar stepped forward to slap the warrior on the back. "We thought you were dead!"

A ripple of voices carried throughout the hall. "You're just in time for the ceremony," someone called out.

"There will be no ceremony," Dayraven snarled.

The hall grew silent.

"That boy, that cursed whelp." He pointed at Rune and looked around at the crowd. "He tried to kill King Beowulf, tried to push him over a cliff. I was there; I saw it with my own eyes."

Rune felt the color drain from his face.

"We didn't kill him when we should have long ago. The gods are still waiting for their sacrifice." Dayraven looked from one person to another.

No one spoke.

"I will be your next king," he said.

Five fully armed warriors stepped out of the crowd.

"Tie his hands," Dayraven barked. "Take the cursed wretch away."

TWENTY·EIGHT

TWO THINGS HAPPENED IN QUICK SUCCESSION. THE BARD whispered, "Keep going!" and reached up to set the circlet on Rune's head. As he did, Ketil stepped forward, drawing his sword from its sheath.

"I was there, too," Ketil called out to the crowd. "I heard King Beowulf name Rune his heir. I saw Rune save the king's life. And I saw Dayraven running from the dragon when his ring-giver needed help."

Sword extended, Ketil surveyed the crowd. Rune watched him, wide-eyed, the circlet slipping over his ear. As he reached up to straighten it, he saw one of Dayraven's men notching an arrow.

"Ketil!" Rune screamed, throwing himself forward, knocking his friend to the floor. He felt the seams of his tunic split open just before white-hot pain seared through his arm. Suddenly, the hall was in motion, men shouting, women screaming, people running, swords clashing.

The moment Rune rolled off him, Ketil was up, flying into the melee. Rune unsheathed his sword, ignoring the old pain of his burned hand, the new wound in his shield arm. He looked for the Shylfings—were they part of this?—but he couldn't see them. The bard stood directly before him. "We have to get people out of here. The side door," Rune said. "Are there more men out there?"

The bard gave him a fast nod, then narrowed his single eye as he looked at Rune's left arm. Rune glanced down at the blood seeping through his ripped sleeve. The arrow wound burned like dragonflame.

"It's not bad. Go!"

The bard went.

Pushing his cloak behind him, Rune leapt onto the dais for a better view. Ketil was fighting a man whose helmet covered his entire face. Near him, Ottar and Brokk faced off against two of Dayraven's warriors, men from the last patrol to return. He caught his breath—there was a body on the ground. Who? He couldn't tell.

The crowd crushed to the sides of the hall, women holding crying children, unarmed farmers standing between them and the fighting. He had to get them out of the hall. Where was the bard?

"Rune! Get down!" Wyn screamed from behind him.

He dropped as an arrow whizzed over him. "Back here!" Wyn said, and he rolled off the dais, almost landing on Wyn, Thora, and Gerd.

"You're hurt!" one of them said, but he didn't register who it was because he was looking at the bard peering through the side door, giving an all-clear signal.

"Listen to me," Rune said, pushing Wyn's hands away from his wounded arm. "We've got to get people out of the hall and keep Dayraven and his men inside."

The three women watched him expectantly.

"Wyn, will you go out the side door and run around to the front? You can slip in and start leading people out."

She met his eyes.

"Go carefully," he said, and watched as she crept along the dais on her hands and knees. She waited for a moment, then scuttled to the door. As soon as she was through it, he turned to Thora. "You don't have to do this," he said. "But I need someone to lead the ones nearer this door back around the dais and out."

"Of course," she said.

"Keep to the walls," he whispered, but she was already gone.

"What about me?" Gerd's voice rose to a wail.

"Gerd," Rune said, thinking. He needed her safe and out of the way. "Will you stay here and guide people to the side door? Some of them will need help."

She nodded wordlessly, but he could see the fear in her face.

"Courage, Gerd," he said, laying his hand on her arm. Then he peered over the dais. Just on the other side, Ketil staggered as his opponent raised his sword for a killing blow. Rune raced around the platform and dove at the man, knocking him down, then leapt to his feet again. Ketil regained his footing and gave Rune a nod of acknowledgment.

Rune kept going. Beside the fire, Gar circled a helmeted warrior, but he seemed to be in control of his fight. Where were the Shylfings?

A groan behind him made him turn in time to see Brokk pulling his sword from a man's body. Rune winced and ran toward the crowd that pushed for the door.

"You'll be safe outside," he said, his voice strong. "Be calm—get the children out. Some of you can go to the side door. Look for Thora!"

A stooped woman clutched at his wounded arm, making the pain flare up. He hissed, sucking in his breath, but she didn't notice. "My lord," she said, tears streaming down her cheeks. "Help us!" Carefully, he detached her fingers from his arm and held her hand in his gloved one. When someone else took her by the arm, Rune turned back to the fight, looking to see who needed help. The Shylfings— where were they?

From the corner of his eye, he saw a bow being raised, an arrow nocked, as a man stepped out from behind a beam. Rune ran, shoving the archer hard, just in time to send the arrow flying harmlessly upward. Then he dealt the archer's unhelmeted head a heavy blow with his sword hilt as Surt ran up, Buri a step behind him.

"We've got him," Surt said as he twisted the warrior's arm behind him.

Rune met Surt's eyes, then raced on, passing Brokk, who gave him a battle grin; passing Ketil, who was binding a man's hands and feet; passing Gar, who still circled the same warrior beside the fire. He could see the orderly line of unarmed people heading for the side door, Thora directing them.

"Cursed whelp," a voice snarled.

Rune whirled, sword in both hands, and dropped into a fighting stance.

Dayraven stood staring at him, his eyes full of contempt. He was an experienced fighter, his bare arms thick as oak branches. Rune's sword was no match for his.

He took a step back, sword raised, wishing he'd taken off the cloak. Now it twined around his legs, threatening to trip him, but he didn't trust himself to let go of the sword to yank it away. He had no shield, no helmet, no coat of mail to protect him. Even his tunic hung in rags, its seams ripped open. He couldn't get his breath.

Dayraven's mail clinked as he stepped forward. Behind his masked helmet, his eyes glittered. No cloak obstructed his movements. Lightning fast, he raised his sword and brought it whistling down toward Rune's head.

Finn's training came back to him and Rune parried. The impact jarred his teeth and sent a surge of pain through his burned hand. He gripped the hilt more tightly. "Don't lose your nerve," he whispered to himself, Finn's admonition steadying him. He took another step back, watching for Dayraven's next move. He dared not attack and leave his body unprotected—Dayraven was too fast for that.

Keeping his eyes on his opponent, Rune shut out the rest of the hall. Sound diminished and all he could hear was his own breathing, ragged and labored.

Again, Dayraven's blade flashed toward him. Again, he parried just in time, stepping back. His foot came down on something, and he tripped, falling backward onto one knee as something metal clinked. *Don't lose your nerve,* he told himself again, lifting his sword, ignoring the fire in his shield arm, the pain in his sword hand.

He struggled to get up, but the cloak tangled around his legs, pinning him down. Dayraven advanced, sword over his head.

Rune swung at the warrior's knees, but Dayraven danced backward, growling as he did.

Rune had no choice but to take one hand off his sword to loosen the cloak. He wasn't fast enough—the folds were twisted too tightly. He grasped the hilt again.

Dayraven stepped forward, keeping just out of Rune's sword reach. He readied his own weapon for another blow.

Rune held his sword with both hands, looking up at Dayraven's blade, preparing to parry it, knowing he wouldn't be able to if Dayraven brought it down with his full strength.

The polished steel came slicing down, and Rune blocked it with all his might. It wasn't enough. Dayraven's blade slid off Rune's and down onto his shoulder. Rune turned his head to the side to avoid the blow, but there was no need. Dayraven's blade bounced harmlessly off Amma's brooch.

Enraged, Dayraven advanced again, and Rune scrambled back as fast as he could, sword in both hands, his wounded left arm shaking with the effort, sweat dripping into his eyes.

Something stopped him—the dais. It blocked his path, keeping him from backing away. There was no escape. He was trapped.

He looked up.

Dayraven stood above him, weapon held high.

Rune tensed for the final blow. Time seemed to slow, and his heartbeat thundered in his ears.

As he watched, eyes wide with horror, the blade began its awful descent.

Then Dayraven's body jerked. Below his mask, his jaw dropped as if in surprise. As his sword came down, Rune parried it easily. Dayraven slumped sideways, falling to the ground.

Behind him, a long, narrow blade in her hand, stood Hild.

Rune dropped his sword, untangling the cloak and scrambling to his feet in time to catch her by the elbow as she swayed.

"There was a hole in his mail," she whispered.

Rune could feel her body shaking—or maybe it was his. "My lady," he said.

White-faced, she looked into his eyes. "I was supposed to weave peace."

Rune looked down at Dayraven's body.

Hild followed his gaze. "Is he dead?"

He nodded.

She looked as if she might be sick.

Gently, he took her arm and led her along the dais, away from the body. When they stopped, she dropped her head, then lifted it and looked at him, angry tears glinting in her eyes. "I'm sick of the killing."

"Hild," he said quietly. "You saved my life."

She swallowed.

"Where are your guards?" he asked.

"Outside. Looking for me," she said. Very faintly, she smiled at him.

Rune gazed at her dark eyes, at the way her lips quirked at the corners before they turned serious again. Suddenly, as if spring had come to a frozen river, he felt a melting in his stomach. She met his eyes, and for a long moment, it seemed to Rune as if he had found the home he'd been looking for all these years, the home he'd never known he lacked.

She looked away, her eyes drawn to something on the ground. She stooped to pick it up. The thing he had tripped over. The crown. She reached up and settled it onto his head, pushing a lock of sweaty hair out of his eyes and tucking it behind his ear. The touch of her fingers sent a shiver tingling through him.

In the distance, somebody shouted his name, and Rune turned to see Ketil by the fire pit, waving his blade.

Suddenly, Rune remembered where he was. What was happening? Where was his sword? He lunged for it, taking in the situation in the hall in an instant. Two men bound, two others lying dead. Dayraven's men. Where was the fifth, the archer?

In the back of the hall, he saw him tied to a beam, flanked by Buri and Surt. And the rest of his own warriors? He scanned the hall. Ottar and Gar guarded the two bound men while Brokk stood wiping the blood from his sword blade. Hemming—where was Hemming? There, with Fulla by his side. Wounded? If he was, he was still standing. Od stood by the fire, a dazed look on his face, and Thialfi and Wyn's brothers were just coming in the door, escorting the Shylfings.

Rune looked back at Ketil. Why was he waving his sword? What was wrong?

Ketil flashed him a wide grin and waved his weapon again.

Relief flooding through him, Rune took a breath and grinned back.

Suddenly, the hall seemed full of people as the crowd surged back through the doors.

From the side door, the bard strode forward. He held

up a hand to command silence, and Rune stared at him, trying to comprehend.

"Wiglaf, son of Weohstan, King of the Geats!" the bard cried in a loud voice. Cheers rose and more people streamed through the doors and back into the hall. Someone began beating the drums, and the sound of glad voices grew deafening.

But Rune barely heard it. He was looking at Hild. As they stared into each other's eyes, he felt his body trembling and he couldn't seem to catch his breath.

Hild inclined her head without taking her eyes off his. "Your people," she whispered. "They're waiting for you."

"They'll be your people, too," he whispered back. The crown slipped forward, over his eye.

She reached up to straighten it, the fleeting smile returning to her lips.

Then she took his hand, and together they turned to face the cheering crowd.

AUTHOR'S NOTE

The last section of the Anglo-Saxon poem *Beowulf* takes place long after the hero's more famous fights with Grendel and Grendel's mother. After those exploits, Beowulf rules the Geats for over fifty years. Then comes the dragon.

When a slave steals a single cup from the dragon's treasure hoard, the creature takes vengeance by fire-blasting Beowulf's kingdom. The king vows revenge and picks eleven of his best warriors—his hearth companions—to accompany him to the dragon's barrow. But during the fight, all of the king's men flee in terror. All except one, that is: the young warrior Wiglaf. Wiglaf reminds the other men of their mead-hall boasts and exhorts them to help the king. None will—they are too afraid. So Wiglaf alone goes to his lord's assistance. Together, the old man and the young one kill the dragon, but during the fight, Beowulf receives his death wound. Before he dies, he names Wiglaf his heir.

In Anglo-Saxon literature—works composed in England between the years 600 and 1066—one of the worst things a man could do was abandon his leader in battle. Dying beside your lord was preferable to the shame of surviving him. Yet in *Beowulf*, ten of the king's handpicked warriors flee to the woods when their lord needs them most. I have always wondered what it was about the dragon that made those men run away, and what it was about Wiglaf that allowed him to withstand the terror. In this book, I have tried to imagine the situation for myself and to answer those questions.

Doing so meant that I had to reshape the story to fit my own purposes, changing many details. Wiglaf's heritage is one of those changes. In the poem, he is indeed a Wayamunding (or *Wægmunding*), just as Beowulf is, and after he alone comes to the king's aid in the dragon fight, Beowulf names Wiglaf, his only surviving kinsman, as his heir. In fact, almost everything that happens during the dragon fight and directly after it is taken straight from the poem. So is the dragon's awakening—after a slave steals a single cup from its hoard—and the dragon's attack on Beowulf's kingdom. The rest I invented.

In the poem, Wiglaf was no orphan and he had no nickname. His father, Weohstan (who did kill Eanmund, son of Ohthere, although I changed the details), was one of Beowulf's men, but he died before the dragon attack.

Amma is invented, as are Hild, Wyn, Ketil Flat-Nose, and most of the other characters. I borrowed names from *Beowulf* and other Anglo-Saxon and Old Norse stories. For example, Dayraven—*Dæghrefn* in Old English—is the name of a warrior Beowulf killed in hand-to-hand combat during a raid in Frisia long before he became king. The feud with the Shylfings, or *Scylfingas,* underlies much of the poem, and in the last lines, there is a sense of foreboding, a feeling that the Shylfings will attack the Geats now that their hero-king is dead. Those familiar with the poem may hear echoes from other sections of the poem within the novel as well, such as Rune's words before the funeral pyre. They are the last lines of the poem:

he wære wyruldcyninga
mannum mildust ond monðwærust,
leodum liðost ond lofgeornost

(of the kings of this world he was the most gentle, the most gracious, the kindest to his people and the most eager for fame)

Although the poem was composed in England some-time between 700 and 1000, it recalls tales and events from the sixth century, a past long distant even then. The story takes place in Scandinavia, not England, in a time before Christianity came to those shores. Just as the poem does, I have combined details from Anglo-Saxon England with those from medieval Scandinavia. The *Beowulf* poet doesn't specify what gods and goddesses his characters worshiped, just that they were heathens, so I have drawn on what we know about Norse religion to invent cultural references for my characters. The result is no more historical than the poem *Beowulf* is.

Dragons, however, occupy a place both in the historical record and in Anglo-Saxon and Scandinavian legend. Beowulf and Wiglaf were hardly the only legendary dragon-slayers; heroes such as Sigmund, Frotho the Dane, and Ragnar Lothbrok (or Hairy-Britches—his hide cloth-ing, boiled in pitch, protected him from dragon poison) also fought dragons. The Anglo-Saxon collection of wise sayings known as *Maxims* includes the truism "A dragon must live in a barrow, old and proud of its treasures." That's where you find dragons in the stories: inside their caves, jealously guarding their piles of treasure. But the historical dragons weren't content to sleep on their hoards. In *The Anglo-Saxon Chronicle*, a sober history recorded by monks, the entry for the terrible year 793 tells us that fiery dragons were seen flying in the air over Northumbria. Did the Anglo-Saxons really believe in dragons? It's hard to say, but one thing is sure—their dragons were evil and destructive, never the kinds of creatures a human could befriend.

Sometimes the dragons had names, such as Fafnir, but the one in *Beowulf* is known by what it does—it's called, among other things, a *hoard guardian*, a *wicked ravager*, a *coiled-up creature*, and a *hateful flyer-through-the-air*.

Names for humans could also have meanings, in the way that the modern name Blanche literally means "white," while Ebony refers to the dark wood of a tropical tree and the color black. With the most common names, people probably didn't think of their literal meanings—when Anglo-Saxon parents named their son Alfred, for example, it's unlikely that they thought of him as being "counseled by elves." Nevertheless, the original, literal meaning underlies many Anglo-Saxon names, giving them an added resonance. In this novel, some of those include *Hild*, which means "battle"; *Gar*, which means "spear"; *Wyn*, which is a runic symbol and a word for "joy"; *Amma*, which means "grandmother" in Old Norse; and, of course, *Wiglaf*, which, in Old English—the language spoken by the Anglo-Saxons—translates literally as "survivor of war."

PRONUNCIATION GUIDE

Eanmund (AY-un-mund): the man Wiglaf's father killed

Ecgtheow (EDGE-thay-ow): Beowulf's father; literally, "servant of the sword"

Freyja (FRAY-yuh): a goddess

Geats (YAY-uhts): Beowulf's tribe

Hondshio (HAHND-shee-oh): one of Beowulf's men who was killed by Grendel

Hwala (HWAHL-uh; the vowels sound like those in *Malta*): Rune's foster father, invented for this story; literally, "whale"

Hygelac (HEE-yuh-lack): king of the Geats when Beowulf fought Grendel

Ohthere (OH-tara): Eanmund's father

Shylfing (SHILL-ving): the enemy tribe (another name for the Swedes)

Skyn (SKIN): one of Rune's foster brothers, invented for this story

Welund (WAY-lund): the maimed smith of the gods

Weohstan (WAY-o-stawn): Wiglaf's father

Wiglaf (WEE-laf): Rune's real name; literally, "survivor of war"

Wyn (WIN): daughter of Finn and Thora, invented for this story; literally, "joy"

ACKNOWLEDGMENTS

If it wasn't for Ena Jones, this novel might never have been written. She was there from the very beginning, and I am in her debt. Others helped me, too: Matthew Kirby asked all the right questions; Megan Isaac, Sid Brown, and Anna Webman generously offered suggestions; and Diane Landolf's editorial skill helped make this a better book. I am grateful to them all—and to my parents for their enthusiasm. Finally, I wish to thank the teachers who shared their deep knowledge and love of the Middle Ages with me, especially Professors Joseph S. Wittig, David Ganz, and Jaroslav Folda.